PRAGUE NOIR

EDITED BY PAVEL MANDYS

Translated by Miriam Margala

BROOKLYN, NEW YORK, USA
BALLYDEHOB, CO. CORK, IRELAND

This collection comprises works of fiction. All names, characters, places, and incidents are the product of the authors' imaginations. Any resemblance to real events or persons, living or dead, is entirely coincidental.

Published by Akashic Books
©2018 Akashic Books

Series concept by Tim McLoughlin and Johnny Temple
Prague map by Sohrab Habibion

ISBN: 978-1-61775-529-3
Library of Congress Control Number: 2017936120

Akashic Books
Brooklyn, New York, USA
Ballydehob, Co. Cork, Ireland
Twitter: @AkashicBooks
Facebook: AkashicBooks
E-mail: info@akashicbooks.com
Website: www.akashicbooks.com

ALSO IN THE AKASHIC NOIR SERIES

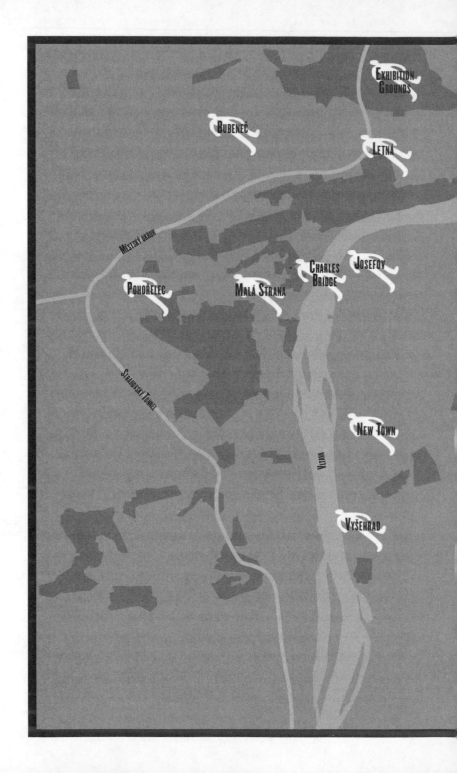

PRAGUE

Vltava

Žižkov

Olšany Cemetery

Grébovka

Hostivař

Pankrác

E65

TABLE OF CONTENTS

PART III: SHADOWS OF THE PAST

PART IV: IN JEOPARDY

INTRODUCTION
Noir? In Prague?

How do you write noir in a city where, until 1990, the profession of private detective didn't even exist? Where the censors cultivated a positive image of the police in both media and literature? Where, in essence, organized crime was nowhere to be found, and the largest criminal group was the secret police? Before you delve in and start reading the fourteen stories in this collection, a heads-up: most of the stories are linked to Prague more closely than the noir genre, especially if "noir" is interpreted, narrowly, as a subgenre of the mystery genre. If, however, the concept of noir is extended and considered a label for literary works that contain elements of crime, danger, and menace, or where main characters find themselves in a critical situation, then you will find fourteen such stories in this collection.

The history of the Czech literary detective story is not very diverse, and the subgenre known as noir appears in it only sporadically. The main reason for this is the forty-year existence of a police state which carefully ensured that the propagandistic image of its repressive elements wasn't questioned in the arts, including literature. And it is precisely noir stories that oftentimes do without the police; if they do appear, it's usually in a secondary (and not always flattering) role.

At the center of noir literature is a solitary hero who must stand up on his or her own to either the crime or to some inner demons. That is a situation unfit for an exemplary member of a Socialist society. It was unseemly and undignified, and as such, official publishers were not allowed to publish many of these narratives. At most they could publish stories set in the corrupt capitalist foreign world and—according to the ideologues—they were supposed to demonstrate to their enthusiastic Czech readers how dangerous and ugly life behind the Iron Curtain was. Czech detective stories in those days were formally modeled after the traditional British whodunit: an even-tempered investigation carried out by a sympathetic policeman. After all, there was no such thing as a private detective in the Socialist regime.

It wasn't until after the Velvet Revolution in 1989 that private detectives appeared in Czech novels. Nevertheless, it was obvious that most of them were based on foreign examples—there was still an inclination to use the classic British model. When Czech authors finally began to write stories in the tradition of the hard-boiled American style, it did result in more naturalistic and action-driven novels. The basic theme of the detective who solves crimes, however, remained unchanged.

But noir in its best form—even if the term itself is still somewhat unclear and used with many meanings and contexts—does not really follow this template. The point is not that the mystery of a cunning murder is always successfully solved by a smart detective, but that the reality of men and women somehow ends up embroiled with crime, in the role of investigators, witnesses, victims, and perpetrators. The endings are not always happy; they do not even always offer a clearly solved case or apprehension of a murderer. On the contrary, the best noirs end tragically, or at least ambiguously. Disillusionment and disappointment are the basic emotions of most noir heroes.

The most popular Czech detective prose from past years uses the concept of friendly neighborliness—these are small stories of small people who sometimes do bad things. This is not surprising given the lack of organized crime in the Czech police state. Its chief representative was a secret faction called the State Security. Particularly the older generation of authors, who were publishing in the nineties and at the beginning of the twenty-first century, could not, or did not want to, break from this tradition.

A more marked change came with the popularity of Scandinavian crime novels, which have demonstrated that even in the countries with the highest quality of life and the lowest crime rate in the world, incredible stories can be developed about gruesome murders and their complex investigations with ambiguous conclusions. And the noir environment has been created there too: entrepreneurial elites and politicians in the Czech Republic interfaced very quickly with organized crime, and the police and justice systems were not pure either, as many scandals in the media documented.

Yet Czech authors do have an advantage: Prague's history in the twentieth century is far more dramatic and colorful than the history of any American city. During the last century, Prague was part of several different states and nations, all of which varied both politically and geographically. First, until 1918, Prague was part of a multinational Habsburg monarchy which ceased to exist following World War I. In 1918, Tomáš Garrigue Masaryk brought a vision of a democratic state of Czechs and Slovaks from America, and thus Czechoslovakia was formed—one of the very few democratic states in Europe at that time. But Nazi troops soon entered Prague, and the independent republic became the Czech and Moravian Protectorate.

The liberation by the Russian army brought only a short restoration of democracy. In 1948, Communists supported by Moscow seized power and established a new despotism which was only slightly milder than the Nazi regime, but which lasted much longer. The Czechoslovak Republic added the word *Socialist* to its name so that its membership in the Communist bloc was clear. The Soviet Union had no qualms about demanding this membership by force in 1968, when the Czech nation tried to break off from the totalitarian regime, and the Russians sent their army to Prague. The Czechs had to wait until 1989, for the fall of communism, to overthrow the regime in a peaceful, democratic way. But even that did not bring the end of the turmoil. In 1992, Slovakia broke off from the single Czechoslovak state, and Prague became the capital city of the Czech Republic.

These dramatic and turbulent historic changes have not just become items in history textbooks; they had real-life consequences for all the inhabitants of Prague. In 1938, it was still a very lively city, where Czechs, Germans, and Jews cohabitated. There was an influx of refugees from European countries where totalitarian regimes had come to power—specifically, from Communist Russia and Nazi Germany. The Nazis then later almost totally wiped out the Jewish citizens. Conversely, in 1945, almost the entire German population was expelled from Prague. After 1948, all major private factories and companies were put under government control, and the smaller stores and shops soon followed. The state confiscated apartment houses and large villas; citizens could not own any sizable properties or businesses. Successful businessmen, large farmers, and even people who simply disagreed with the ideology of the regime ended up in prison if they hadn't already saved themselves by escaping abroad, which was forbidden and punished. Everything was dictated by the Communist Party—which was, in turn, directed from Moscow. It wasn't until the nineties that the victorious democratic movement led by Václav Havel tried to redress these historical injustices, and started to return property and a good reputation to all those who had been robbed by the Communist regime.

It is good to realize this context because many of the authors of the stories included in *Prague Noir* work within it. Historical twists and their intersection with the everyday lives of Prague's inhabitants are a theme of the stories included in the section called "Shadows of the Past," most notably in Kateřina Tučková's story "The Life and Work of Baroness Mautnic," and in Markéta Pilátová's story "All the Old Disguises." Chaim Cigan's (alias Karol Sidon) piece "The Magical Amulet," although I included it in the section "Magical Prague," has similar themes. This section depicts another important feature of Prague, renowned for the many magical stories and macabre legends from its many historical periods. According to connoisseurs of folk tales, every one of Prague's historical districts, which luckily experienced no destruction in any of the European wars, has a high concentration of ghosts and phantoms per square meter. That's also a reason why this side of Prague can't be omitted.

Unlike novels of social criticism or magical realism, Czech crime novels have so far been translated only very rarely (here one has to note an exception: *Innocence; Or Murder on Steep Street* by Heda Margolius Kovály). As I have already mentioned, the history of the Czech literary detective story has not been—thanks to the social and political circumstances of recent history—voluminous, and on the whole not of high quality, although one can find many pearls. Perhaps the most interesting (and darkest) in this regard is the work of Prague-based, German (mostly Jewish) writers Gustav Meyrink, Franz Werfel, and ultimately Franz Kafka (the novel *The Trial* does, after all, contain a criminal plot). But this type of Prague literature was erased in the year 1939, and there was nobody to continue the tradition.

This is why I decided to approach authors who do not solely write detective novels, but do use, more or less, the genre's props and methods. The first is the maestro of Prague mysteries, Miloš Urban, who already has under his belt one purely noir novel (*She Came from the Sea*). Then we have Petr Stančík, who's been very successful both here at home and abroad with his latest novel, *A Mill for Mummies*, a captivating, humorous antidetective story based in nineteenth-century Prague. Kateřina Tučková likes to use the investigative method in her best sellers; the stories in the triptych *To Disappear* by Petra Soukupová also have criminal motifs. The novel *Tsunami Blues* by Markéta Pilátová is a Czech woman's variation of the excellent spy dramas by Graham Greene; Chief Rabbi Karol Sidon, under the alias Chaim Cigan, has started to publish a tetralogy, *Where Foxes Bid Good Night,* a thrilling story set at the end of the Communist regime, and infused with criminal and surreal elements in an alternative reality. Sci-fi stories by Ondřej Neff often contain noir plots, and the popular writer Petr Šabach likes to depict witty tales about outsmarting the criminal element.

Fortunately, in recent years there have emerged novels by new authors who have breathed fresh air into the genre, sometimes from unexpected places. University professor Michal Sýkora writes carefully constructed books inspired by current British police procedural novels; Štěpán Kopřiva has emerged with perhaps the best of the Czech hard-boiled school, *Rapidfire*; and Jiří W. Procházka, alongside his partner Klára Smolíková, has introduced a detective series with the novel *Dead Predator*. An erstwhile policeman writing under the pseudonym Martin Goffa has transferred his police experience into literary form with a few novels and a collection of stories. Michaela Klevisová has found her niche in psychological detective stories, where who was killed and how is not as important as the portraits of the characters and their conflicting ambitions and motivations. Even a respected author of children's books, Iva Procházková, has written an excellent detective thriller.

Prague Noir is a colorful collection in which some of the stories are linked only loosely to the noir genre ("Epiphany" by Šabach, or "Olda No. 3" by Irena Hejdová, whose neighborly themes put her closer to more classical writers like Karel Čapek), while others are examples par excellence (particularly "Three Musketeers" by Goffa). "Amateurs" by Štěpán Kopřiva is of the hard-boiled school, while "Percy Thrillington" by Sýkora is a classic detective story. Some of the authors draw from their previous books: Petr Stančík revisits the hero from *A Mill for Mummies*, the unorthodox Commissioner Durman; Petra Soukupová varies the motif of a sudden and unexplained loss of a family member, which was typical in her stories from *To Disappear*; Kateřina Tučková examines the history of a woman marked by the wrongs of the Communist regime; and Markéta Pilátová's "All the Old Disguises" recalls, again, the globetrotting stories of Anglo-Saxon authors.

Ondřej Neff offers a romanetto in the tradition of a classical writer of Prague horror, Jakub Arbes; Miloš Urban writes an over-the-top action story set on the Charles Bridge; Jiří Procházka ventures into the world of circus folk in an amusement park; Chaim

Cigan looks into the past of a Jewish family; and Michaela Klevisová contributes a delicate story about the closeness of an unexpected and irrational danger.

I see *Prague Noir* as a chance for Czech authors to introduce themselves to international—especially Anglo-Saxon—audiences at a time when there are fewer and fewer translations into English being published. Czech literature of the twentieth century has quite a few world-renowned authors (Jaroslav Hašek, Bohumil Hrabal, Václav Havel, Milan Kundera, etc.). Our literature of the twenty-first century, however, barely touches this platform. One of the reasons must surely be that the fame that the Czechs gained from the Velvet Revolution has passed, and what's left is Prague's reputation as one of the biggest tourist magnets in the world. Contemporary Czech literature is vivid, vibrant, and informed by contemporary world literature which—thanks to active translators—is usually available in Czech very fast. It is global and local, poetic and humorous, filled with stories from the past, present, and from imaginary worlds. And it is waiting for when, in addition to all the enthusiastic Czech readers—according to global statistics, the Czechs, along with Canadians and Norwegians, are the most diligent readers—it will also gain a greater international audience.

Pavel Mandys
Prague, Czech Republic
November 2017

PART I

SHARP LADS

THREE MUSKETEERS

BY MARTIN GOFFA

Vyšehrad

It's fall, the end of November—disgusting and bleak. Only a few moments ago it was still raining, and for most of the day, waves of fog swept through the city. In the place where I am waiting right now, however, this kind of weather seems fitting. Perhaps there is no sort of weather that would not suit this place. Hot weather is bearable here; snow comes across as majestic; cold and rain only emphasize its mystique, so that you can almost hear the clatter of horse's hooves and the clash of swords and shields.

During the day you love this place, and at night you fear it. But it beguiles you just as light does for moths. Once it ensnares you, you will forever be coming back here. Just like me.

When I moved to the city twenty years ago, the small window in my kitchen offered a direct view of the castle walls. It was less then a day after that I was atop them, above all the surrounding roofs, walking along and watching the river and the blocks of houses below. A few years later, just a short distance from here, I was standing there with my bride right after the wedding ceremony, still in our wedding clothes. We felt not only as if Prague belonged to us, but the entire world, and all that was living, was ours too.

Well, here I am again, alone as I almost always am these days. That woman has been gone for a long time, and the child that I wanted to show all of this beauty to one day, she decided to have with somebody else. But none of that is Vyšehrad's fault. It has witnessed millions of similar and worse fates.

My breath turns to mist. When I walk, the wet grass softens my steps. Below me I see strips of lights, but up here, by the castle walls, it's dark. I took care of a few lamps last night, and just as I imagined, so far nobody has fixed them. The conversation which is going to take place here soon is best accompanied by darkness. I don't even know what time it is—perhaps midnight—but time means nothing to me. Not now, for sure, and most decidedly not here. But it's futile to try to explain. Those who know this place know what I mean; those who do not wouldn't understand.

Twenty or thirty more minutes pass. Around me there's only silence, while the city fusses with its ordinary life. I'm awaiting footsteps—the crunching on wet sidewalk gravel. Time passes, but I know that I will eventually hear it. I'm not afraid. I fear nothing. In fact, I feel strong; stronger then ever. As if those thousands of souls lying in the cemetery just a short distance behind me are protecting me.

I lift my hands and breathe into my palms. I could put my hands into my pockets, but I want them free, I feel better that way. I should have taken gloves, it occurs to me. Finally, I hear somebody approaching. The soles of shoes are crushing the fine gravel, and the sleeves of a jacket swoosh with each movement of the arms. I am standing on the grass under a tree, and the man—who walks by only a few meters away—cannot even see me in the dark. He walks slowly, almost languidly. He reaches the ledge of the wall, looks around, and lights a cigarette. He's waiting for me. The moon hasn't risen yet tonight, and under the broken lamps I only see a silhouette. The glowing cherry of a cigarette moves from the waist to the mouth, and then back; again, up and then down. He seems calm, looking somewhere into the distance, waiting. I look him over for a minute or two, and only then do I leave my cover.

"Hi, Dan," I say. He jerks slightly, but once I am close to him, I can see that his face has formed into a smile.

"Evening, Bary," he replies, putting the cigarette into his mouth and offering his hand. I do not like that nickname, but that has never phased him. Today, however, there's no time for pettiness—more important things await us.

"Long time no see," he adds as we shake hands. Yup, long time. Three or four years, perhaps. But as if that time lapse didn't exist, when I told him where to meet me, he remembered immediately.

"We could have seen each other a week ago, but you didn't come," I remark.

"A week ago?"

"At Anton's funeral," I remind him.

He turns his face toward the city and puts his hands on the railing. From the cigarette he holds between his index and middle fingers, a piece of glowing ash falls off onto a wet stone, and is immediately doused.

"Yup, there."

"Yup, there," I repeat.

"You know, Bary, I . . . I had to leave the city, and then later . . ." He trails off.

"Let it be," I say. He's lying; I have known that for a long time. He's always lied, god knows why. Maybe it seems easier to him than explaining or defending something.

"Dana has kept his ashes; she still doesn't know what to do with the urn," I continue.

"Hmmm," he mumbles, and inhales the cigarette. He knows Anton's wife as well as I do.

We're silent for a while. A wind has picked up and it moves the treetops at our backs.

"So why did you want to talk to me?" Dan asks. Apparently he's already dedicated the required amount of time to the memory of his friend.

"It has to do with the funeral, actually. Well, more like because of the things that preceded it."

"Like what?"

"Do you know at all how he died?"

"Hmmm," he grumbles again in what I take to be acknowledgment.

Anton was forty-six. In August, his lungs started to feel as if they were on fire. Later, the same feeling erupted in his belly. In September, he lost fifteen kilos; in October, ten more; by the beginning of November, he was hospitalized. Those were the last two weeks of his life.

"I visited him in the hospital, Dan."

"You did? I couldn't. I couldn't deal with seeing him like that."

Is he lying even now? Maybe yes, maybe no. He throws the glowing butt into the abyss below. As the air hits it, it sparks for a last time before it disappears from view, like a small comet.

"He wanted to talk to me," I explain.

Dan's face turns toward me. "He wanted to talk to you?"

"Yeah." I watch his hands, which he's putting into his jacket pockets. Does he have a gun? I can't be sure, but even if he does, we're just talking.

"You should have seen him. He looked like an old man—only skin and the skeleton underneath. He was unable to utter a complete sentence, that's how tired everything made him."

Dan turns toward the wall's ledge and spits over it. "Cancer is a bitch," he hisses through his teeth.

"That it is." I nod and wait for him to ask about Anton's reason for wanting to talk. But he's silent; only slowly and lightly nods his head.

"He apologized to me," I say after a while.

Dan's movements become even slower until they cease completely. "Apologized?"

"Yeah, apologized. For that."

"For what?" he asks carefully, but we both catch the change in his voice.

"You know for what, Dan." There's nothing in the sentence that should scare him. It's a simple statement of fact. "He apologized for all the shit I had to go through. And also for Jakub."

Now he stands with his face turned toward me again. I'm looking into his eyes indifferently, perhaps even placidly, without any spite. His hands are still in his pockets.

"Anton told me that you knew about it," I say, and this time I turn my face toward the city. I stand sideways next to Dan, my hands visible to him, and what I am saying sounds ordinary and boring. I do not want a confrontation and I hope he understands that.

A few seconds pass. If there's anything in his pockets that would scare me, for now it remains in its place.

An old roadster shot out from a forest road and screeched out onto the pavement in front of a moving armored truck. The truck veered to one side, its right wheels losing the support of the reinforced highway shoulder; in a moment, it was lying on its side like an animal unable to extricate itself from a sophisticated trap. The engine was still running and the wheels were spinning.

Another car, a gray station wagon, materialized from somewhere, and its driver and passenger jumped out to join the men in balaclavas who had gotten out of the roadster. There were four of them: three men with shotguns, and one with a machine gun. They all aimed inside the truck, where two security guards were crouching behind the reinforced glass. One had a bloody smear on his forehead; the other was holding the top of his head. As the shock of the impact wound down, they noticed the gun barrels aimed directly at them. How many shots could this glass withstand? Who here, in the middle of a forest, would come to help them? Nobody. Surely not fast enough to save them.

The men outside continued to aim and yell. The two men inside finally did what they had to do. The third member of the crew was in the back, in the cargo space. He was not able to stand up to the aggressive power move either, especially since the impact and the resulting fall to the floor had caused a dislocated shoulder. When the boxes full of money were being transported from the truck to the gray station wagon, one of the gangsters suddenly raised a gun and aimed it at his head.

"Why, Dan?" I ask.

"What do you want to hear?"

He lights another cigarette and I put my hands in my pockets. So far it looks like a truce.

"Why didn't you tell me about it then?"

He leans his head back and exhales a column of smoke. "Why?" he repeats my question. "And what would you have done, Bary? Would you have agreed, if we came to you with the idea?"

"You could have fucking given me a chance!" I'm losing it a bit, I should calm down. I have to keep my head cool; yelling will lead nowhere.

"We simply were not sure. Don't look for any other reason in it."

"You had no right to decide for me."

"Let it go," he says wearily. "It's all gone now."

"Gone? It depends."

"Look, Bary, I am sorry about how it all went wrong. First Jakub and then your problems, but—"

"*Problems*? That's what you call it?" Again, I'm raising my voice—but I can't help it.

Only when we got out of the fucking truck did the hell start for me. Jakub's death, the police investigation, nightmares, depression. Pills, alcohol, and more pills. And finally, a six-month stay at a psychiatric ward, when I could no longer deal with the recurring nightmares of four gun barrels in front of my eyes.

"Shit, Bary, I . . . Will it help you if I apologize like Anton? Hardly."

"You, apologize? And how about Jakub? Will you apologize to him too?"

We're looking into each other's eyes, our faces almost touching. We're both agitated—I can see how he breathes fast, his nostrils widening with each exhale, but I am not afraid of him. In the past, I used to be scared of nightmares, but if you can survive this, nothing can ever frighten you.

A man in a security uniform was standing with one hand raised, the other hanging limp against his body. Even the smallest movement caused such pain in his shoulder that his eyes teared up. One of the balaclava-clad men was sitting in the driver's seat of the station wagon, pumping the gas pedal; two others were in the process of transporting the last boxes of cash; the fourth was waiting, his shotgun cocked. Then the shot rang out and dozens of lead balls deformed the face of the security guard beyond recognition. As his body started to collapse, the murderer was already on his way to the getaway car.

I do not stop watching him. He's waiting for me to say something, but I remain silent. After a while, he can't take it.

"What do you want from me, Bary? What the hell do you want?"

I still wake up at night from time to time. I have a feeling that a huge, rusty roadster is charging toward me. I still remember that impact, just as I remember Anton's reaction, when he turned the wheel sharply to the right. Or . . . perhaps the impact made him lose control of the wheel. I can't say for sure. Just as I can't explain why it was him who drove, when it was my turn. It is peculiar that I don't remember it, because the police asked me about that a few times.

What do you want from me, Bary? What the hell do you want? I hear it as an echo.

"I want my share, Dan."

"Your share?"

"Yeah, my share. Compensation for the pain; satisfaction. Call it what you will."

"Bary, for god's sake . . . it's been five years!"

"So?"

"So? How much do you think is left? We got peanuts; back then we were only cogs in the machine."

Sure, just cogs in the machine. Dan, the dispatcher—dispatching the cars full of money, and once we drove out, he informed the balaclava-clad men about the chosen route. Anton, who was supposed to assist so that the transport of the cargo would go smoothly. And then, finally, me and Jakub—two fools who did not know about anything and found ourselves in the middle of a storm in which one lost his life and the other lost his sanity.

"You should have warned us. This was a con, Dan."

"Would it have changed anything?" he mumbles.

"Jakub could have lived." I am looking at him, but he does not react.

I don't know whether Jakub did anything to defend himself back then. Anton and I were lying facedown by the trees at the edge of the forest with our hands tied behind us, and we couldn't see what was happening behind the car. Or at least I didn't see it. I dug my face into the dirt and closed my eyes. I had no idea what to expect. I was quiet, and I even prayed silently that I would survive. Then when a shot sounded out of nowhere, I did not understand why I was still alive.

Dan is silent—I have no idea what's going through his head.

"We were not sure with you," he says after a while. "But Jakub . . . he would not have been able to digest it."

He's right about that. At least as far as Jakub is concerned. Jakub felt as if he was the last one in the world with a sense of justice, so sometimes it was unbearable to be around him. I don't know what I would have done if Dan and Anton had come to me. But I am sure about what Jakub's reaction would have been.

"Moreover," Dan says, "you knew his family. It simply would not have ended well."

Sure—Jakub and his family. Four brothers growing up without parents, the youngest of whom originally worked with the police but then transferred to a security firm, perhaps to compensate for the dirty tricks the remaining three pulled for a living. When I met them at his funeral, my hands started to shake.

"Maybe we could have avoided it, Dan."

"Bullshit," he answers.

"You could have done it some other time."

"We didn't plan it! We were only pawns, I told you that already."

"Anton said that you brought those people on."

Dan takes a drag of his cigarette, and the smoke he exhales dissipates in front of my face. "Yes, that's true. Those were contacts I had from the past. He had not met them at all, except . . ."

Except for those three eternal minutes on the highway in the middle of a forest; the longest three minutes of my life.

"It bothers me a lot, Dan," I say. "A whole fucking lot!"

He goes silent again, maybe waiting for me to continue.

"You did not give us a chance. That's the worst part—you did not give us a chance, after all that we had been through."

"Go fuck yourself, Bary," he snorts. "What had we been through? Do not turn us into the three fucking musketeers. Maybe that was Jakub's idea, but . . ." He shakes his head. Another cigarette butt goes flying. The wall ledge we are standing by barely goes up to our thighs. If he pushed me, I would fall twenty meters down to the wall's base. But today I have no fear. I feel at home here; in this place, I have experienced everything one person can experience. I feel as if my feet have rooted into the million tons of dirt and rocks on which I am standing. As if, even if Dan tried to push me, I would not budge. Not one inch. I used to sit on this low wall at times when it did not matter to me whether or not I fell. In one hand, a bottle, usually; in the other, a cigarette; and in my head, buzzing insects. And now . . .

Dan is watching me and who knows what he's thinking. But just as I am not afraid of him, he might not be afraid of me.

The silence is suffocating us both—for different reasons, but with the same intensity. Only a couple of meters away from us, two inconsequential and transient beings, stands the centuries-old tower of St. Peter and Paul's Basilica, rising toward the dark sky. Its bells, tolling their welcome during the day, or mourning every passing hour, are silent, just like the two of us.

"I want money, Dan."

"It's been five fucking years!"

"So?"

"I have nothing left."

"Do you know what I do now? I slave away in a warehouse. I haul boxes for peanuts. I already lost my apartment. I roam around, renting one place after another, waiting until I can dig myself out of this shit somehow."

"And what do I have to do with it, Bary?"

"Who is going to hire a guy who's spent time in a nuthouse?"

"Shit, I . . . I said I'm sorry, so what more should I do? I simply don't have any money left!"

"I want my share, Dan. Only my share—nothing more, nothing less. Shared fuck-up, shared money."

"I've told you already—we're not musketeers. We've never been."

We've *never* been? Okay, probably not. But still . . .

Four cops, in cahoots from their initial training. Uniforms, pistols, cars with lights and sirens. Mostly Anton and I were partnered, and Jakub and Dan, but sometimes we mixed things up.

We disciplined drivers, chased petty thieves, collected junkies from parks; it was a routine job. After ten years, Dan was the first to give up. He found a job with a security firm guarding department stores and banks, and transporting money. In the following two years, all three of us joined him.

"I'm serious, Dan."

"And I am seriously telling you, again, I have nothing left."

He is brusque and uncompromising. This time I know he's not lying. But that changes nothing.

"I don't care." I shake my head.

"I told you everything I wanted to," he closes the discussion, and puts his hands into his pockets again.

"And I am telling you—you need to take care of this. Do what you can."

"Don't piss me off, Bary!" he hisses, and takes a step toward me. In his agitation he takes his hands out of his pockets again, but they're empty. "There's nothing left, don't you get it?!"

He turns to leave, so that I really get it.

"You squander two million," I place my palm on his back, "but for me—who, other than Jakub, ended up in the deepest shit—you don't even have spare change?"

He turns to me again and his eyes are only a few centimeters from mine. "I didn't get any two million," he says. "I have no idea what Anton told you, but it was far less."

I watch him. He's upset; he's speaking with emotion and points a finger in my face.

"Okay," I nod, "calm down. He told me exactly the same thing."

"What?"

"That it was less."

It's starting to drizzle. The droplets are cold. A few of them land on my face.

"So then why do you keep talking about two million?" Just a moment ago he was staring daggers at me; suddenly, there's something else in his look. Uncertainty, alertness. He takes a half-step back, perhaps without realizing it.

"He got that money, but you know that better than me. Supposedly, you exchanged part of your share for a favor." As I speak, I tense up a bit. I try to ready myself for the blow which, so far, is not coming.

"What the hell are you talking about, Bary?" His face, tone of voice, eyes . . . everything confirms what Anton said.

"He told me that you traded a portion of the money for Jakub."

He's quiet and stares at me with piercing eyes. For a while I can stand his look, but then I turn my face toward the city again. I want him to see that he does not have to fear me.

"I do not want to judge you, Dan. I don't know what was between the two of you."

"Shut up! Shut up, Bary, you never—"

"It doesn't matter to me!" I yell at him. "I don't fucking care, do you understand? Jakub is gone, has been for five years, and I have to take care of myself. Here and now!"

He's quiet. He's standing beside me, breathing excitedly, and he does not seem to notice that the rain has become heavy. It seems to me that the trees in the park lean closer to us and barricade all escape routes. As if they are forgetting their friendliness with which, on sunny days, they hide lovers on the local benches.

"What exactly did Anton tell you?"

"It doesn't matter. I just want my share."

"What the fuck did he tell you?" He's seething. I know these states of his. He's dangerous like that; he has trouble controlling himself.

I inhale. "Apparently, Jakub found out that you had been involved with one of his brother's women, and he wanted to tell him. At least according to Anton. I am not quite sure. There had to be something more, but apparently you got scared, so you used the robbery to have him killed. That's why you got less money."

"Shit, Bary . . . surely . . ."

"I've already told you that now I have to take care of myself. How did you put it? That we were no musketeers? Probably not. Jakub can't help me anymore, but you can."

I expect him to look down, but he peers into my eyes. I withstand his gaze because if I dodge it, I've lost.

"What do you want, Bary?" he finally asks, tiredly, staring down at the ground somewhere beside my legs.

"You know that already. Compensation. Satisfaction."

"Compensation, satisfaction." He grins, but his façade is already crumbling. I feel it from his every pore, every word.

"Exactly."

He's silent for a while, but then he slowly looks up at me. "How much?"

"How much?" I echo.

"Yeah, Bary, how much?"

I'm looking at him and almost imperceptibly nodding my head, as if just for myself. "I don't think it's about money anymore," I say.

Surprised, he furrows his eyebrows. "No? Then what is it about?"

"You probably wouldn't understand, Dan."

"Don't piss me off, Bary! You hear me? Don't piss me off! What is it you want then, if not money?"

This time I am silent. I watch a man I do not know, whom I have never known. He's standing in a soggy jacket, rain droplets trickling down his face and hands.

From the dusk behind him, three figures emerge.

"Hello, you son of a bitch," says one of them through clenched teeth, and Dan turns sharply. He wants to back away, but there's nowhere to go; behind him, only the low ledge of the castle wall.

I am slowly turning and leaving.

"Bary! Fuck, Bary!" I hear behind me.

Jakub's brothers will also want to know the name of the shooter and his companions. Even through the droning patter of the rain, I hear the crackle of the stun gun.

Will I finally sleep without nightmares? God only knows. Maybe I've just replaced them with new ones.

But sometimes you simply have to see things through.

AMATEURS

BY ŠTĚPÁN KOPŘIVA

Hostivař

It was true love. He knew it with absolute certainty. Not only did he suffer from all the physical symptoms—his heart beat wildly, his stomach tightened, and phenylethylamine sizzled in his brain like scorched oil. His psyche wasn't spared either—the feeling of harmony and trust was so strong that it left Huk off-kilter. As a consequence, he felt permanently unbalanced, and he had to force himself to concentrate at all times; push himself to focus on every task, and constantly remind himself that he could not afford to make any mistakes. Particularly on a job like this one.

He got up earlier than usual. He put on shorts and a T-shirt; slid his feet into worn-out sneakers. By the door, he checked a barrel with leftover hydroponic water and grabbed a digital pH tester, toothbrush, and toothpaste from the table.

Suong was still asleep. She was lying on a mattress in a corner of the office—only a strand of her black hair and one bare foot poked out of the sleeping bag. By this time in the morning she was snoring quietly. Huk couldn't even look her way without feeling electricity under his skin.

He opened the door quietly and slipped out into the warehouse. It measured 490 square meters and was empty except for a construction frame hanging from the ceiling to the concrete floor. In the frames were stretched sheets of foil: on the back, black; on the front, white; the trusty, reflective Orca Grow Film. Huk lifted the flap in the corner that served as an entrance and stepped into the greenhouse.

The heat slapped him in the face with a ringing twang.

* * *

During the past seven years, the Vietnamese have completely overtaken large-scale cannabis cultivation, Bartoš claimed. *Not that the Czechs were pushed out completely—many of our citizens are still involved in growing cannabis on a small scale, in all sorts of indoor boxes, but all that is incomparable to the scale on which the Vietnamese mafia operates. They rent warehouses on the outskirts of Prague where they can grow not hundreds, but thousands of marijuana plants. That means earnings of twenty to thirty million korunas from one harvest. The Vietnamese mafia has the means to conduct this type of illegal business: infrastructure, international contacts, human and material resources. With time, the mafia has also acquired very solid know-how. For example, at the beginning, many large grow operations were uncovered due to their very high electricity consumption—whether they used it illegally or paid for it, the Czech utility company would always find out. The moment the Vietnamese realized that, they reassessed their methods. Today, they make no such mistakes, and the quality of their product has improved. The Vietnamese mafia originally used slave labor—if that poor soul imprisoned in the greenhouse had food delivered through an elevator shaft, that would have been a sporadic luxury. Okay, maybe not so sporadic, but the moment that the mafia discovered that a gardener's specific knowledge could influence the quality of the product, they stopped the practice. Today, they only hired people who knew how to measure pH, use substrates and fertilizer, what to do when the plants lacked magnesium or phosphorus. To put it simply— they were experts. No amateurs allowed.*

The warehouse had three exits: front, back, and through the loading ramp. Huk used the back one. In the small space between the warehouse and fence, the trampled grass pretended to capitulate, but was really lying in wait for the enemy's attention to weaken so that it could attack with wheatgrass and cat's tail. Right by the fence, a Babylonian tower of rotten wooden pallets was dramatically crumbling, and an electric motor was quietly rusting through. But most importantly, the electrical heart of the large greenhouse was parked there: two diesel Volvo Penta units, each with a capacity of 450 kilowatts. They were on for twelve-hour cycles; in addition to the metal halogen lighting of the warehouse, they also powered fans and vents. Huk urinated by the fence and walked to the outside water basin. He washed his hands, wet his toothbrush, and squeezed out a bit of striped toothpaste. He could have done all of that inside (there was a toilet and a shower next to the office), but he did not want to wake up Suong—he wanted to let her sleep as long as she could.

The Hostivař morning smelled like rain and hot exhaust fumes. Huk was standing by the fence, brushing his teeth, and through the wire fence he gazed out at the empty lots, metal enclosures, and cracked asphalt that stretched all the way to the train tracks. Hypsman's industrial park, the rotting factory quarter dating back to the first republic, seemed to have disappeared into an architectural vacuum. Here and there the oblong façade of the Prague Glassworks stood out as part of the new development, or the wheat silo of a steam mill; metal scars on the highway glistened—the fragments of railroad trailers that now went nowhere. The steam mill hadn't worked for ages, and the nuclear accelerator that used to be there was gone too. The mill had been turned into movie studios before the Protectorate; they made such seminal pieces of Czech cinematography as *The Little Mermaid* and an ad for the shoe brand Baťa. Today, they were shooting *Street* here.

Currently, the main technology used to uncover marijuana growhouses is thermography, Bartoš explained. *Even if the boys get an independent energy source, sophisticated filters, and other fun stuff, the building will light up like a Christmas tree through the infrared camera aimed from a helicopter. The most sophisticated polystyrene insulation will not cover up heat. In this way, NPC uncovers around sixty Vietnamese-run greenhouses every year.*

* * *

Before she left, she'd hugged Huk tightly and kissed him. And again—it was not only the physical contact, the touch, that crackled with static electricity. It was as if Huk's nervous system was tuned to receive other frequencies. He perceived the apexes of her brain waves, her swinging polyhedron of emotions, her energy stimulated by caffeine, and perhaps something more—suppressed tension.

"Are you okay?" he asked.

Suong disengaged, and smiled. "Of course."

He remembered when he'd first seen her. He thought such a pretty girl would not even look his way. But the moment he pushed through her superficial persona, he understood that Suong never believed in first impressions. She always carefully examined, weighed, and thought out everything—and once she decided, she acted directly and briskly. It was one of the many things he loved about her. When she exited the building, she turned one last time to look at him over her shoulder. She brushed back her hair and gave him a final glance. In that moment, Huk thought he could stand there forever; his legs apart, in the doorway to the prefabricated hall, the entrance to the illegal Vietnamese marijuana growhouse wide open; and he would simply keep looking at her.

He slammed the door and turned the key.

Suong heard the door banging behind him. She heard the double click of the lock but she did not turn anymore; she continued walking up the driveway, past the always-open gates that had become overgrown by a bush of hawthorn, out from the grounds toward the main street. She walked past the bus stop, where a retired-looking man in a Manchester hat was waiting; he looked her up and down but she was used to that and ignored it. At the corner, she turned. She did not go far, only to the white truck parked by the sidewalk.

She tried not to think about what she was doing—not necessarily because she felt guilty, but simply because it felt better. In fact, she was sure of this: despite the fact that it tasted like betrayal, it was no betrayal at all.

Suong banged on the side of the truck, knowing that Dan could see her in the rearview mirror. The door slid open and Emil's thatched head peeked out onto the street, glancing both ways. "So? How does it look?"

"Good." She was surprised by her feeling of disgust at herself. Fortunately, the feeling dissolved fast.

"He doesn't suspect anything?"

"That one?" she said. "Dude—he eats from my hand. I have never met a bigger idiot. An exemplary piece."

"Clever girl." Emil smiled at her vacantly and shifted so that she could get into the truck.

She closed the door behind her.

Emil slammed the truck door and turned to his snitch, observing that, in spite of what was about to take place, Suong was remarkably calm. Emil hated the cliché about Asian self-control (this was not his first operation, so he had seen more than enough hysterically screaming Vietnamese), but he had to give it to Suong—she knew how to handle herself. And also, she knew how to bargain. Twelve percent from the take? Just thinking about it made his chewing gum turn bitter. But there was nothing he could change: it was her mark, and it was she who had slept with the gardener, the dirtiest job.

"Do you know how many plants there are?"

"A little under a thousand. Let's say about nine hundred." Her clear Czech, complete with a Prague accent, had always fascinated him: all those wide-open vowels and adjectives decorated with twisting *eys*. Suong was a model second-generation Czech Vietnamese. Her parents came to the Czechoslovak Socialist Republic at the end of the 1980s, thanks to the agreement between socialist countries on educational apprenticeship visits, along with tens of thousands of other Vietnamese. That agreement was one of the main reasons why the Vietnamese community in the Czech Republic had such a strong historical background. Suong was born in Prague, grew up there, and went to school there. Her accent both irritated and attracted Emil. Just as Suong herself did.

"Nine hundred plants?" Emil multiplied fast. "After drying, that could make three, four million if we sell to Vizier."

"So much? Dude!" Bombay was beside himself, as if this changed anything for him. Everybody knew that however much he earned, he'd be broke within a week. Emil allowed him on his team only because he'd been with them since the beginning. It was not clear, however, how long this arrangement would last. What once began as a hobby had morphed into a full-time professional job—and getting rid of Bombay would be a necessary farewell to their amateur past. Bombay's psychotic history played a huge role in this decision. Even though all three of them had been users—Emil, Dan, and Bombay—only Bombay ended up with a psychological disorder. He had realized this when, riding a tram, he started hearing other random tram riders conspiring to kill him. Like any true math and physics grad, he approached the situation using disjunction elimination. He stole his father's voice recorder, and taped the voices of his would-be assassins. Clearly, that was precisely the correct technological filter that needed to be inserted between reality and perception: when Bombay listened to the recording at home later and discovered nothing but trite banalities, he committed himself the next day to a psychiatric hospital. Since then, he'd been all right—more or less.

Right now he was sitting on the floor of the truck, smiling like a village idiot and emptying crumbs from an Ikea bag. Emil and Dan preferred mountaineering backpacks: not only could they fit more product in them, but their hands were free during the operation. This was quite an advantage at the moment when their only means of defense was thrashing around with a sawed-off mop handle.

Sure, a mop handle was not the most sophisticated mode of

persuasion, but it was, unfortunately, necessary. Emil never really understood why the gardeners put up such stiff resistance when attacked. The product was not theirs, after all—it belonged to the Vietnamese mafia—and that was, in Emil's opinion, another example of an organized system that deserved to be robbed.

"So?" Suong asked. "What's the holdup? Let's go!"

Dan, sitting in the driver's seat, turned his head.

"Let's go," Emil confirmed.

The truck pulled away from the curb.

Robbery of the Vietnamese growhouses happens more often than you'd think, Bartoš smiled. *Most of the time, the culprits are Czechs or Slovaks. Not surprisingly, the same historical development occurred in the Czech Republic as in the rest of Europe. Organized crime had been overtaken by a multinational conglomerate—mainly the Russians, Ukrainians, Nigerians, Vietnamese, and Kosovo-Albanians—and the Czech underworld had been downgraded to support services or had dissolved into smaller groups that are now trying to piggyback on the international syndicates. From this point of view, the Vietnamese are an ideal target because their community is the most closed off, and so they cannot always identify the culprits. In other words—it is a relatively easy way to get loaded, and while doing that, a Czech criminal may still consider himself important.*

They backed the truck behind one corner of the hall so that it was not visible, but it was close enough for them to jump back in and speed away. Emil and Bombay pressed themselves against the doorframe, one on each side. Suong banged on the metal door.

"Sweetie?" she called out. "It's me. I forgot something, let me in please."

There was a short, absolute silence; Emil heard only the soft thump of his own pulse between his ears. Then the lock clicked twice and the door opened.

Bombay's mop handle whizzed in the air.

The strength of the blow surprised them all. Most of all Suong, who had assumed that they would only nudge Huk to push him out of the way, but Emil was startled too. And judging by the astounded look on Bombay's face, he was surprised by his own strength as well.

To note how stunned Huk was by the attack would be unnecessary. The wooden rod struck him right in the face. Due to Bombay's height, the blow landed above his eyebrows, on the lower part of his forehead.

There was a sharp crack, Huk's head jerked, the handle broke—and Huk flew back two meters.

Emil and Bombay had trained so they did not collide in the door. Bombay went in first and behind him, Emil slipped into the hall. Dan ran in third. Suong entered last.

Emil looked over the warehouse—the foil construction of the greenhouse, the walls, bags of substrate, plant pots, fertilizer, dirty garden tools—he had seen all this many times. Then he shifted his attention to the gardener, who was sprawled on the floor. "What is this?" He pointed to the guy. "Suong? How come that—"

He didn't finish, because the gardener kicked his feet out from under him.

It was more of a reflex than a planned counterattack.

Huk was lucky that the rod hit him on the forehead, the hardest part of the skull: if he was hit three centimeters lower, his nose would have been broken—the bone pushed through his face and into his brain.

Even if he got lucky, it didn't necessarily mean that Huk was able to think or plan in any significant way. His entire sightline was overtaken by roaring pain; his skull pulsed like thunder; something hot was leaking from his eyes (perhaps tears, perhaps blood); his brain was paralyzed, and the figures around him turned into shadows behind a curtain of red mist. From afar, he heard that beanstalk of a man yell something at Suong, and intuitively he kicked out at him. By lucky happenstance, he managed to fell the giant.

With his blurry vision, he saw the tall man crash to the ground—but right away, another movement flashed past him. It was the same guy who had hit Huk before. He had now grabbed the fire extinguisher from the corner and was standing with spread legs above Huk, lifting the extinguisher above his head. Clearly, he was planning to finish what he hadn't been able to accomplish the first time around. He was definitely ready to send Huk into the world of two-dimensional objects, and Huk was just helplessly lying at his feet. Paralyzing pain cut through every cell in his body, and he was not able to move at all.

Bombay swung the extinguisher.

And Suong hacked into his back with a nicely sharpened hoe.

Bombay squeaked. He let go of the extinguisher, which bounced off the concrete right by the gardener's ear and flew off into a corner. Meanwhile, Bombay was startled, swiveling around and trying to reach the hoe which waggled between his shoulder blades.

"That's enough!" Emil yelled from the ground while Dan caught Suong from behind and grabbed her hands. "Stop that amateurish idiocy!"

Finally, Bombay successfully dislodged the hoe from his back.

"So? Are you going to explain yourself, Suong?" He gestured toward the gardener. "How come he's not Vietnamese, huh? How come he's not a gook? What's going on here?"

"Go to hell, you asshole," Suong spat.

It was not a very comprehensive answer—but in a sense, it was enough for Emil. Therefore, he did not protest when Bombay attacked Suong with rage in his face and a bloody gardening tool in his hand.

In that exact moment, something small and white and blue flew in through the door. It was a cylinder, and it was turning in the air.

Huk was probably the only one who recognized what it was,

even in his state. He covered his ears with his hands and closed his eyes as tight as possible.

It is true that we were not all that gentle handling those idiots, conceded Bartoš.

When ten mini grenades explode under your feet, each with the intensity of 160 decibels, it shakes you up quite a bit.

And when, additionally, there are four tear gas grenades of chlorobenzalmalononitrile—CS gas—it really is something to cry about.

And that, approximately, was Emil's reaction. Even if he could not remember exactly what had happened, he suddenly found himself on all fours—tears streaming from his eyes, snot in his nose, skin burning like it was on fire, ringing in his ears. The entire world was swinging in the discs of white smoke and Emil was suffocating and vomiting on his hands. He perceived the figures in black uniforms as if from a distance. They came out of the smoke and yelled at him to lie down on his stomach and put his hands behind his head—to lie down and not to stand up, so hurry, hurry—now, you asshole! He did as they ordered him to do and sank down in his own puke, and he felt the policemen pull his arms behind his back and fasten plastic handcuffs on his wrists—he now knew for sure that he was out of the amateur league.

Huk was ungluing his eyes slowly and painfully—it took some time to get his vision sharp enough to see the guys from the ESU, who had infiltrated the hall through all three entrances and were now standing above the bodies on the floor. They were securing Emil and Dan, and calming the resisting Bombay. One such figure clad in black was even standing above Huk, offering him a hand. "So how is it going, Huk?"

He took the offered hand and let himself be pulled up to his feet. Because of the gas mask he couldn't see who the person was—

was it Pergl or Fiala? "Good," he croaked. "I'm okay."

"Really?" said Pergl or Fiala. "Your face is all bloody."

"Oh well," Huk answered, "they hit me with a mop."

The tear-gas haze was breaking into cotton candy–like tufts, and a man from the team who had been recording the entire operation pointed outside. Solemnly, Major Bartoš himself marched into the warehouse along with some VIP from the Ministry of the Interior. They both wore bulletproof vests and gas masks. Bartoš was explaining in a low voice that this Vietnamese growhouse had been secured three weeks ago, and they had used it as a decoy. First Lieutenant Břetislav Hukvald—he pointed at Huk—had pretended to be a gardener, and together with his informer, they'd lured the gang right into the trap. The VIP nodded his head in awe and looked as if he wanted to shake Huk's hand, but Huk ignored him, because, finally, he saw Suong.

He approached her at the same moment she started walking toward him. They fell into each other's arms, and Huk felt relief enveloping him, perhaps even euphoria. Not just because they got Emil and his group exactly as planned, but because Suong had just given him definitive proof—she had lured them and betrayed them for him, for him and nobody else. It seemed to Huk that everything around him floated away, disappeared and lost its meaning—Major Bartoš and his posse, the ever-so-important VIP and the team member in charge of recording (who was just then recording bags filled with substrate, being mindful not to catch the group of colleagues on the recording who kept on beating Bombay with batons as he was still resisting, swinging the hoe wildly, yelling that they would never get him, ha ha, he knew very well all of this was just a hallucination . . .). Huk was not taking notice of any of that—only of how he now held Suong, and how she held him, and how both of them were shaking.

It was true love. He knew it with absolute certainty.

DISAPPEARANCES ON THE BRIDGE

BY MILOŠ URBAN

Charles Bridge

"So, everyone pay attention," the technician said, and then paused dramatically. "A camera with a chip is fine, but these ones have their own kind of intelligence and, to top that, are high definition. This means that they can independently count the number of people on the bridge; they can remember a face which they then know to distinguish from a hundred million other faces. But what's more important, they can identify a criminal even if he is not in their memory yet. And you can then zero in on that person and probe him."

Soukup looked around at the audience and gloomily admitted to himself that his lecture hadn't yet made the kind of impact he would have expected. *The police are probably too dense to appreciate this kind of technology.*

"The cameras can identify the criminal based on what?" Officer Vacek asked.

Based on shit, thought Soukup, though out loud he said that it's based on the concentrated look on one's face—but absolutely not based on skin color, because the European Commission for the Improvement of Monitoring Technology is particularly sensitive about the issue.

Vacek looked at his boss and they both turned the corners of their lips down. Well, if the European Commission watches it . . .

The technician continued his lecture. This was his fourth one—the first was with the city police at the castle; then in the Old Town Square; next in Malá Strana. But here, it was more interesting: the cameras—twelve of them altogether—monitored the Charles Bridge, where the migration and fluctuation of people is great, comparable to the area under the Eiffel Tower or Piccadilly Square. Not that the sea of people here was identical—the bridge couldn't support such masses—but the movement was similar. He touched the monitor and the number *679* appeared in the upper right corner. It immediately changed to *682*, then *674*, then shot up to *711,* because from both sides platoons of tourists came marching, following their guides. From the Old Town Square side came Koreans or Chinese; from the Malá Strana side, what looked like Italians.

"One day it'll crumble under the weight of all of them," Matlach, the shift commander, said.

"I hope soon," Vacek responded. "I can't bear to see that bridge anymore."

"Our cameras will watch it for you," Soukup assured him.

"Turn off those stupid numbers, it gets on my nerves how they keep on changing," Matlach grumbled as he put his lips to his electronic cigarette. "It's like I'm watching gas consumption in real time while driving the car. Then I don't really watch the road; I stare at the dashboard instead. I wanted a car without it, but apparently they don't sell those anymore."

"That's great that you don't have to smoke outside," Soukup remarked. "If you excuse me, I'll have one out on the sidewalk."

"That's unnecessary, we have a police backyard here." Vacek nodded at his boss to make sure he was okay with it. "I'm going with you."

"To the backyard?" said Soukup. "Where the inmates walk around in shackles? I'm not going there."

"Come on, smart guy."

Vacek hoped that he would not be sorry for having a cigarette with this kid.

"That was great," the young man laughed in the backyard, and lit his cigarette without offering the light to Vacek. "How your boss wanted to turn off the numbers. An old brain simply can't track both at once—the numbers and the images."

Vacek shrugged. "You can't fault him. Those cameras only remind him of his looming retirement."

Soukup was inhaling his already exhaled gray-blue smoke. He had gotten used to the fact that a few policemen could be smart, but the majority are fatheads who have no technical foresight or sense of humor. This one was trying to be approachable, but to him he was just as dead as the old boss. "I also don't think those cameras know everything," he tapped ash into a broken cup placed on a beat-up chair, "but if they announce that somebody is sticking a hand into somebody else's pocket or handbag, then I think it's useful."

"It's clear to a robber that we're here to stop him," Vacek commented. "We also stop thugs, vandals, and those idiots on the bridge who climb on the baroque sculptures. I am not worried about that. But what if one person supports another, for example? What if people simply walk across hanging onto each other, or maybe they just want to take a picture by a sculpture? What if the camera sends us to get those people too?"

"That has not yet happened. Your other departments would already be complaining. Until you get familiar with a new thing and you really learn how to use it—and that sometimes takes a long time with the police, please excuse me for saying so—we have enough time to work the bugs out. We'll fine-tune the software and send it to your cameras. Often you don't even notice; you simply can't keep up."

If this brat wanted to demonstrate to Vacek that he had a far better and more sophisticated job, he had been quite successful. The constable realized that his cigarette didn't taste all that great and he killed it in the cup. "How exactly will the arresting camera work?" he asked.

"When it sees a pickpocket in action, " Soukup answered with a serious expression on his face, "it shoots an electric beam at him which, over a long distance, will incapacitate the pickpocket until you arrive."

Vacek raised his hand to scratch the crown of his head and the boy jumped, startled. They both knew it was all just drivel.

"Such cameras are very expensive—the criminal department will get them; the city police cannot afford them," Soukup added, and hurried back into the building.

Vacek imagined he was holding a throwing knife and that he would launch it at the boy and then watch it sink between his shoulder blades. The kid would be tremendously surprised right before his death; cloudy eyes full of reproach and self-pity.

Vacek returned into the operations room. Matlach was already waiting for them, and right away asked Soukup to go through the entire presentation again, using PowerPoint. The young man shrugged indifferently and began. Vacek, who remembered it all, stared at the monitor. He had to admit to himself that the image offered by the new cameras had the same definition as a good TV screen.

Shot: the Charles Bridge from the Old Town Tower side; the immediate space between the Pieta on the left and the Calvary on the right. Vacek couldn't help but look away every now and then from the colorfully clad selfie-takers toward the dark, still sculptures that stood in resigned silence above the unstoppable bronze river and a vibrant mass of promenading foreigners. With his finger, he tentatively touched the screen to enhance a beautiful detail of the Pieta. Some woman is kissing the hand of Jesus, just taken from the cross. He didn't know who it was. The other figure would be Mary—the mother mourning her son, that eternal old Virgin, he laughed to himself. Then there was a man—probably an angel— but who was the girl kissing the hand, as if offered to her by the dead? It could be Mary Magdalene, who sang so wonderfully in the musical he had seen the previous year. Understood—one doesn't kiss only the *hands* of superstars. Then he aimed the long-distance eye toward the sculptures right across the way, where there was a golden glinting inscription. Vacek knew quite a bit about that: it was Hebrew and it meant "the God of multitudes is holy." *And he had a saintly patience*, he said to himself, *that God of multitudes*. It was at this inscription where the city police had intervened twice already, and he personally took part in one. Once a ginger-haired American Jew, wearing a black jacket and white shirt with a hat on his head, threw a sponge soaked in black paint on Christ. He had concealed the sponge in a plastic bag. The sculpture had to be expertly cleaned, and the American—content with himself—willingly, almost gaily, paid the fine. Perhaps he had come to Prague only to do that. Another time, a Filipino who came on a chartered trip attacked the Calvary. When he saw the inscription in the language of the Jews, without thinking, out of pure Christian passion, he climbed the cross to break off the letters. His foot slipped and so he grabbed the letter on Jesus's left side and remained there, hanging. The sculpture has an electronic fence, and Vacek was there in exactly three minutes and nine seconds—he timed himself on his Casio G-Shock watch—and carefully, almost like a rescue squad, brought the small Filipino down from the cross. Before he realized it, at least a hundred people must have taken pictures of the scene. That same evening, he saw himself on social media; the story even made it onto the news. He expected to be promoted after that, but it never happened.

Soukup finished the presentation and Vacek stopped reminiscing. Matlach dryly said that the cameras were excellent but also very expensive, so the number of interventions on the bridge would now increase, even if half of them were false alarms.

Some of the officers left and Matlach sat down beside Vacek. He leaned on his shoulder which somewhat startled the constable, though he was also pleased.

Matlach admitted that it would take him some time to learn to work with the new cameras. In his opinion, there had already been plenty of innovations and the inventing should stop for at least five years, so that ordinary people could get used to it.

Soukup protested that Commander Matlach was a commissioned officer, and so he didn't need to gape at screens; he had people to do it, like Mr. Constable here. And right away, he began quizzing Vacek on how to zoom, and how to use the electronic focus on face shots to immediately search the archives for offending persons.

Vacek almost began telling him off but Matlach took it in stride and said that he intended to learn it—come what may. Soukup suggested that in this case he could explain the system for the fourth time. But the boss only waved his hand and pointed to a chair where the boy was supposed to park his bottom for the remainder of the day. Should the officer here during his shift find something unclear (all those pixels were, after all, somewhat treacherous), then he should explain everything to him in detail.

Soukup sat down and danced his fingers on the display of his cell phone. Vacek switched two of the cameras onto a full shot of the central part of the bridge. One set of lenses recorded the entire long runway. Another set, like an invisible spider, nosily moved all over the tourists: arms, jeans, heels, cameras, cell phones on selfie sticks, scruffs, and faces; when somebody started laughing, you could see all his or her teeth and the tongue down to its root.

Then a shot of Jan Nepomucký, that familiar shiny bas-relief and frequently fingered cross. They're still there; nobody had stolen them and no pilferer with a concentrated look on his face was taking anything out of the pockets of the assembled and promenading people. The numbers in the corner of the monitor stopped; the cameras, however, continued recording and the crowd flowed from one sculpture to another, from a street vendor to a portrait painter and an enamel jewelry vendor; from the orchestrion on wheels, to a moving barrel organ, all the way to the jazz band with eight players. In that moment, nobody entered or left the bridge, which was confirmed by the first and last screens. That lack of change is rare, and had been proven by students from the physics department. Especially during the high season, at the apex of tourist turnout between ten a.m. and midnight, the time period when nobody entered and nobody left the Charles Bridge was surprisingly long: an entire seven and a half minutes.

The police had this data and Soukup was aware of it, and now he was helping to configure the cameras and was teaching their use and operation to those forever unsavvy cops.

Currently he was entertaining himself with an app his friend had come up with. On the display of the cell phone, a naked young woman appeared, and he looked up. He wanted to make sure nobody could see his display over his shoulder. Good, nobody could spy on him. But when his eyes slid on the monitors in front of Vacek and Matlach, something stopped him in his tracks. He watched for a while and the chewing gum fell out of his mouth. He stuck his finger on the sculpture of Nepomucký.

"Eighteen seconds. Rewind it on this monitor and then again forward, play a loop. Over there, let the camera run."

Vacek rewound the recording and then hit play. Then he saw it too: a woman with a red hood. Peculiar clothes in such hot weather, even if the hood was attached to a T-shirt with short sleeves. In any case, the woman looked more conspicuous than the people around her. She didn't have any luggage, not even a purse. She wasn't holding a cell phone; she didn't have anything in the pockets of her tight white pants—that's the detail Vacek had to enjoy, checking out her butt. For a fraction of a second she turned, leaning against the stone fence. Vacek and Matlach peered at the lenses of her big sunglasses when unexpectedly, their view became obstructed by a large group. The people dispersed after a while, and that's when it all became peculiar: the woman in the red hood had disappeared. They played it one more time while scanning the side monitors as well to keep checking the live feed. Soukup divided the screen of the middle monitor so they saw the live feed in the upper half, while the bottom half repeated the scene with the vanished

Red Riding Hood. Nobody complimented him for it. Using his cell phone, Soukup took a picture of the last frame of the woman, when she looked toward the camera through her sunglasses.

"Have you tampered with this?" Vacek asked, puzzled. "The super-clever camera deleted that woman long-distance?"

"The police expect reliability from its business partners. Even if you're so young, you should understand that, young man," Matlach commented.

But Soukup shook his head. "What do you mean *tampered?* That's ridiculous—we're a serious, reliable business. In my opinion, that woman fell into the water when we couldn't see her. An unsuccessful selfie. Or she's a junkie and she jumped in. Perhaps she thought she'd fly. Or—"

"Stop it, you're not here to—"

"Or somebody pushed her."

"But then somebody on the bridge would have seen it, right?" Vacek protested.

"People would make a huge fuss and the phone would already be ringing off the hook. Look—everybody on the bridge is completely calm, and down there . . ." He tried to aim the cameras on the surface of the Vltava River, which worked except it was impossible to get a shot of right under the bridge. Therefore, they concentrated on the action on the bridge, their eyes gliding from one sweaty head to another. Everything was calm; slow movement, wandering from one souvenir vendor to another, endless picture-taking. The saxophone player by the sculpture of St. Ludmila had just wiped his forehead with a checkered handkerchief and exactly eleven people took a picture of him.

"The answer is probably quite simple," Matlach said. "She simply took off the hood. We do not know her hair color. Too many people, not the best view. So what? She was hot, took off the hood, and left."

"You got it, boss," Vacek said, and ignored the gesture made by his colleague who had been silently listening to their conversation from the adjoining table: she put her fingers into her open mouth and pretended to vomit.

"No red T-shirt left from there," Soukup insisted. "Are you colorblind? We would have seen her—with or without the hood."

"Perhaps she took off the T-shirt as well."

"She didn't wear anything underneath—maybe only a bra. Look, here . . ." The monitor zoomed in on the woman's torso in such detail, that, indeed, between her shoulder blades, the outlines of a bra became visible. "You have to send somebody there—right now," Soukup urged.

"There's no cause to suspect any crime has taken place." Matlach shook his head. "The cameras are not almighty. That woman left, that much is clear, but we didn't see it and neither did that miracle of yours, so get used to it. I have people out, but right now they're on Mostecká Street, near the Malá Strana square where some sort of jerk parked right on the sidewalk and is arguing with them."

"So you go," Soukup challenged Vacek. "It'll do you good to move around a little bit."

"You do your job," Vacek replied coldly. "You still haven't demonstrated the night vision to us."

"During the day? Yeah, that would be really practical." Soukup got up without a word and left the room.

"Where are you going?" Vacek called after him. "Stop! We're not finished yet."

They heard his steps on the stairs, then voices downstairs. Then—silence.

"I could run after him, a bit of training would really do me good."

"Oh, let him go." Matlach waved his hand. "He's pretty good, isn't he? If only he weren't such a little fucker . . . We'll finish the presentation when he comes back."

"And will he?" Vacek searched the monitors and in a short while pointed at the Jan Nepomucký sculpture—and at Soukup under it. "Look where he hurried off to."

"That was expected," Matlach exhaled.

The young man stopped, looked into the camera, and saluted them officially—with his palm turned toward himself. At the last moment, he pulled his fingers into a fist, the middle finger last. A challenge to follow and a vulgar gesture in one.

"So here we have an insult to the police and a recording as proof," Vacek interjected and watched Soukup backing into two groups of tourists led by a guide. He disappeared from view, then reappeared; he stopped at a puppet vendor to whom he explained something animatedly. He pointed to the place where the woman with the hood had last been seen.

"A real Sherlock," Matlach grinned. "He should have joined the Criminal Investigations Department."

"Him?" Vacek said. "He would make fun of the police force and then they would beat the crap out of him." One of the tourist groups turned toward the sculpture and created a small gathering around the guide and puppet vendor. Those two could be in cahoots and had the tourists stop exactly there, as if the artistically represented martyr was only a minor attraction of the Prague show; the major attraction being to get the tourists to purchase a few silly overpriced souvenirs.

The guide talked; the tourists listened. Somebody with his back to the camera was looking over a puppet of a devil when Soukup inserted himself into the group, repeating "Sorry" or whatever it was he was saying, trying to force his way into a clear space. Then he disappeared suddenly as if somebody had just tripped him. He was nowhere to be seen.

Matlach and Vacek both laughed; but then nothing special happened. The guide took the group to another sculpture and the vendor turned his attention to other prospective clients. Soukup had disappeared.

"Did you see it too?" Vacek said.

"Well, I'm watching it with you."

"Exactly like that woman." *High-tech cameras aren't worth shit,* he thought, *if they can't even watch out for one girl and one brat on the Charles Bridge.* "How about the patrol on Mostecká Street?"

"I'm sending them now." Matlach gave a few short orders via a transmitter.

"And can I . . ." Vacek didn't have to finish.

"Get over there, fast. It smells like some sort of setup. Be careful!"

Dripping with sweat, Vacek ran through Karlovka, and right in front of the bridge he stopped at the bookshop behind the sculpture depicting the Father of the Land. He had known the bookseller from the times when, as a city police constable, he used to patrol there. Now he left his hat there and ran under the arch of the Mostecká Gate. Ba   ton, a can of tear gas, gun, and handcuffs, all hanging on his belt. Tourists yielded to him with respect and attempted, hurriedly, to take a picture of him. Excitement in Prague.

Vacek tried to contact Matlach, but the boss was right then dealing with the URNA rapid-response unit. So the colleague who a while earlier had scoffed at his ingratiating behavior answered his call. She assured him that they had everything under control and she wished him good luck because URNA had declined to intervene on the bridge—they even laughed at Matlach. The poor soul was now negotiating with the regional commander.

Vacek checked out. He passed the Calvary sculpture and came up to Nepomucký. Seven Asian women were all touching his shiny bronze appendages. If Vacek had more time, he would love to watch that for a few more minutes.

He was in a hurry, zigzagging around, dodging tourists; he tripped on a small boy and let the mother admonish him. Soukup was nowhere to be found.

When he was near the end of the bridge—where there was no river underneath, just Malá Strana—he stopped by the stone lions near the St. Vitus sculpture. The dapper youngster watched him with his eyebrows raised in amusement and a smile suggesting playful eternity in the tender, almost feminine face. Vacek was startled by how much this saint resembled Soukup. Even in the hot weather, he got goose bumps realizing the resemblance and his sweaty shirt sucked onto his back like a cuttlefish. A crowd enveloped him, another travel expedition. It occurred to him that he recognized some of the faces—he had seen them on the monitors. He looked for the guide to admonish him—after all, others must be able to get across the bridge.

There was no guide and no children anymore, only adults with peculiar expressions on their faces. People snatchers . . . ?

They jostled him so much that he had to yell at them. As he was pushed to the fence, he realized that he was about to tumble into the Vltava. He reached for his transmitter but couldn't find it—somehow, they had clipped it from him, along with his cell phone. But he could still feel the tear gas can and gun. He tried to figure out whether the police cameras could see him here, and where exactly he should aim his SOS gesture. And at whom he should aim the gun, because he was not about to shoot into the air. Or—no, not yet. To shoot at people was still premature.

"Stand back. Stand back!"

Nobody listened to him. Was it possible they were all foreigners? He felt like an idiot. He realized that in the middle of this crowd the cameras would not see him anymore, he would have to be a head taller; he knew that he had disappeared from the monitors his colleagues were watching. He raised his hand with the can of tear gas and pushed the button. He would be choking with them, but at least he would make them disperse.

But he didn't choke. He was inhaling a beautiful scent which immediately calmed him down. He breathed through a handkerchief that was thrust over his nose by a strong hand. Surprised, he realized he wasn't holding the can of tear gas anymore, or the gun. And that was good—he had never developed a proper relationship with guns and he had always dreaded the thought that one day, he would have to shoot. His knees buckled. He was thankful to be surrounded by throngs of friendly bodies. He couldn't fall down, not even if he wanted to.

He was leaning against so many kind and attentive people.

Vacek was lying in a large room, with a headache and a dry mouth. It surprised him that he was naked and that they hadn't tied him up, though he couldn't quite move any of his limbs. He managed to turn his head onto his left ear.

He wasn't even surprised to see Soukup, lying just a meter to his left, also naked and not yet awake. He remembered everything up until the crushing crowd under the St. Vitus statue. He started swearing aloud at himself. But his voice was thin with fear which only added to his dread. So he berated himself quietly: *Idiotdummiemotherfuckerassholepolicepieceofshitnowyou'rescrewedyoudeserveityoustupidsonofabitchfuckingfuckerthey'lldisolveyouinacidthosecocksuckerswillthrowyouintothevltavayouarenotgoingtogetoutofthisshitthisisamajorfuckup* . . .

It was not quite dark yet, but not light either. The source of the tiny bit of light was impossible to identify. He moved. He wanted to sit up but he couldn't. His skin was pulling. His back, butt, legs, and arms were glued to the faux-leather surface of the mobile hospital bed. A horrible thought occurred to him—that the entire backside of his body was covered in superglue and now, as he was trying to escape, he'd tear off his skin. The glue smelled fruity, like jam or molasses. When he looked at his forearm, slapped on the board, and tried to roll his hand off, he noticed a small, dry smudge. He tightened his muscles and moved his hand slightly, but the substance pulled it back. He tried six more times, and each time he had to give up. His escape plan was scrapped.

In complete silence he could hear only his shaky, panicky, fast breath which he tried to calm down, but his terrified heart sabotaged this endeavor. Then he heard something else—a trickle of water, then dripping. Then again only breathing. He turned his head as much as he could to the side. He could only see the naked, pale young man. He looked at Soukup and pondered whether he

felt sorry for him too, or only for himself. He wasn't able to answer the question, but he was sure about his hatred. After all, the
asshole got him into this mess to begin with. Nevertheless . . . the
boy had behaved courageously, and if Vacek hadn't followed him,
the embarrassment would probably have been impossible to bear.
Suddenly, the boy jerked and moved his leg. He lifted it by the knee
and stayed like that. *He can and I can't?* Vacek was envious. Then he
noticed that the surface underneath Soukup's knee was wet.

He watched the liquid flow first to the knees and then to the
feet. A thin trickle and drops; the knee lifted. Urine was dissolving
the glue.

He, likewise, had nothing but his body and its functions. Vacek focused on his bladder—hoping the depressing atmosphere of
the room would do its magic. He imagined he was in a boat cabin
slowly sinking in seawater. It worked, although not quite as he had
imagined. He sucked in his belly and shook his hips so that he
could aim the direction. He tried to pee slowly; he needed to get
the moisture between his calves, knees, and thighs. The tempera-
ture of the liquid cooled off rapidly, and it surprised him how the
feel of it soothed him. It occurred to him that he had just acquired
a special knack for pissing.

Again—the trickle on the floor; now he had to try to lift his
knees . . .

Somebody entered the room and he went motionless again.
He heard steps from behind. Even if he managed to turn his head
a bit, he wouldn't be able to see anybody. He did, however, smell
cigarette smoke.

"Give me some too," he said without thinking, and his request
was granted. A cigarette was inserted between his lips and he inhaled baked tobacco as deeply as possible. He started coughing,
spit out the cigarette, which continued smoking by his hair and ear.
Somebody picked it up and held it in the air. A female hand. Again,
he got a puff, inhaled and exhaled twice more, and then—nothing.
The cigarette disappeared.

"Pig," a woman's voice said. "And that boy too. Her—no. A lady from England—that's so obvious."

"What lady?" he asked in a hoarse voice.

The woman walked around the bed and he could finally see her.

Perhaps forty, but thanks to her slim figure, she looked younger. A pretty woman; the type who could have been in modeling years ago, and if not, her figure was certainly still great. Dismissive, cold, shrewd. She looked as if she were ready to hit him between his eyes, but there was also a look of resignation. Oh no, this one would not beat him. Unless she planned on bringing in a tough guy to do it for her, that is.

But first, she could talk. Would she? *Please, God—let her talk!* That's the first step to some sort of reasonable solution. The atheist Vacek begged a nonexistent deity.

She looked at him and said: "You shouldn't have gotten involved, pig, especially not the boy. You're nothing special—but he's such a waste." She lit another cigarette.

"So at least save him," Vacek attempted. "He's not even twenty-five. You chloroformed him, so take him somewhere, throw him into a ditch, and let him live, okay? You don't even have to put any clothes on him in this hot weather."

She shrugged. "Maybe he's not asleep and he's only pretending. And it wasn't chloroform. I blew scopolamine into both of your faces."

"Scopolamine?"

"Something like that. And you so obediently laid down, though the guys had to deal with you then. How much do you weigh? At least two-fifty, right?"

"Only two-fourteen."

"You barely fit into the cabinet for the trinkets we sell by the sculpture."

"I fit in that? Well then, I am not so fat."

"To transport clients we also use a fake barrel organ and orchestrion, but you couldn't fit in there. She and the boy could."

"So she's a client?"

"And what did you think, you fool?"

"A sicko who lets herself be kidnapped in the center of Prague, stuffed into an instrument box, and brought into this cell?"

"In a way so that your cameras do not see it. But they did see it, didn't they?"

"Not how you intoxicate and secretly kidnap them. But this young IT superstar realized that the woman pretty much fell inside the bridge. Or . . . we aren't in it, are we?"

"Who knows?" She scrunched her nose. "Yuck, I'm getting sick."

"And what am I supposed to say?"

"It's your urine, so you breathe it as long as you have to."

"What do you plan to do with us?"

"Am I supposed to talk to a corpse?"

"Try."

"So listen, narc, Ex-in Tours is a travel agency that you probably haven't heard of, right? You are not—and never will be—our client because you're gonna get it for free. But others pay happily. Euthanasia can take different forms and when money is important, then the Czechs can offer the most luxurious product. Our package offers lodgings in the Royal Lime Tree hotel in Malá Strana, a guided tour of Hradčany, a degustation dinner at Plútó—not to be mistaken with that hole in Letenská with the same name. This Plútó is situated in the oldest gothic cellar in Rybová Street. Then, the actual walk on the Charles Bridge, where everything ends. We take care of the check out, since it's our hotel."

"And this hotel is also yours, right?" He glanced at the ceiling. "I will not be served any dinner, however."

"And you won't get the guided tour of Hradčany, either. Plus, you walked across the bridge already."

"Which still does not mean you have to get rid of the boy too. Even if he is a spoiled brat."

"Unfortunately, it does. He's woken up already, and is only pretending to be asleep."

Vacek turned his head toward Soukup, who had yanked free a wad of hair that had been glued to the table. The young man hissed in pain, but at least he could lift his head a little.

Soukup tried to pretend he was in a daze. Vacek now saw another body behind him. It was the woman with the hood. It was under her head and she was still dressed.

"Why are we naked and she is not?"

"Scent trail—should somebody be looking for you. As they already are. And your uniform would also complicate everything further. Don't worry—everything has been incinerated already. Janet here was supposed to have everything behind her so why glue her to the bed? The dissolving glue is only for fast transport . . . And for cases like the two of you dicks. You interrupted my work so I didn't manage to give her the golden dose."

The owner of Ex-in Tours bent down and then straightened up, a garden hose in her hand. He thought she'd beat him with it, but she turned the water on and started to sprinkle him. He swore but that did nothing. Then she showered Soukup as well. He managed to keep his eyes closed but based on how he moved and shook, it was clear that he had woken up.

"Stop it," Vacek said, teeth chattering. "This isn't Guantánamo."

"You guessed right—urine does dissolve this sugary glue, but water doesn't. It didn't occur to me that you would piss yourself on purpose. My mistake, nothing to be done about that now. There will be no more washing, not even after you're dead."

She started to roll up the hose when, beside Soukup, Janet woke up and shrieked.

"Shit," the woman swore. "You see what you did?"

Janet sat up and looked in disbelief at the two naked, wet men. "What's up?" she asked in English. "What's this? Who are these people?"

Mrs. Travel Agency now had a full syringe in her hand and was affixing a needle on it. "It's normal situation here, don't vorry, be happy, and it's okay like vos agreed," she said in such broken English that even Vacek recognized it.

"Not this way," Janet protested. "It was not supposed to be like this. I don't want to have anybody here. I don't want to be awake, for chrissake! Why am I awake? Why are they naked? This is all wrong, you moron!"

Soukup had stopped pretending and now shivered on the bed. He was gaping at Janet and the woman who was approaching her with the syringe.

"How am I supposed to inject her now?" She was upset. "Tell me that, you idiots. She saw Hradčany from the bridge and was ready to die. She wanted it. Everybody wants it. Every suicidal dope who cannot do it himself. What am I supposed to do now?" The arrogance and aggressiveness had left her; only despair remained.

"Get away from me!"

"And another travel company welcomes bankruptcy," Vacek said to deflect attention toward himself.

"No! No!" Janet jumped down from the bed, ran through the room to the door, and pumped the doorknob in vain. "Let me go! Please? I've changed my mind. I don't want to die anymore. Certainly not like this."

"If she doesn't want to, she doesn't want to," Vacek said. "Product returned, cancel the order."

"I'll cancel you, motherfucker."

"You have to let her go, otherwise you'll definitely be what you have been from the beginning in the eyes of the law: a mass murderer. I really doubt that Janet will let you inject her."

The woman towered above him. He saw her from below, disappointed and devastated, but also unrelenting.

And so he continued: "Where are those guys who brought us here? They could deal with the three of us easily. Except they have no idea that this is the end for Janet here, right? Or only some know about that? Did you brainwash them with your adventure-tourism bullshit? That's why they're not here and you are. If you're not able to inject Janet, she'll attack you—perhaps even kill you, what do I know—because as I am listening to her, she kind of likes living. And if you do kill her and then us, which means a murdered policeman plus a barely adult young man, you better know that our guys will finish the job and you'll end up in jail with a life sentence in a cell six times smaller than this. Do you want that? Probably not. So let all three of us go and you'll have mitigating circumstances. I'll speak up for you too."

His words didn't have the impact he was hoping for. But if he had succeeded in saving Janet and gaining some time, the main result was that the attention of the confused woman with the syringe full of heroin or some other shit turned toward the one who had caused the least problems.

She approached the young man and looked at the syringe as if she were gauging if it were necessary to inject him with all of it. To kill this mouse, only one-tenth of the dose might be enough?

Soukup was weeping now. It was impossible to comprehend his babbling. Vacek understood him deeply and was thankful that the boy was not paralyzed with fear and was making at least some sounds, even if they were unworthy of someone who was the master of modern technology.

Precisely—*was*. Vacek quietly and painfully unglued himself from the table; his back was the worst. But he managed to remain quiet. He got up and dropped his legs down. He congratulated himself on the successful removal of the glue. Dissolved using internal resources.

Janet, wide-eyed, was watching him. He put his finger to his lips—almost gluing it to them. The woman was not aware of him yet. She was hunched over Soukup like a vampire binding the victim with an embrace. The boy was jerking on the bed—both legs freed but not his arms.

Hitting the woman from behind might not work out. So a

blow to the side of her head sent her to the floor. Instead of being content that he had defused her, he became worried that he'd broken her cranial bones. He really didn't want that.

"And another business plan down the toilet." He started laughing, but immediately stopped when the door opened again. Vacek was not like most policemen—he was well read. That's why this reminded him of a scene from Poe's story "The Pit and the Pendulum"—the ending, where an officer extends his hand to the poor wretch and saves him. *Deus echt machina,* or whatever it's called. Who else but the good old Matlach would extend his hand to him? But the man in the door was not Matlach. It was one of the miscreants from the bridge. And he was not extending his hand—he had a pistol.

It popped and then Vacek was lying on the floor, but he was not wounded. Soukup and Janet cried out at the same time. He hid between the beds, beside the woman. He checked her for a gun. Perhaps a pocket gun. But where would she put it? Nearby, there was the syringe, with the needle still fixed to the plastic top. The guy quietly walked around the beds; Vacek was sliding as far as possible away from him while Janet was experiencing her worst nightmare. Leaning on the wall, she started to heave and throw up. Perhaps remains of the degustation menu?

Soukup became quiet and listened for a moment. Then he saw the man with the pistol and started to sing the old song saying that he was not a policeman and was there by mistake.

The man found his boss. "Did you kill her? That can't be!"

"Not me!" Soukup shrieked.

"Ten thousand per person, she promised. And I brought in three. So thirty thousand. Who will pay me now?" he sputtered into the young man's face.

Your fault, Vacek thought, *fixating on money all the time. It doesn't pay.* Stealthily, he scooted near the man barefoot, and when he was about a meter from him, he jumped on his back and jammed the needle into his right ear. The needle sank in deep, and he pushed down on the piston with his palm.

He had never heard such a ruckus. He was focused on holding the man's hand with the pistol aimed toward the floor, away from anybody else. For good reason—the guy shot again, two shots, both bullets ricocheting off the floor; one hit Janet in her knee, the other one just missed her. Janet fell down and her shouts almost drowned out the shooter's. With his left hand, Vacek yanked the syringe out of the guy's ear but the needle remained inside. Vacek still had him locked by his neck, while also holding the man's wrist with his right hand. As he had no more hands to use, he relied on his teeth and bit the finger the guy was using to poke at his ear. It surprised him how easy it was. His aim was precise—the knob on the finger; two joints were gone, or more precisely, they were in his mouth. Salty and sour, torn human flesh, tendons and blood. He spit it all out on the guy's neck and felt how his body started to give up. He held the man until he was lying on the floor. Vacek grabbed his pistol, aimed it at his head, and realized they were both smeared with blood and that the guy's face was completely white and he was probably dead already. Heroin meant for the client had been administered to this thug.

There was pounding on the door, a rumble and roar. The door flew open under the power of a metal ram. Vacek dropped the pistol and put his hands up. URNA had arrived. He closed his eyes and hoped that his colleagues would not shoot him.

When the mayhem calmed down, Matlach stood in front of him and looked as if he had never before seen a naked cannibal.

"A bit late in the day," Vacek couldn't help himself.

He watched the police doctor check the guy's pulse. The doctor shook his head, then headed over to the owner of the travel agency, said, "She's good," and moved on to assist the wounded Janet.

"Sorry." Matlach smiled and wrapped him in a blanket and patted him on his shoulder.

"Where are we?"

"In Malá Strana, in some old warehouse. We're a few minutes from the bridge."

"I'm still pretty much stuck, can someone unglue me?" Soukup asked, and they turned to him in surprise.

It occurred to Vacek that he could recommend to his friends from URNA an immediate and very effective dissolvent.

THE DEAD GIRL FROM A HAUNTED HOUSE

BY JIŘÍ W. PROCHÁZKA

Exhibition Grounds

The ceiling fan in the pub creaked to the irregular rhythm of my heartbeat. And it was noisier than my alarm clock—the alarm clock under my skin. I lit another cigarette to even out the beat of my heart.

"Listen—are you Štolba?"

"Yeah, the boss said it was him."

Two tables of the pub were taken up by the carnival people. There were nine of them. Beyond the windows, a snowstorm and Matěj's carnival raged. Matěj's Pilgrimage in Prague presents a conflation of four hundred years of traditions and religious celebrations with modern-day consumerism, cheap thrills, and robbery of all kinds. Pickpockets, petty thieves, fortune-tellers, and everything in between; children with cotton candy and parents with cameras and paper hats. Every year, hundreds of thousands of people visit this juggernaut of entertainment. And the same number complain how the merry festival becomes more expensive and screechy every year. Dozens of merry-go-rounds, hundreds of shooting galleries in caravans, stands with sausages and mustard. Eurobeer and the lethal combination of Fanta-Cola-Sprite everywhere.

I was ignoring the crap from the bar. I was waiting for somebody.

"Hey, old fart—I need something from you. The boss called!"

I was sitting at a table with a stale beer in front of me. Behind me, a coat hanger; above me, a fan.

"Hey! What's up? Don't you hear me?" bellowed a tattooed man from the carnival group.

"Arnold, you dummy, go talk to the detective yourself! Or are you afraid of him?"

In a glass ashtray, I built the Pyramid of Cheops out of cigarette butts. The approaching Arnold looked to be about forty. Tall, muscular, and sullen, with dirty-blond hair. Almost like me. He came up to me and leaned on the table. His arms were as large as my thighs. On his chest hung a gold chain thicker than the one on the Tower Bridge. I raised my head.

He was staring at my eyes. Sharply, as all the worldly guys do when somebody ignores them.

"Didn't you hear, shithead, that I need to talk to you?"

"I didn't hear enough to answer you," I replied.

The door behind the bar creaked.

Everything around the door was illuminated like those colorful pictures of saints. An individual exuding the dignity of the Dalai Lama and the toughness of Vito Corleone entered the grimy pub. Merry greetings sounded from the table with the carnival people. The shepherd came and with a magnanimous look examined the room in a nicotine haze. Arnold was still staring at my face.

I was silent. What was I supposed to say to that walking steroid anyway?

Baffled, the hulk turned. "Dad, he's still ignoring me."

"Try to greet him, Arnold," the elder advised. He was about seventy, gaunt as a fakir. This was a man who, with all of his 130 pounds and a pipe, managed a huge circus-carnival family. He wore a leather jacket, gold around his neck, gold in his left ear, and, surely, gold in his heart. And he was sad. "And only then offer him our proposition," he added.

"Did you hear the big boss?" Arnold slammed his fist on the table. The top butt fell off the pyramid. I was sorry about that. That one was the toughest to position.

"Here's your new beer, Štolba." The server, Julča, circled the hulk.

"Thank you, sweet Julča."

"We need something from you, snooper." The giant pushed the frothy drink to the side. The two tables near the bar fell silent. Arnold again slammed his fist on the table, causing beer to splash on the cheap flower-patterned tablecloth. Goodness, why does he do that, the oaf?

"Did you lose your tongue?" he hollered into my face.

"God, what an idiot," came from the group of travelers. That was the big boss.

I watched Arnold's scarred hand, bigger than that of the brown coal digger in the Mostecká Basin. It was scratched and scuffed like the hands of all carnival and circus men. These guys build their autodromes and centrifuges and circus tents and merry-go-rounds in rain and sleet. Their hands are as scarred as their souls.

I slammed his palm on the table and flashed my other hand. The opaque blade of the Konol knife hacked between his pointer and middle fingers. He held them close to each other and now a jackknife was sticking there. From the pointer and the middle fingers, a drop of blood leaked out. I pulled the knife out from the table and put the sharp edge to his neck. I saw the travelers scurry our way, together with the bouncers. I was expecting them. I had experienced those types of SOBs in the hundreds, but that was back in my previous life . . .

Back then, I was still alive.

Behind the jittery guys with jittery jackknives, Don Corleone came up. "Arnold, you're not doing it right." He put his hand on the guy's shoulder. "This is our Mr. Štolba, right?"

"I don't remember you adopting me," I said.

"Good day." He smiled at me. But he was still sad. He reminded me of a gravestone wet with rain and lit up with circus neon. With the tip of his thumb, he touched the sharp edge of my knife. Gently, he pushed it away from Arnold's throat.

I liked him. It takes a confident person to play with a knife's sharp edge at somebody's neck with his bare palm. On his wrinkled face one could assume a smile, only thanks to a slight curvature of contour lines around his eyes, mouth, and nose. His gray eyes were hidden between wrinkles as bottomless as the state's debt.

"Please excuse my awkward entrance. Arnold really tries, but he is a tad dumb. Right, boy?"

Arnold clutched his bleeding hand. He wasn't answering. It was his son; that was as clear as a sunny day.

"Yeah," I nodded. "You shouldn't let him go out without supervision."

The man slipped Arnold behind himself, to safety. He sat down across from me. The chair creaked. I'm not sure why I felt like everything there was creaking . . . the fan, the chair, personal relationships, communication, the tap on the right side. All that creaking, a badly oiled world.

"Allow me to introduce myself. My name is Ferdinand Goodwill Traveler and I govern a successful traveling company."

"That sounds like a phrase from Wikipedia."

"From what? I employ more than seventy people." Perhaps he expected me to fall off my chair. I only burped and wiped my mouth.

"So?" I slid the knife into the sheath on my belt. I may have retired, but I still wear my equipment, including a Glock in an underarm holster.

"I have plenty of money," he said. "And it's urgent. Very urgent."

The guys were still standing behind their big boss. The rhinoceros on the right had a scar across his cheek; the thin man and the fatso on the left beautified themselves with about twenty earrings each. Mr. Fatso was also proudly exhibiting a nose ring in his splayed boxer-like nose.

"And these are your bodyguards?" I took a sip of my beer. The froth had already thinned.

Ferdinand shook his head. "No—family. You have met Arnold already, a weight lifter, acrobat, and animal keeper. These two—who look like Laurel and Hardy—are Laurel and Hardy. One works in the shooting gallery, the other with carousels. They are also both clowns in the circus. And Hardy is a tamer too. This is House. That scar on his face is from our lioness Elsa. He's a keeper, and in charge of feeding. And all the rest—cages, supplies, and such."

They nodded their heads as Ferdinand introduced them. "Lads, wait for me at the table. Thanks." And the space emptied.

I leaned forward with my elbows on the table. I put my chin in my palms and gazed at him.

"What so very urgent thing do you want me to do for you? What horrible thing has happened to you?"

"My daughter was killed."

"Hmm. That's not good news."

"You have this entire evening."

I was looking into his gray eyes. Waiting.

"Twenty-five thou?" he ventured.

"Do we have something to drink to it?" I raised my pint.

Don Ferdinand waved at his people. "Bring me my favorite!" In his hands appeared shots of liquor.

"I say . . . the matter with your daughter . . . that really deserves a shot," I offered my sympathies.

"This may be the best condolence I've received in the last few hours."

We toasted. In this, I will certainly support this circus tradition.

"How about the police?" I put the shot glass on the table.

"Shit no!"

I did not ask more. It was clear. This crime was not covered by the regular law. Nomadic men have had their own laws for hundreds of years. Certainly, every small robbery is gratifying, but they are a far cry from the extortions of the banks and financial institutions of today. In fact, we're talking about only one law: an eye for an eye and a tooth for a tooth.

No nifty lawyers. No corrupt judges—of whom there's a surplus in this country. Each one of them with their deep pockets wide open to payments. These are, however, travelers—with their bizarre but nevertheless pure justice. Nothing more, nothing less. Something that those belonging to so-called proper society will never understand.

I refused Ferdinand's offer to cover everything I had ordered and I paid my bill. I can still pay for goulash and a couple of beers. And that twenty-five thou will take me through an entire month.

We went outside. It was half past eight, and it was sad.

The March storm had calmed down. Here and there, the playful wind spit a few lumps of snow into our faces. On the pedestrian island by the trams in front of the Industrial Palace, pairs of boys and girls huddled together like in a Himalayan storm. The flashing neon lights in front of the Industrial Palace lit up the caravans and groups of attendants. The wealthier families enjoyed huge centrifuges, twisters, boosters, and bungee jumps; the poorer citizenry had to be thankful for merry-go-rounds, shooting galleries, flying ducks, and bouncy castles.

But they all enjoyed it. And that was the point.

The booze tents were overtaken by the golden youth of Prague. The dumbest kids in the smartest schools.

Don't hesitate—visit a unique Prague attraction!
The last extended ride! Do not swing the gondolas!
Cotton candy! Dutch attractions! Enter the Haunted House!
Zombies, skeletons, murderers, and living corpses are awaiting you.

There really were corpses here. More precisely, one female corpse. Nonliving.

We walked inside the Haunted House past the cash register with a crying cashier. Her green eye shadow was running down her pudgy face. I was worried that the deluge would short circuit the electric tracks.

She lifted her head and gaped at me.

She had to know something.

They turned the lights on inside, which spoiled the effect of the phosphorescent walls of monsters. Visitors to the Haunted House drive in on one track, seated in blue and yellow carriages. They pass latex figurines splashed with artificial blood, with axes hacked in their heads and spilling guts. Most of the exhibits are turned on by the carriages themselves. They drive through mechanical slats which activate the sounds and electric motors in the skeletons and vampires. Everything bellows and brays and bobs. Everything grins—except for one girl.

A pretty, slim, and leggy girl hung in the air about thirty centimeters above the track. She was impaled on the large lever. The tracks here fork out into two circuits. The other one is used to park carriages. The wooden lever sticking out of her back was wet, and the girl was bent like a bow. The lever substituted for an arrow.

"Oh my god." I was practically speechless.

Don Ferdinand, gray-haired, lined, and wrinkled, stood beside me. Behind him were the corpulent, once-pretty woman from the cash register and the four men from the pub. Above it all, as if sitting on a throne, was a lit-up skeleton with an artificial vulture with a hand in its beak. From behind, we were watched by a zombie with bulbs instead of eyes. On the left, the muscly Arnold, and right behind him, a curve. In the niche with the virgin with cut-out eyeballs, the wide-shouldered Hardy with his pierced boxer's snout was dwarfing us, and beside him, blubbering Laurel with the vine of earrings was shivering. He had a small red heart tattooed on his neck, with tears running down. They were all adorned with gold chains, rings, and earrings. The rhinoceros-sized House was there, with the scar on his face. They were all there.

I kneeled down by the pool of blood. Then I looked into the girl's face. "What was her name?"

"Rosalina."

Rosalina was a blond girl with a dragon tattoo on her neck. Her body was lithe, butt firm, thighs like Aphrodite, with graceful hips. Rosalina could have stayed there the way she was. She would fit in with all the bizarre scenes better than the girl with gouged-out eyes. Another luxury attraction among the zombies.

Don't hesitate—visit a unique attraction!
A Haunted House with a real dead girl!
The last extended ride . . .
And do not throw those hamburgers at the exhibits!

For goodness sake—what is that stench? Where do I know it from?

"What do you use for upkeep with all the tracks and monsters?"

"The usual—used oil. And we clean it from time to time," Hardy answered. I inhaled the stench again. That was no oil or thinner. But it was chemical sure enough.

"She was on drugs," I asked without a question mark.

The big boss almost took out his razor: "We are travelers, Štolba! You know us, and know that we do not do the shit non-Roma do. We are worldly!"

"I'm just asking. That's why you hired me, after all."

Don Ferdinand was standing among the phosphorescent and flickering figurines. To see a father above his dead daughter—that's a vile thing that is damn hard to delete from your memory. In reality, you can never delete it, even if you used to be a cop. That's the stupid police routine that never becomes completely routine. Demons stay with you forever. And that's why you lose your dear ones. Friends. All of them. And your former friends then say: *Look, hasn't he always been a bit off? And cynical? And that black humor of his . . . prick.*

Fuck yourselves. All of you.

It is also shitty when you tell parents something they do not want to hear. Such as that their beloved child uses meth and coke. They do not even admit smoking their own joints back when they were students.

"Yes," Ferdinand answered, "that's what I've hired you for." He spoke concisely and clearly. I like this type of person even if today they're considered living fossils. I am an old policeman who gave up his badge nine years ago. I am a tyrannosaurus with a Glock and a jackknife. I try to be fair. And that vexes quite a few people.

"Do you have your own doctor of some sort?"

"He's behind you."

I turned. The planks creaked. Ah, that was the guy with a scar on his face. Typical MD. He wore a violet hoodie with an English flag and the inscription, *Cambridge.*

"I am a doctor."

"I know. You're House. I'm eager to see what outstanding medical school you graduated from."

"Fuck you. What can I do for you, Mr. Clever?"

"You know . . . time of death, signs of violence, rigor mortis."

"Everything I put together is here." He handed me a tablet.

I whistled. I skimmed with my finger. I nodded my head. "Good, doctor. Very good, House."

I was looking over the face of the olive-skinned girl. Not even the terrible grin on her face could detract from her beauty. But it was as if the beauty—even postmortem—was still experiencing a brutal, slow death.

They took Rosalina off the lever. Do you know that feeling when you're taking the chicken and tomatoes and bacon slices off a skewer? Taking a human off a skewer is worse.

The girl was lying down between the tracks, and should the carriages with visitors drive around, she'd become a horror star. She was wearing a sexy minidress or nightie (I don't have a good grasp on this area), as if she'd been getting ready for a hot tub or bed.

"Okay, then. Let's roll, people." I got up from the cadaver. Some turned away. And hunched.

Ferdinand lifted a hand loaded with rings and bracelets. All gold. And he beckoned me.

Everybody froze.

"I need to know where you were at the time of the murder,"

I began. "Do not ask, *Why me?* I don't care about that bullshit. I want your alibi, and if anybody tells me that he was jerking off in the caravan or that some girl can swear you were together that evening, you're very unlucky."

"How come?" House asked. "The testimony of any witness is valid, unless they're family."

"Bravo, doctor." I turned toward him and rubbed my fists. They cracked.

"That *Cambridge* is rather silly." I walked up to him. "Lean toward me. So that I can whisper something to you."

The travelers watched me with suspicion. Ferdinand nodded to the doctor. The scarred guy tilted toward me.

"So that you understand," I couldn't whisper, "to me, you are all one family. Clear? You're gypsies, right? And you're very proud of it. So what now?"

"So we're one family, our alibis are not valid, and we'll try to tell you what you are looking for," Arnold spoke up from the back.

"Thanks, Hulk."

"Do you know what I like about you, Štolba?" Ferdinand said.

"My honest face?"

"How delicately you communicate with people who have just lost their sister, daughter, and cousin."

"Yup, I am excellent at that." I lit another Marlboro. "Apropos, Ferdinand," and now I really softened my voice, "why do you suspect your family? Anybody from the outside could have done it."

Ferdinand hugged me around my arms and took me a bit farther away from the group. "Could have. But the house was closed the entire day for maintenance. Only us who are standing here were there," he whispered.

I nodded my head and thought of the girl. That lever was stuck in my head. And a peculiar wound in her belly. And scuffed palms.

"House, can you?" I gestured as I walked back to Rosalina.

The guy with colorful tattoos kneeled down beside me. He waved away the smoke from my cigarette and lit his own.

"What do you think about that hole in her belly?" I asked.

"Peculiar, irregular. As if somebody kept moving her around on the lever. And then here, the straight cut. They jerked her sideways or something? I really have no idea."

"To move and twist the girl—there could even have been two of them. It's better to murder in pairs."

"Two murderers?" Ferdinand took the floor. He looked over his family members—Laurel and Hardy glanced at each other. Laurel burst into louder sobs and Hardy became even more vexed.

"Maybe a murderess." I sat down in a carriage. "These days, women demand the same jobs as men."

Almara, the cashier, snorted.

"There could have been two of them who lifted her and impaled her on the lever," I continued. "Or one big guy; a giant of a man." I looked around me.

The wide-shouldered House beside me, Arnold the hulk, and Hardy the pit bull all stopped liking me. Pity.

"But we still do not have the most important thing. That which is more important that any of your alibis," I pondered.

Ferdinand Goodwill Traveler dropped his head into wrinkled palms. "Shit." He must have thought about this from the second he found his daughter. I looked at him and he nodded. He put his hand on my shoulder. "Štolba, would you like dinner?"

"Do you have meat?"

"Always. We are hunters, after all."

"Maybe you still are, Ferdinand. The rest of us—we hunt only in supermarkets."

He just shrugged his shoulders.

We went outside. Among the moving crowd, there were about fifteen people standing around the Haunted House.

Ferdinand stopped. "Motive?"

I nodded: "A dead girl in a haunted house—there could be motives enough for three horror movies."

"For me, it is enough that you find the one."

* * *

The caravan reminded me of a hotel suite, including the leather chairs and a plasma TV taking up half the wall.

"Štolba, one more thing about my family." Ferdinand handed me a plateful of food. It was spicy, meaty, and intoxicating, and it came with fresh bread. *God, I thank you for the bounty.* "They were all moving around the house all day long. They had all sorts of work they had to do in there, but to be clear—the back of the house is made of sheet metal, corrugated iron, and an asphalt roof. Anybody who wants to could get inside."

"For now I would concentrate on those who were demonstrably there, Don. And if everything fails, then you will keep the money. To suspect a random visitor of murder—especially since all of you were moving around, and Emanuela was at the register—that's idiotic. To find that shithead in one evening among the millions of Prague residents—that I really cannot do."

"I understand. But one of the neighbors could have killed her too. On one side, there's a Russian merry-go-round and autodrome, and on the other, there's a chain carousel," Ferdinand protested, even if he didn't believe all that much in what he was saying.

"What about those druggies from the fountain? There's a whole lot of them. Wasn't Rosalina selling them drugs?"

"What drugs?"

"Methadone, meth—whatever you call it."

"Štolba, we are carnival people. We have our carousels, shooting galleries, and centrifuges. And rum and beer and cigars." He leaned on the table with his hands and the veins on his arms stood out. Above him, the Virgin Mary clasped her hands. She cried over baby Jesus on a 3-D Chinese painting in a flower-patterned frame.

"The girl was not using drugs," he uttered, resigned, into the emptiness. "And I have already told you enough."

"Can I finish this marvelous food?"

"Bon appétit."

He was watching me with his gray eyes. I felt like he was reconnecting my brain synapses and altering my perception. The circus Dalai Lama engulfed me with his eyes.

"Štolba, try to find other motives. Could you?" The wise eyes had suddenly lost their color as if he had rinsed his eyeballs in paint thinner.

"Jealousy, cheating, money, extortion, competition, business, risk, drugs, or revenge," I mumbled more or less to myself.

"Would you like seconds?" He got up from the chair.

"If I can . . . it's delicious."

"The real Hungarian goulash. And by Hungarian, I mean Hungarian."

"Doctor, where were you at the time of the murder?"

"What do you mean, Mr. Snooper?" House was angry. Something was off with him.

"What was your relationship with the girl?"

"Uncle. So what?"

"Did you love her?"

"Probably not." He rubbed his eyes with his palms. "Of course I loved her. Always! Can you understand that?"

"I'm starting to. You loved her the way only an uncle can love his sweet, young, but mature niece."

He nodded, wiped tears with the back of his hand, and snorted. And then he got it. "You snooping shithead, what do you—"

"Dare to suggest?" This time *I* got vexed. "I dare to interrogate you because your niece was murdered. Should I note that you have no alibi?"

"I was in the menagerie," he said, calming down.

"And your witnesses are trained monkeys? Or zebras?"

"Shit—do you have any idea how messy it is in a circus during each performance?"

"I actually do have an idea. That's why I'm asking you."

"Laurel was there with me."

He left. He couldn't even slam the door, so he settled with breaking the cane that belonged to a poor zombie.

* * *

"I didn't do anything," Laurel teared up, twisting his mouth the same way as his namesake from silent comedies.

Oliver Hardy muscled up beside him. Stooped, obstinate, ready to attack. Like I said—a pit bull. "Apparently, you can be quite heavy in your dealings with others," he remarked.

"You heard well. And just between the two of us—has anybody asked you anything?"

Hardy took out his switchblade. The blade came out.

"Should I aim at your belly or head?" I asked. I didn't even take out my Glock.

"No! No more violence!" Laurel howled. He was either drunk or high, which worked for me.

"What are you yapping about, you stupid idiot?" I did not say this—Hardy did.

"How much violence have you experienced today, kid?" I smiled at Laurel.

"Well . . . that . . . like . . . when sweet Rosalina was impaled. Here . . . everywhere." He spread his hands. "I was always worried about her . . . And now this."

"And why didn't you defend your sweet Rosalina?"

Hardy hissed, and if he had a scar on his face, it would surely have become an incandescent red.

"Let him be, you fuck."

I turned to him. If he wanted to, he could sweep the monkey cages with me. But that's not the point. Whoever is stronger is never the point. "Hardy, you know what?"

He leaned over and put his large hand on my shoulder. He was as menacingly quiet as possible.

"Har-Hardy, he's aiming at your balls," Laurel stammered.

In the weak lighting, the Glock was almost impossible to see. Hardy couldn't stand me; I couldn't stand him.

"Do not slow down my investigation," I whispered. "Do not get in my way, ever. Do you understand?" I put the Glock back in its holster. The angular guy blinked and nodded.

"And now, kid, tell me—why didn't you help your Rosalina when you were so afraid for her?"

"Because . . . because I couldn't!" The boy looked desperately at Hardy.

"He wasn't in the Haunted House. He was with me, in the menagerie," Hardy answered for him.

"With House? Well, there were quite a few of you, like at a funeral."

"Oh go fuck yourself. And you, come with me, bro." Hardy hugged Laurel and started to leave.

"So—together again, right?" I looked at Arnold. A man bigger than the Petřín Tower and as majestic as the Charles Bridge at full moon. He was glaring at me, vibrating lashes and protruding ears. "Can you cut down the sack depicting a hanged man?" I asked him.

He didn't cut it down. He jerked it and tore down the rope from its nail in the ceiling.

"And now throw it on the lever. It's about three meters from here, right?"

He flung the sack and struck home, right on the metal lever. The sack slid on it down to the floor. "I do this at every performance. Do you want me to fling you there too?"

"Not to forget—where were you at the time of murder? And do not tell me the menagerie."

"We had a break. Before, I was lifting our acrobats, and after the break I went to lift weights. Rubber ones. Inflated."

"Where were you during the break?"

"I went to the caravan for a pick-me-up."

"You were alone in the caravan, I assume."

"No. I have Ornella there."

I scratched my nose.

"A turtle," he added.

"Well, thanks for your help, Arnie."

"What?"

"Send Madam Cashier here."

"And that's it? After flinging the sack and Ornella's alibi?"

"That's it."

I went out to gather my thoughts. I lit a cigarette and watched the hustle and bustle all around. The Industrial Palace towered above the caravans, centrifuges, carousels, and swans. It was lit by a million bulbs. The structure, with its art nouveau design, was a slap on the ass to all the curlicue Parisian buildings. Even our Eiffel on Petřín is prettier, only scaled down to one-third size. And nobody can compete with our fairy-tale Industrial Palace. Not even the castle from the Disney logo. Damn, we have the most beautiful world kitsch. And in front of it, every year until the end of times, eternal: Matěj's humming carnival. And I, instead of sipping beer from a plastic cup and eating a sausage with mustard at a kiosk, investigate the murder of a girl. A few more things I needed to ask occurred to me. I went back to the Haunted House—to the cash register.

The cashier was waiting for me.

"So what do you want from me? Should I confess to the murder of our sweet girl?"

"Yeah, that would save me a lot of work." I was looking at my notebook in the flickering light.

She spit on my notebook and face. I wanted to spit on her too, but instead I just wiped off my face with a jacket sleeve.

"Mrs. Cashier, what if you told me who you saw here that evening and what was going on around the house when they murdered the girl inside?"

Emanuela stared at me. Her rouge-red lips shook. And right away, she burst into wails: "Sir, please—find the son of a bitch! I will strangle him myself!"

"I believe it."

"Who could have done that to her? Our sweet girl had a tough life anyway. The poor girl went through everything that a circus girl can go through." She continued sobbing and the sea of tears reached our ankles and kept rising. "I saw all of our men here! Today, they were all crazy. And despite it all, she was so happy." She smiled now through her tears. Her green eye shadow mixed with her black mascara.

"Anything interesting? Did you hear anything—an argument, any other sounds?"

"No, but—" She stopped. "You can see it for yourself. How could I . . ." She trailed off.

From the cracked speakers near the carousels, autodromes, shooting galleries, and swans, disco music from the eighties howled in concert with the bawling of ushers and the roar of the masses. She couldn't have heard all that much. But she stopped. Twice.

"You're right. It's terrible." I stroked her arm. "But you did hear something else too, didn't you?"

She rubbed her face with chubby fingers and ended up with a Joker mask. She nodded, and started crying even more—I thought that would have been impossible.

"I'm not sure. I heard something breaking. Nothing more. I went quickly to the house, but nobody was there. It could have been drunks. We have heaps of broken bottles here."

This could work.

"Listen, Emanuela—can I call you that? Was Rosalina always dressed so skimpily?"

"You know, she's our girl. A cool, snazzy carnival girl. In the circus she was a flying acrobat, and girls do not overdress for that. For children, it's the acrobatics; for dads . . . a peepshow."

"But she was not due to perform. Don't tell me she went to the Haunted House like that, in a skimpy nightie."

The cashier's eyes bulged, which added another level to her already picturesque face. She understood now. "That was not a skimpy nightie. Rosalina didn't wear it for her performances. Mr.

Detective," she sobbed, "somebody had to bring her here already dressed like that, right?"

I gripped her shoulder. The clever Mrs. Cashier.

"One of ours, right?" She buried her face in her palms. And remained so. The tears had risen to the high-alert level.

"Štolba." Ferdinand was submerged in a leather chair in the caravan's living room. "I'm sending people out. They don't need to watch the Haunted House." He spoke heavily and kept his eyes fixed on the thick carpet. "You really think that . . . ?" He looked up at me again.

"I don't think. I need that proof. I have something, but I can't get it before midnight."

"Look, do you seriously want to tell me that in three hours you found the killer of my little girl?"

I bowed my head. I knew that he had tears in his eyes. Not only because of the sorrow. Ferdinand banged his fist on the table.

"Should I call those four right now? Or not until the staff finds what you're looking for?"

"I would wait. Shall we have coffee?"

"And if they don't find it?"

"They will. You sent thirty of them. They'll examine everything within the radius of two, three kilometers. It can't be on the other side of Prague, after all. The murderer had to return to the circus show. And everybody was there. But if it is not found, would a confession be enough for you?"

Don Ferdinand lifted himself from the chair. He sauntered to the coffee machine. "Štolba, you must be one son of a gun," he said, then turned holding a cup of coffee.

I lifted my hand. I aimed my finger at him, and with my arm made a movement as if I were shooting. "That's why people like you, maestro, hire me."

"Sugar?"

"No, but I do have the killer."

"Really—no sugar?"

Emanuela lit up the Haunted House. She had fresh makeup on and was as colorful as a rainbow. Again, the snazzy madam from the cash register. Hardy had a pit bull look and was gazing at the large lever. Laurel had stopped crying. He watched the carriage tracks. Arnold's eyes were fixed on the sack he threw at the lever. House ping-ponged his eyes from the lever to me, Ferdinand, and the others. The big boss was on the phone behind the coffin with Dracula.

"We can start," he uttered when he finally finished the call. "It's your turn now, Štolba."

"I know that one of you has committed murder," I began *my* circus performance. "I do not need to listen to any speeches. The only speech will be mine, you carnival trash."

"Dad! Why did you invite this idiot?"

"This motherfucker needs a beating."

I had them. I took out my Konol knife from its sheath. Policemen like this knife very much because it's practical. The spooky lighting of the house flashed on the blade. I walked around them. Laurel conjured up from somewhere a butterfly knife. Hardy readied a switchblade. Arnold waved brass knuckles around my head. In House's hand, a jackknife flashed.

"Good stuff. Mikov?" I tapped my knife on his. The blade disappeared.

"I am a killer because I have a Mikov?"

"Honestly—you lead the list, doctor. Show everyone present the fatal wound of your beloved and only love, Rosalina. And can you affirm in front of everybody how much you loved your young, mature niece?"

House pursed his lips, teared up, and looked at Ferdinand.

"Štolba," Ferdinand addressed me so quietly that I barely understood him, "in the family, we have clan and relational connections which you, even though you know us, could never understand."

"Very well. Let's go back to the wound." I raised my hand. "To the structure of the fatal wound. Your tablet please, House."

Doc walked around all the men with his tablet. I scanned them, and embedded in my memory every facial twitch. The Lord's last supper: one of them had betrayed his own clan.

"Laurel, how about meth? Can you fly?" I pointed the knife at him.

The skinny kid looked around, startled: "What are you talking about, sir? I have no idea, sir, what's on y-your mind? For god's sake, don't look at me like that! He's a devil! And he's trying to divide us! Let's kill him! Kill him! Kill him!" He was waving his butterfly knife around.

"Fine job with the knife." With a careful move, I extracted the butterfly knife from his hand. "Do you know that Rosalina, in addition to the hole made by the lever, has a knife wound?" He blanched.

"Perhaps it was *this* knife." I waved his weapon in front of his eyes, then set it down on a nearby table. "And maybe it was because of the meth she didn't want to sell you. Or because she asked for a higher price for the goods."

"No!" Laurel collapsed.

Ferdinand rubbed his forehead with his palm. "Is this really necessary, Štolba?" He looked at me with his weary gray eyes.

I slid the blade of the Konol over my throat. I nodded. And closed my eyes.

"Do you want a good kick?" Hardy walked right up to me. He glanced at Laurel and then back at me.

"Hardy, you're so dumb that you could kill anybody, just like that. Right?"

"You—anytime, snooper."

"Rosalina as well? For example, when you discovered that she was supplying Laurel with meth?"

A deep silence descended on the Haunted House.

"Shit, Štolba," Ferdinand spoke up. "You're taking it too far."

"No, he isn't," said somebody from the left. It was House. "Laurel has been using meth for about three months, Dad. We wanted to help him. Rosalina too. But it was impossible. And we knew what you would do if you found out. Don't be angry, please."

"He killed Rosalina?" Ferdinand walked up to the vibrating body. "This oaf?"

"No, he didn't. Because he was here when I talked to the girl," the cashier interjected with exhaustion. "He left and sweet Rosalina was still alive."

"Thank you," I said. "And if we know that it was not Laurel, we thus know it was not Hardy either."

"And how's that?" Hardy was nervous, but mainly he was worried about his brother.

"Because your hands are not cut."

Hardy put the knife back into his pocket and lifted his calloused, scratched hands. He couldn't understand why, but he did it.

"Arnold, House, Laurel, show your hands! The other side too," he said, instead of me.

Arnold reacted first. "I have them cut by this son of a bitch. By him—the same one I asked to solve the death of my sister," he sobbed.

"It was me who sent you to him," Ferdinand added. "Before I went to the pub."

"House, examine Arnie and tell me whether he has any other scratches besides the ones from my knife?"

Arnold stood. He didn't move.

"You have no proof of anything," Laurel squeaked from the floor. I looked over the faces of all present. It's good when you have thirty years of experience investigating murders. Then it is quite clear to you.

"You, who call yourselves—in your own jargon—travelers," I began, "*guys without fear and drugs*—you cook meth here. I came a couple of hours ago and smelled a sour chemical stench. That's generated when meth is made. I sniffed around Rosalina and I could smell it. For the stench to be that intense, it could not have been the result of just production but of an accident. For now, we can call it that."

"What did I tell you, Štolba? We do not make it and we do not sell it."

"Not everybody, maestro. Not everybody. Emanuela, what did you hear after the performance?"

"Glass breaking. I thought that it was drunks being wild."

"Should I kick through the wall behind which there is supposed to be a parking track for carriages? Somewhere near the lever? Near the lever with Rosalina where I smelled that junk?"

Hardy didn't say anything. He picked up an iron rod from the ground by the track and started to whack the walls of the Haunted House. There was fury in his action; there was hate in it.

"So where do you have it?" Nobody tried to calm him. "Where?"

Behind the three panels on the left—nothing. But behind the second panel to the right of the lever with the sack—something.

"What is it?" The big boss Ferdinand looked like a boy whose friends had stomped on his glasses.

Behind the wall, there sat a closet with an upturned table. Along with everything else needed to cook meth. Some of it was broken and scattered on the floor. But there was no burner, no flasks. Only shards. And a motive.

"A smashed cooking room," House answered his father.

"How do you know?" Ferdinand turned to him. "It's your work, or what?"

"I watch TV, Dad. On the news they give more tips about cooking drugs than any drug dealers do."

Ferdinand looked at the shaking Laurel. That boy had been experiencing disgusting withdrawal symptoms the entire time.

"Who was supplying you? With whom did you deal?" Ferdinand knew how to articulate a concise query.

Laurel was covering his head with his hands and was cowering in the fetal position: "I was selling it to the kids at the fountain.

That's why they go there! I wanted to help the family! He said we'd help everybody with it!"

"Rosalina surprised your cook," I said. "We probably cannot reconstruct the entire discussion, but I can imagine how it went. Accusations and threats that she would tell Ferdinand. An argument in the cooking room, a fight, broken glass. And she certainly told him that he had betrayed his family's rules—your community's rules—and hers as well. And then she ran away from him."

Emanuela sobbed: "Sweet Rosalina ran out of the house. She was in her performance costume. She was distraught. But nobody followed her."

Ferdinand peered into the cooking room behind the wall of corrugated metal and plaster.

"Arnold, show me the scars from Štolba."

The muscleman didn't move at all for quite a while. Perhaps he thought we couldn't see him.

"Arnold, could you show me the knife?" I asked as kindly as I could. "As long as I have known you travelers, for more than thirty years, you have always carried fine knives or razors on you— or now, more modern carpet knives. But you, Arnie, did not pull a knife on me. Not even in the pub when everybody drew their knives. Not when I asked you to cut off the sack with the hanged man. Not even now, when I pulled a knife on you. You only threatened me with your fists."

Arnold's breathing quickened.

"You have no knife," I went on. "Do you think we'll find it in Rosalina's caravan, where you followed her from the Haunted House after she threatened to expose you? To tell how you made Laurel distribute the shit? What did you do when she hid from you? Were you afraid she'd call Ferdinand? Another argument followed—that's when you stabbed her, so that she would finally be silenced?"

Ferdinand watched Arnold and me. He was as gloomy as the sky just before a storm.

"And then you brought her here, in that nightie and impaled her on the lever?" My last question floated in the air.

The reddening Arnold resembled a melting furnace.

"One moment!" Doctor House was perhaps even smarter than I had thought. "Arnold's clothes would have to be bloody if he brought her here. In the caravan, there would have to be evidence of the fight and . . ." Hurray. He got it. "Shit, did anybody examine her caravan?"

In the meantime, Ferdinand's phone rang.

"Sure, bring it here. All of it. But we may not need it anymore."

It was clear. It was clear to all in the Haunted House. The missing knife. But I was not done yet.

"Arnie, do you know what bothers me about you?" I decided to take him down completely. He hunched, the shithead—one could almost feel sorry for him. "That you did not throw Rosalina on the lever like that sack."

Even though there was silence, I could hear the boiling of adrenaline from all sides. A waterfall of adrenaline. They were awaiting my every word.

"You put her on the lever and let her slide down while the girl was still alive."

"Štolba, for god's sake," Ferdinand moaned.

Emanuela shrieked. Laurel pulled himself together and stood up.

"Why else was the wound so wide open?" I turned to face all present. "House and I wondered too. As if somebody was buffeting Rosalina on the lever, turning her around. Unfortunately, it's much worse. The girl herself caused that terrible hole in her belly. And that's why her palms were scuffed. She was fighting for her life as long as she could. Until the last moment."

"No! I didn't do it!"

That was fast. Everybody was surprised but they were still watching me.

"You positioned her carefully," I pointed at the lever with the sack, "so that the rod was inserted right into her knife wound. Which you did not quite manage. And then you left her. Alive, she slowly slid down and suffered like an animal. She was resisting using her hands, pushing them against the ground, and that's how she remained poised thirty centimeters above the floor. That's how it was. You're a son of a bitch, Arnie. You are a murderer."

Arnold, confused, looked around. "You can't believe that story! People, you won't put this on me!"

Dark silence in a dark haunted house. Outside, the carnival thundered, and here, silence thundered. The hulk looked around. He was searching for an exit route. He wanted very much to run away into the roiling masses outside. And run farther and farther away.

And that's what he did. He started like a steamroller. Unstoppable. Fleeing from the damned Haunted House. He stomped and thrashed his fists around . . .

There was a *swish*.

Laurel had thrown his butterfly knife and hit with precision.

Arnold touched his neck. Confused, he looked over everybody and staggered out of the house.

Behind him, a bloody trail followed.

"Štolba," Ferdinand said to me later in the pub, "here's thirty thou."

"You said it would be twenty-five."

"That's okay. Let it go."

I did let it go. I took the money. "Thanks, Ferdinand."

The big boss smiled and disappeared in the cigarette smoke.

He also disappeared completely from my life. I have to admit—sometimes I miss him. He was one of those men who are rapidly waning from our world. And you know yourself that there are no more men like that being born.

Two days later, I was sitting at my spot at the pub, again arranging cigarette butts in the ashtray. In the *Prague Daily*, I learned that at Matěj's carnival, an animal had fatally wounded a drunk keeper in the cages.

Interesting.

"Will you have one more beer, Mr. Štolba?"

"Thanks, dear Julča."

"Not at all."

PART II

Magical Prague

THE MAGICAL AMULET

BY CHAIM CIGAN

Pankrác

Since he'd started studying in Prague, he had wanted to treat himself to *Hamlet* at the National Theatre. He could afford only a standing-room ticket, so all he could see was the front portion of the stage; what was happening farther back on the set he had to imagine. Therefore, he did not see how the director solved the problem of Hamlet's ghost when he appeared to his son at the beginning—asking him to avenge his murder committed by his brother and the queen, his own wife and Hamlet's mother.

Naturally, in the ghost of the murdered king, Max saw the ghost of his own father who had been killed by the Nazis. But the deep vindication which he experienced avenging that murder brought him to diametrically different thoughts while riding home in a tram. When he was thirteen, he was helping a man who lived on his street in the Journalist Houses to translate books from Yiddish to Czech. The story the man gave him to correct was his own, and he'd written it in Czech. Max thought the story was peculiar—not only due to its awkward Czech, which he had to correct. It was as if the story was from another world, and he was not all that impressed by it. After all, Mr. Polakovič fought the Nazis in the Svoboda army and could have talked about more interesting things than nomads without a leader wandering through a desert.

If Max were writing a novel, he would write about the life of his father until his heroic death; unfortunately, he did not have enough material for it. He himself did not remember his father. Based on his mother's sketchy information, it seemed that she married him—a much older man, and a Jew to boot—more out of pity than love.

They discussed other things in addition to the story—things that were not possible to talk about otherwise. Max was interested in global politics: why the Marshall Plan was rejected, the Korean War, the atom bomb, and so on. He also wanted to know whether Hitler would have won the war if Stalin hadn't gotten military assistance from the United States. Mr. Polakovič answered his questions diplomatically—yes and no, or not at all. His stepfather, on the other hand, always had answers ready, but one could not believe him. They argued often because he didn't like that Max went to see Soviet military films. According to him, most of the Russian soldiers didn't even have shoes and their officers led them by the thousands against German tanks; human life had no value for the Bolsheviks. "Their mantra was," smirked his stepfather, "there's *a lot* of us!" He also said that without American help, Hitler would have killed all the Jews in concentration camps.

But what could he know about the situation in the Soviet Union if he spent the entire war in concentration camps—first in Germany, later in Russia? In the summer, when they went fishing, he overheard his stepfather telling the water bailiff that he was a colonel in the Svoboda army, trying to impress him so that he would let them fish without a permit. That's why it never occurred to Max to write a novel based on his stepfather's stories, even though he would certainly enjoy it. He talked about Mr. Polakovič as one of those Polish Jews from the Journalist Houses who had joined the Communists during the war. In reality, he was just jealous of the fact that Max would talk so much with Mr. Polakovič, whereas with him, Max would only argue. According to his stepfather, the "Polish Jew" was simply using him; otherwise, he would have to pay somebody to edit his story.

The boy was not entirely self-centered. He did realize that the old man talked to a boy from the street only because he could not talk about similar things with his friends from the Journalist Houses. Somebody else might rat him out. Maybe that was the reason why Mr. Polakovič never invited him to his apartment after their walks.

Max was curious about his living situation, and he would have liked to look at the Jewish books that were being published in the Soviet Union. Yiddish is written right to left using Hebrew letters and he was interested in this. Mr. Polakovič said that the same writing was used to write the Torah, which is more than a thousand years older than the New Testament.

At the end of February 1956, when Max was almost fourteen, he learned for the first time from Mr. Polakovič about the atrocities in the Soviet Union. He was surprised—they didn't walk toward Vyšehrad, as they always did on the main street past his school, but instead they turned right, past the Garden Store, toward the Na Děkance stadium. Mr. Polakovič led him to a barren pear tree, which had been growing there on the small, snowy, clay-filled patch of land. From here, Mr. Polakovič had a panoramic view. He leaned on his cane and, looking left and right, talked to Max for about an hour about the Soviet Communist Congress that condemned Stalin's atrocities, including all the trials of Jewish doctors, and a mass murder of Polish officers in Katyn. While he was telling him all of this, quietly and excitedly, leaning toward Max, his face turned completely blue with winding red capillaries under the skin.

"Katyn?" the boy said.

"You know something about that?" asked the old man.

"Me? No. Not at all."

His stepfather did sometimes talk about Katyn. He said that the Germans deported them there and then they had to bring out the bodies from mass graves, dredge hundreds of already decomposed corpses from the mud. He would not hear Max's argument that surely the Russians would not do such a thing. After all, the Polish fought on their side during the war, and the Russians liberated them. Those corpses must have been Soviet war prisoners who were shot by the Germans and now they wanted to get rid of them. Mother ended their argument, as always, and his stepfather had the same obstinate look on his face as Mr. Polakovič did when Max criticized one of his stories.

Max did think of things other than just politics, but with Mr. Polakovič that was their only topic. Max continued seeing him even after the story which, with his help, had been published in the *Jewish Yearly*.

"Of course, without any mention of your assistance," his stepfather teased. The Suez crisis was being discussed in the press and so Max again argued with him, because he was worried that there were thousands more Arabs than Jews.

It was a somewhat clumsy turn in the discourse. More importantly, soon after, a nephew of his father came to visit them. He was the son of his father's sister from Bratislava, which would have made this a significant event even without what it eventually led to. Despite the fact that his father's nephew was born in 1916, like his stepfather, and was twenty-six years Max's senior, they were cousins. That's why the boy could stay after dinner for the conversation in the living room with his cousin, mother, and stepfather. In addition, it was Saturday and there was no school the next day. Max could not remember what his father looked like because he lost him when he was still very small. His father had been killed by the Germans in Theresienstadt, and Max knew him only from photographs. But he believed that Fred looked like him, and so he felt a little as if his father were sitting there with them. Therefore, he was not really listening to the conversation. His curiosity was piqued when he overheard mention of an amulet that Max's father was supposed to be in possession of, as a protection against evil.

It was a magic amulet, inscribed by the learned Trnavian rabbi Simon Sidon, Fred was saying, and the lives of many in his family had been saved thanks to the amulet, during both war and peace. According to him, even if Mom disagreed, it saved Max's father's life too during the First World War—he came back with no injury, which was a miracle. If only he'd had the amulet with him when the Gestapo took him, the poor man would have survived that war too! Mom kept shaking her head: "That's ridiculous, Fred. My own father also fought in the war and he returned just like hundreds of others did. And it is not true that Willy came back home uninjured from World War I. He went deaf from all the explosions. And I never heard about any amulet from him."

"I think," interjected the omniscient stepfather, "that whether somebody survives or not is decided not by God or an amulet, or by being an engineer or a famous heavyweight boxer. I know what I'm talking about because I saw them dying like flies—within a month they were all dead. Even a boxer who had biceps like mountains."

He (and this Max believed) had survived only because his body had been made resilient by hard work. Plus, he was not scared of anything, even if he had no education and no exceptional accomplishments to speak of. Max still did not understand how this amulet was linked to his cousin's visit; he only understood that Fred had come from as far a place as Bratislava because of it. That would explain why he would not leave without it. Max had never heard his mother mention that his father believed in talismans, never mind having possessed one. His cousin sighed, saying he needed it badly even though he didn't even know what it looked like. All he knew about it was that it was magical and it had Hebrew writing on it. He even said to Max's mother: "The fact that Uncle did not discuss these things with you is understandable! You are, after all, a Christian, and this is a family secret. Perhaps he didn't want to show it to you, and when he needed it most, it was too late." Suddenly, Fred pointed above the boy's head toward the library. "What if he hid it in a book?"

"It's not in the books, I would have noticed," Max assured him.

"That's true—he has read everything, especially those health books with pictures," his stepfather added sarcastically.

"And you know what? Why shouldn't we look?" Max's mother sided with Fred. "We'll divide the bookshelves and check every single book." And so that the boy wouldn't think she was ignoring him, she added: "Max can go through the bottom shelves." She stood up from the sofa. "Besides, I cannot remember the last time I dusted those shelves."

Because Max was kneeling as he was going through the books and the rest of them were standing, they forgot about him and discussed things he really shouldn't have heard.

"Oh please, don't try to convince us that you have a right to it because you're family—just stop that, okay?" his stepfather said. "You're in trouble and you need to get out of it, am I right?"

That's how the boy learned that his cousin had decided to immigrate with his entire family to Israel and he dearly needed the amulet, because Israel was at war with the Arabs.

"Oh my God—what if they send you to Suez?" blurted Max's mother, holding a dust rag.

"That's precisely why I was hoping I would find the amulet somewhere here." Fred sighed and put back the copy of *The Valley of Decisions* by Davenport that he had been searching through.

Later, his stepfather said: "If it was ten years ago, you'd be good enough for them even in your fifties, but today they have younger ones. I would not go there even if they promised me gold. It will all end badly, anyway. If not now, then very soon. You cannot believe the French and British. They'll betray Israel as they betrayed us in 1938 before the war, and as they always do with the Jews. In the end, they will throw all the Jews in the sea and you'll be happy that you stayed with your family sitting on your ass in Bratislava."

When they had checked all the books to no avail, Fred sat down near the bottom shelves with glass doors and noticed Max. For a while, they simply peered into each other's eyes. "Nope," Fred finally said glumly, "the Jew has no choice today. If he stays here, his daughters will marry Aryans and he will have no Jewish grandchildren, only some crossbreeds. In Slovakia, they would for sure baptize them. There, even Communists believe in God. In America or England, they would marry goys."

The boy put the lid on the box of photographs he was looking through. "I am no crossbreed," he said defensively.

"Well, be happy about that," the stepfather rejoined. "If your dad had married a Jewish woman, you'd have ended up the same way he and my entire family did."

That night, his mother prepared the bed in Max's bedroom for Fred, and Max slept by the window on a pullout couch. Max asked a lot of questions about his father but he didn't learn anything new, only that he was a skier and, when he was young, he had been a boxing champion in Slovakia. Later he moved to Prague because of some actress, and from then on he and Fred didn't see each other much.

"That was my aunt," Max said.

"Hm," Fred grunted. The only thing on his mind was the amulet. "They would not deny me it," he meditated, lying in the boy's bed.

"What will you do?" Max asked. And when he didn't get an answer, he said: "I think they need plumbers in Israel."

"Why do you think so?"

"They're needed everywhere, right?"

"Do you want to be a plumber?"

"No! I will be a writer."

"So why do you talk about it?"

"Because of you. You would not be able to make a living as an agronomist. There's only desert."

Max woke up early, at dusk. First he thought that the light was on in the hall, but that was the dawn. Through the grainy glass door in the hall, the early-morning light created a beautiful mosaic of colors, from light blue to pink. Then he heard his mother and stepfather talking quietly. With one hand on the door handle, he stopped and listened to them. Suddenly, without him even moving, the room fell silent. In the light, he observed a diminishing shadow on the glass so he closed himself fast in the bathroom. He peed and flushed the toilet. When he came out to the hall, his mother stood by the living room door already—or still—dressed.

"It was just Max." She turned toward her son and said: "I got worried that Fred became sick."

"I am a Jew," he said.

"Come here, give me a kiss." She reached out to him.

He felt her probing gaze as he kissed her on the face. When he was small, he believed she could see right through him. With time, he understood that she could not and he could lie without being uncovered. That was a great discovery in his life. But now she had no reason—why was she suspicious again?

"I wanted to tell you later, but since Fred has already broached the subject, I'm going to tell you now," she said. "Do you know what Daddy told me before they took him away? He sat down on the shelves—just like Fred did last night—and he said very solemnly, with his Slovak accent: *When our Max is grown up, he cannot marry a Jewish woman, and if he does, then she should be baptized.*"

Max returned to his room but couldn't get back to sleep. His head was full of everything he had heard that night. It all came back to his mother's look when he kissed her. *Maybe she thought he was listening behind the closed door*, he said to himself. And what were they talking about the entire night that she was still wearing the same dress? His curiosity got the better of him and—barefoot so as not to wake up Fred—he opened the door and stepped out into the hall again. On his tippy toes, he walked past the closet and stopped in the corner by the living room door. He wasn't surprised to hear them discussing the amulet again. But it hurt him to realize that they had lied to him and Fred.

"You should give it to him if he came only for that," he heard his mother say. "At least the thing will be out of our house once and for all."

"And what do I tell him? That I had it hidden in the safe?"

"I could tell him it was in the kitchen."

"Sure, with all the pots and pans. Or better yet, in the bathroom! Don't be dumb. He's forty—what would they do with him in the army? He would not believe you anyway, and what would he think of us then?"

"I'll tell him that it has been tucked away behind the glass in the credenza since 1939, and that we had no idea about it." Her voice was firm. "Perhaps between the two telegrams from Helena that she had sent me from the ship. What do you think? I hadn't known about that at all until one morning when I was getting coffee cups. It just occurred to me to have a look and what do you know, Fred—I found this! You know, if we don't give it to him and then something happens to him, it would be on our conscience until we die. Certainly on mine."

Suddenly, the door opened.

The boy, scared, pressed himself against the wall and stopped breathing.

"I'm going to wash the dishes from last night's dinner," his mother said, too loudly, as if she wanted Fred to hear. Passing by Max, she entered the kitchen and turned on the light, as the morning light was still dim. Max watched her through the partially opened kitchen door, cleaning plates from the table and putting them away in the sink. He would so very much like to know why they had to look through all the books the previous night if his stepfather had the amulet hidden in the safe behind a painting of ships. But that would mean asking his mother, which was out of the question right then. It was far more important to get back to bed without her noticing him.

Finally, she turned her back and stood near the credenza. He noticed she slid aside the glass behind which were those telegrams she had mentioned; then, very fast, he got back to his room, to his makeshift bed under the window.

When he woke up, he remembered dreaming that his father was alive. He did not die—they did not kill him—but he knew that his mother had remarried and, therefore, he had lived the entire time in Germany and did not let anybody know. They were all sitting in the living room—his mother in the chair by the window, near the huge lampshade, and his father and stepfather across from him (Dad looked like Mr. Polakovič). They were trying to figure out what to do, since she had ended up with two husbands. The best solution would be for his father to move to the neighboring apartment—that way, Max would be able to visit him anytime he wanted to. Sadly, it was only a dream. But maybe not entirely; he was able to remember, just between dreaming and waking up, that he'd had the same dream before and could return to it again.

Then he noticed the bed in which his cousin Fred had slept. The bed was empty and that reminded him of the amulet. The thought that he had fallen asleep and that Fred had already left with the magical amulet belonging to his father made him alert. He was in luck—all three of them were still sitting in the living room and Fred was staring at the table between them.

"Good morning," Max announced himself.

"Wash and brush your teeth!" his mother ordered.

"I have already washed," he lied.

"Then go dress and don't run around here in pajamas."

Because he was worried that if he left they would never show him the amulet, he ignored her and entered the room. Before they got a chance to say anything, he moved to the coffee table between his mother and Fred. His stepfather was sitting on the sofa, dark circles under his eyes; he put his huge, work-hardened hand far out on the table. He looked so guilty that Max had no doubt that under his hand, he was hiding the amulet.

Their visitor had nothing to hide and was vindicated as it became clear he had been right all along. "Feel free to show it to him," Fred laughed. "Imagine—your dad slipped the amulet behind the credenza glass and your mom came upon it this morning! Do you want to have a look?"

Max stared at his stepfather's hand.

"Show it to him already," the mother pressed.

He lifted his hand and under it, on the white crochet doily, was a yellowed square in celluloid, smaller than the matchbox vignettes Max had been collecting. Max's face betrayed his disappointment. Firstly, he had imagined the amulet would be much bigger, maybe a little worn since it was so old. And most importantly, he expected there to be magic signs on it, which clearly were not there. For the life of him he could not figure out why they had all been arguing so hard about it the night before. In the morning, when he overheard his mother talking to his stepfather, who said he'd had it put away in the safe, he still thought the amulet was very valuable and that his stepfather was hiding it so that he could sell it later. His mom, however, earned respect in Max's mind because she had decided to return the amulet to his father's nephew. Still—how valuable could this tiny card be?

Fred was clearly satisfied. He took the amulet in celluloid and, holding it between two fingers, showed it to the boy. "Should you ever, God forbid, need it, Max, write to me in Israel and I will send it to you," he promised.

The hard, small card was covered with small symbols of a writing Max could not read—probably Hebrew, which is read just like Yiddish, from right to left.

"Do you know what's written on the card?" he asked his cousin.

"I do not speak Hebrew, boy. But in Bratislava, I will ask a rabbi to translate it right away."

"Some spell," his stepfather chimed in dismissively.

It now occurred to Max: "Listen, I know a man who speaks Hebrew and he lives nearby. He translates from Yiddish and he is Jewish. I'm sure he'll translate it if I ask him."

"Who is this?" Fred asked the stepfather.

The stepfather only shrugged and, surprisingly, had nothing negative to say about Mr. Polakovič: "He's a decent man." They must have been very curious about what magic this card, with its short text, was hiding.

Fred hesitated as he pondered whether or not to entrust such a valuable thing to Max. "Do you promise to come back right away? And not to go anywhere else?"

"Where would I go?"

"Well, I don't know—to your girlfriend so that you can show off . . ." He finally handed over the amulet in the small transparent bag.

"I don't have a girlfriend." Max shook his head and hurried to dress.

Now he was really interested in seeing what Mr. Polakovič would do when he rang the bell—whether or not he'd let him into his apartment. His home seemed to Max far more mystical than the amulet itself. Soon, he was running up the street toward the Journalist Houses. But it was Sunday and the building was locked. By the door, however, there were buttons with the names of tenants and a microphone. Pushing the *Jakub Polakovič* button meant that Mrs. Polakovič could answer. She had never learned Czech well; she mostly spoke Russian. But if he returned without his goal accomplished, he'd be embarrassed. So he pushed the button and waited. Fortunately, Mr. Polakovič answered the intercom and when Max said that his mom had sent him, the door lock rattled. The door opened by itself, and when he entered the building the door closed behind him. It was like entering another world. There were many windows so the building was full of light, like a palace.

Mr. Polakovič was in a very good mood when Max came in. He wore a housecoat, and underneath, pants and a shirt. So Max had not woken him up. The smell in the hall was completely different from the smell in his apartment. He took Max to his room where, under a window on an office table, there was a flat portable typewriter made of brown Bakelite. There were also two phones, an open book, and a stack of papers with writing on them. Above low bookshelves, overfilled with books, hung many framed drawings and photographs, and on one of the cabinets there was a lit-up old radio. There was no bed or sofa so there had to be a separate bedroom, a kitchen, and probably a child's room too, Max thought.

"Who is this?" Max pointed to a colored pencil etching right across the door. Based on the attire, it could have been Mr. Polakovič's grandfather.

"That's Jicchok Lejb Perec, a great Yiddish writer."

"And this?" He moved on to the photograph.

"That's Salom As, also a great Yiddish writer."

Then the boy's interest was piqued by the portrait of a young man, which reminded him of a reproduction of the portrait by Alois Jirásek that hung in the corridor in his school. Under the sketch was the signature *Max Švabinský*. "And who is this?" wondered Max, since such a famous Czech painter would surely not paint portraits of famous Yiddish writers.

"That's me."

"You knew him?"

"I still do, he lives in Dejvice."

"But you're so young here!"

"I too was young once, you know."

"Well, yes, but you are a foreigner!"

Max had thought that Mr. Polakovič immigrated to Czechoslovakia after the war. But he learned that Mr. Polakovič had actually lived in Prague before the war—until 1942—because he had Romanian citizenship. He worked for a Romanian import-export business. The biggest surprise, however, was that when Max finally handed the amulet to Mr. Polakovič asking him to translate it, the man looked at it and said, "I've seen that already," and returned it to him. "There's no magic—it is a priestly blessing which you can find in the Bible. It's behind you, on the table. I can find it for you. I also showed it to your father."

"What? To my father?" Max couldn't believe what he was hearing.

"Back then, I lived right above you, where the Povroznuks live now. I even saw you as a newborn, when we drove your mom and you from Doctor Ulman's maternity ward. As a foreign diplomat, I was allowed to have a car and the Germans couldn't do anything about the fact that I was a Jew; not until the end of 1942."

"And why is that?"

"Because Romania was one of Hitler's allies. But you know that, right?"

"Why did Dad show it to you?"

Right then, Mr. Polakovič started to squirm in his chair by the radio, as if Max's visit was of no interest to him anymore. But

Max could not leave—he had more questions now than before he came in. So he stubbornly sat down on the chair at the table and tried to explain to Mr. Polakovič what he'd learned last night, and what happened in their apartment. Even though Mr. Polakovič was looking at him attentively, he did not appear to be listening to him at all. He clenched his hands against the chair armrests so hard they shook, and then the shaking moved into his face. His left eyelid started quivering as if he had a tic. Max didn't know whether Mrs. Polakovič was home, but he became so scared that he couldn't even stand up. *If Mr. Polakovič dies of a stroke*, he thought, *the last image he'll take with him is my face.*

But then the possibly dying man suddenly recovered, leaned toward the radio, and started to adjust a knob. He slowly turned the radio dial, and then a tune sounded. But it was not Radio Free Europe or the Voice of America that Max's stepfather listened to. The male voice sounded agitated and spoke a language that Max had never heard before, though he did catch the words *Kol Jisrael!* Instantly, he understood everything. Now he understood why the old man was so nervous! Every day at the same hour, he listened to Israeli radio. When Max told him that his mom had sent him, Mr. Polakovič thought it wouldn't take long and he could still catch the radio program. Then, Max figured, he got worried about revealing that he was listening to the Israeli radio show and he became agitated—in the end, he simply gave up and turned the radio on.

While the program was playing, Max skimmed the Bible. It was an old Czech translation and there were words he could not understand; it contained the New Testament too.

When the program was over, Mr. Polakovič tuned the radio to a different station and then turned it off. Without commenting on what had just transpired, he asked the boy for the Bible and put his glasses on. As if nothing odd had happened, he answered the question Max had posed half an hour before: "Your father wanted to know what the amulet said before he lost it. I also thought, just as your father did, that it would be some magical formula, and we were both disappointed that it's only a small square of parchment with a priestly blessing. Here we go." He pushed his glasses to the end of his nose and slowly read: "*May God bless you and protect you. May God always watch over you and be merciful. May God always be with you and give you peace.*" He exhaled and fell silent.

The boy felt that Mr. Polakovič hadn't told him everything. He remembered what he had heard, and asked: "If it was before you left, and then they took Dad two years later, why did he think he would lose it?"

"Promise you will not tell anybody." The man looked up from the open book after a short while. "Do you promise?"

"Yes."

"Your father carried the amulet with him throughout the entire First World War, and because he trusted its power, he later—in 1942—gave it to your stepfather when he learned he'd be deported to Theresienstadt."

"What? He gave it to him?" The boy jumped out of the chair.

"Your mother asked him to do that. At least that's what he told me. Josef was the only child of our landlady. She was already a widow and, understandably, she worried because he had been prone to problems since his childhood. He played cards and mixed with the wrong crowd. But your mother believed that she'd be able to protect your father until the end of the war since she was a Christian, and so she persuaded William to give up the amulet. They couldn't know that the respite would protect them only until 1944, when Jews from mixed marriages also started to be targeted. But at least your father saved our landlady's son, and you should be very proud of him. Of your mother too—she was a very beautiful woman."

Only then did Max understand what he'd witnessed the night before and why his mom and stepfather were so secretive about the amulet. They would have to acknowledge that his stepfather had survived the war at the expense of his father! Fred, too, talked about it—if his father had had the amulet when the Gestapo took him, he would have survived that war too. When he now imagined how they murdered his father in the concentration camp, he didn't feel his throat tighten and his eyes didn't become teary as had always happened; he was overcome by pure anger. Anger directed at his stepfather, mother, and God. If God existed and orchestrated everything like that, why didn't he at least make sure his mom would marry somebody else after the war?

Since then, in Max's mind, a whole lot of years had passed. In reality it had only been six. The reason his mother had persuaded his father to give the magical amulet to his stepfather became curiously clear after he watched *Hamlet* in the National Theatre. There could be no other backdrop but the lustful love of a young woman for a man much younger than her husband. The most peculiar thing was that he felt as if he'd known about this since his childhood. He just couldn't admit the consequences which befell him—still reeling from the bloodshed at the end of the tragedy—during his tram ride home through the poorly lit city.

Two years prior to seeing *Hamlet*, his half-sister had been born and his parents moved the sofa bed to her bedroom. He slept on a bed by the kitchen window leading to the balcony, right across from the credenza. Any new mail had always been slid behind the credenza glass, and when he returned home late that evening and sat down on his bed, he noticed there was a letter from abroad. He got up to see who'd sent the letter to his parents. It was stamped *USA*, and it came from New York. The sender was *Freddy Goldsmith*. Before he realized that this was his older cousin who'd emigrated to Israel, he noticed that the addressee was *Mr. Max Deutsch*—he himself! It was black on white, in a light-blue tissue-paper envelope. He was even more surprised when, opening the envelope, the amulet and a hundred-dollar bill fell out.

The first portion of the letter explained why Freddy had moved to the United States. In Tel Aviv he had built a successful plumbing business, but he'd always known that he'd have far more opportunities in America. In fact, he did it all for his daughters, who he successfully married off to Israeli Hungarians (Jews born in Israel) from good families. He and Vera had five grandchildren from their daughters, but both sons-in-law lived under the threat of a war breaking out. What's more, there was a terribly humid climate for a period of six months every year in Tel Aviv, and Vera struggled to breathe due to the heat. And so on, and so forth. A whole lot of bragging; the number of branches his business had, and how if he were not retired and didn't give all his property to his daughters, he'd be a multimillionaire by now. At the end, with fairly unintelligible language, he indicated why he believed that Max was going to need the magical amulet far more than he or his sons-in-law. Max understood this from the news. Like a true American, his cousin probably thought the same as his stepfather—that if Khrushchev didn't remove the rockets from Communist Cuba, America would completely erase Cuba, the Soviet Union, and quite possibly Czechoslovakia from the map.

But Max was far more interested in the amulet than in Fred's bragging. Not because he thought he'd have to go to war or because he feared a nuclear war, but because the amulet had found its way back into his hands on that particular day. As if he hadn't gotten it from Fred; as if his father's ghost was thus telling him: *If you have ever loved your father—then avenge his extraordinary murder!* The sudden appearance of the amulet and the timing would certainly support that. But in reality, his mother did not kill his father—he suddenly resisted the voice in his head—she only persuaded him to give the amulet to his stepfather.

He put the letter away and, holding the amulet, sat down under the light at the kitchen table. He remembered what Mr. Polakovič had told him about the priestly blessing, and he tried to remember the awkward old-Czech translation of those three sentences. It could have been from the Bible of Kralice they studied at school. Peculiar that he bought the Bible of Kralice—had it in his book collection, and read all sorts of things from it—but this passage he never looked for. He peered closely at the small card and tried to read the faded words from right to left. The letters reminded him of the keyboard on a child's piano. He looked at a letter—and it rang out. If he wanted, he could have played the words until he could grasp how to pronounce each one and what they meant.

It was as if he had just woken up. He lurched and realized that something very peculiar was happening to him. Instead of seeing the letters, he was hearing their voices. It was as if the voices recorded what Mr. Polakovič told him so long ago, when he read it for Max from the Bible, and now he was saying it with two voices, in slow motion, in both Czech and Hebrew, so that even Max Deutsch could understand. And when at the end it sang the letters שלום, a true peace came over Max. Everything fit—all he had ever thought, all that had ever happened to him—including his mother in the hall, who was now watching him. He knew that she was there watching him, but he also knew that he couldn't look up from the amulet. He had to wait, until his anger at the two people in the living room from his childhood disappeared, and God would grant him peace.

MARL CIRCLE

BY ONDŘEJ NEFF

Malá Strana

The guy just laid there, with the chisel of a jackhammer stuck in his crushed chest. His face was covered with dust and pieces of brick. He looked as if he'd been crucified— his hands thrown apart, his head a bit to one side. His dead eyes stared at the top of the arch, strongly lit by a halogen lamp. I felt sick, and quite possibly like my stomach would proceed from the stage of protesting to the stage of vomiting, if the dumb girl behind my back didn't stop shrieking.

"He got what he deserved, the piece of shit. He shouldn't have meddled in things he knew nothing about . . ."

She wriggled and twitched, giving a hard time to the two men holding her. One was a security guy, the other a construction worker, a hulk of a man with hands as large as shovels.

"Shut off, cow," he urged her politely.

Shut off—that's a good one, I thought. Probably a Ukrainian who's trying to speak like a native Czech. *Shut off, really great.*

I noticed the look on the engineer Vavřinec's face. *What else is going to happen? What else is awaiting us?* I could read it in his eyes. A death in the workplace and a hysterical girl, that's truly a murderous combination.

We both knew her. Her name was Adéla Turková. A fanatic believer in the sanctity of anything historical. She belonged to a group that called themselves the Trace. When something is being built in Prague, first the conservationists come running like a pack of hyenas and behave wildly, especially when somebody tries to fix something or, God forbid, build something in the historical center.

But even the most callous conservationist—who will comment on the shade of the lightning rod cover in the corner of the inside courtyard of an art nouveau house in Vinohrady—is helpful and tolerant compared to anybody from the Trace. And that Turková was, among all of them, the worst berserker.

"You'll all croak—and you deserve it, every single one who dares to touch the thread will die . . ."

The *thread*, that's the favorite notion of those nuts. The past, according to them, does not disappear with time. It establishes a fine thread, tying various elements into one living organism. A city like Prague—founded around a former ford in the times when the English, following Caesar's invasion, painted their asses blue— is knotted all around, in every which way, with the thread. The activists from the Trace loiter around any hole in the ground so that they can sniff out and rescue that thread of theirs. When they learned what was underneath that former Jesuit Palace adjacent to the Church of St. Nicolas, they rambled around Malostranské Square like red ants. Rotunda number five! In Prague, there are four Roman churches with a circle platform, that's why they're called rotundas. This St. Wenceslaus was a found treasure, hence the indignation of the Trace group. Most of them had given up with time, except this Turková. Security had a very clear order not to admit her into the building, but she always found a way to get in and make a scene. She would do anything—like dress up as a dachshund so that she could suddenly appear where she should not be at all.

Like, for example, on a construction site in the moment when a jackhammer killed Vasil, a foreman. When the police arrive, because doubtless somebody has called them already, and the ambulance as well, they will for sure ask Turková what in the world she was doing at the site of the tragedy. They'll ask me too.

Both of us were here—we could say—on business. She wanted to create a scandal; I was supposed to uncover what had been going on at the construction site. My name is Peter Wagner, and it would be difficult to explain what it is I actually do. I write for various magazines and translate; I draw an additional income from tutoring annoying kids in German. But mostly I am a skeptical psychotronic—that's how somebody once described it. I am interested in all paranormal phenomena. I've been tottering around them for the past twenty-five years. I know all the dousers, clairvoyants, telepaths, and telekinetics in half of Europe. I have tried to start believing that they really can see the future, and move objects long distances, and cure cancer. I have not been very successful, and that's why I belong in the category of skeptics. On the other hand, I am unable to dismiss them because sometimes they do guess things correctly, move something, or cure something. I keep asking myself—*What if?* Also, these people are quite fun. Wackos, all of them. I use them for my small zoo of idiots.

This I am not telling anybody, naturally, so people know me as a psychotronic. And as such, the engineer Vavřinec—in charge of the reconstruction of the St. Wenceslaus Rotunda—turned to me some time ago. Apparently, strange things were going on at the reconstruction site, as if a poltergeist was raging there. Injuries. Unexplainable breakdowns of machinery. The cement mixer opens by itself and crushes a worker. The fuse board radiates a blue glow. The wooden stairs fastened by five-inch nails suddenly collapse like a house of cards. Injuries, but small. A jackhammer rammed into a chest, that's a new one.

An interesting happenstance that I arrived to the place of the accident right at this moment. Vavřinec had asked me to come and his voice sounded very serious on the phone. But that was before he learned about the death on the construction site. Why, though, has this Turková materialized here?

No time for riddles. Paramedics ran in, led by a doctor, their reflective vests shining in the blaze of construction lamps, like glitter on Christmas ornaments. Even two policemen appeared; they took pictures of the accident and especially the chisel of the hammer rammed in the chest. A policeman has to have a strong stomach.

The doctor confirmed death and the paramedics wanted to remove the hammer. It wasn't easy to do, because the chisel was lodged so deeply that they had to turn on the hammer to dislodge it. The dead man started to shake and his head wobbled from side to side. That was a substantial spectacle; even Turková stopped shrieking for a while.

The paramedics removed the body, then other policemen came in. Somebody dragged Turková away and Vavřinec pulled me into his office for coffee. His hands were shaking, just about spilling the hot liquid.

"What was all that about?" I asked.

He offered me a shot. I didn't say no.

"Why didn't you tell me—"

"I did not know."

"That there's a corpse down there?"

"I called you because last night . . . there, inside . . . were those weird sounds again. Banging and also howling. But a corpse . . . that was there in the morning. The guys came in for their shift, it was open, and poor Vasil was lying there."

"An accident?"

"How can somebody kill himself with a jackhammer? Bullshit. It's impossible. Somebody had to do it. Somebody pinned him down like a bug onto a corkboard," the construction manager said, with both gloom and fear in his voice.

We were sitting across from each other in an ugly room, more like a closet. Beaten-up table; on it, a computer with an outdated monitor. On one wall, there was a board with blueprints and pictures. The St. Wenceslaus Rotunda had been discovered when the palace was being reconstructed in 2003. It was well known that the remnants of a thousand-year-old church could be somewhere there. According to the old records, the rotunda was demolished down to its foundations in 1683. It had already been weakened, also thanks to the fact that in 1628 they began to erect a baroque church on the site, and into its brickwork they built a marl circle as the foundation for the altar. Everything was nicely documented in the pictures on the board. Architectural historians thought nothing had been left of the rotunda. It was not until 2003 that it became clear that something was, after all, preserved. Most of what was left were the remnants of the original Roman floor. They discovered seventy-four tiles—three shapes arranged in five rows. The tiles are either hexagonal, square, or triangle. The hexagonal ones have no glaze; the triangular ones have from brown-violet to almost black glaze. The hexagonal tiles depict lions and mythical creatures called griffins—half eagle and half lion.

Engineer Vavřinec led the reconstruction. Naturally, it is impossible to reconstruct the rotunda in its entirety—the palace, situated above it, would have to be taken down. Nevertheless, inside the palace there will be a room that will become a testimony to the Roman history of Prague. Its floor will be reconstructed too—specialists will make replicas of the original tiles and they will rebuild the entire floor as it looked a thousand years ago.

"What were the sounds?" I asked the manager.

He was shaking his head. "I myself did not hear them. The guy from security called me. He thought the cement mixer turned on by itself."

"That's impossible."

"Of course it's impossible. He woke me up at three in the morning. I told him to go turn it off. He said he was afraid. I have to say this all makes me nervous too. That's why I called you in the morning."

"Before you discovered the horror?"

"Of course." He looked me in the eyes. This coffee cup banged the small plate when he tried to lift it by its handle. "Do you think something can be done?"

"Stop the construction."

"That's not possible. I was thinking of other things. Perhaps you know some people who know the ropes . . ."

"Magicians?"

"You think I am nuts. But this is not normal!"

"Why don't you let it be? Why don't you get a different job?"

"I don't know. I have other offers, but somehow I have come to like it here. You understand—the fifth rotunda in Prague. And before that, there was even something else. We found a fragment from the circle made of marl. A very odd discovery, there's nothing else anywhere like it. The stones are very peculiarly carved; toward their center, they are smooth, the outside is natural. Scientists are at a loss. They say they're older than the foundations of the rotunda, perhaps dating back to pagan times."

"Okay, but because of that you want to be accused of work-safety negligence? They can blame the death on you!"

His eyes were haunted. "Mr. Wagner, I thought you'd be able to help me . . ."

Four days later, Orlík called me. He's the captain at the CSI and it doesn't matter what his real name is. We're friends and sometimes go on motorcycle trips together. A few times I've sent a clairvoyant his way, always with plenty of caveats that clairvoyance is fraud. He was never upset with me, and it seemed that he was satisfied. We met up there at Hradčany, in the At the Black Ox pub. He asked me about Adéla Turková. I told him I didn't know her that well. An activist from the Trace. Very nutty.

"An aggressive type?" he asked.

"Just a girl."

"I heard she slapped you."

How did they hear that? It's been two months; she waited for me when I was returning home. I live in Žižkov, Dalimil Street. It was almost dark and there are not many lights in front of our house. She was pressed in the corner and she lunged out at me with that shriek of hers. I didn't tell many people, perhaps two or three, one of them Vavřinec. At him, she hurled a flowerpot.

"Slapped me? She only yelled at me."

"Could you tell me more?"

"Is this an interrogation?" He was starting to get on my nerves, which may have been a bit frayed already.

"I simply think you could help us out."

"With what?"

"It was murder, Peter. You have an alibi, we know that. But you do belong to the circle of people connected to the construction. Are you absolutely in the clear?"

"And why shouldn't I be?" I replied.

"There's a lot of stealing going on at the construction site. The Renova Company. Special construction works. There's stealing going on at every construction site, but these historical reconstructions of old objects . . . It's difficult to stick to the budget. They scratch the brick wall and there's a fresco from the thirteenth century. And in a snap, the construction costs half a million more."

"But there's nothing you can do about that, right?" I was very curious what he was trying to imply. He's turned out nicely, hasn't he? My good buddy Orlík! So why would you believe a policeman?

"Do you know that the Renova Company is one of the major sponsors of the nonprofit organization Trace?"

"I did not know that."

"Every complication means the construction becomes more expensive, and it's in the interest of construction companies to make the budget grow."

"That makes sense."

"The Trace will make sure there are complications and the company makes more money."

"What do I have to do with that?"

"Maybe you know something about those complications."

"Yes—machinery defects, fuses, weird sounds."

Orlík raised his eyebrows. He sat there in his motorcycle jacket, the froth in the beer in front of him slowly thinning. "A poltergeist tale."

"You think Vavřinec and Turková killed Vasil so that Renova can make more money?"

"You'd be surprised what people do for money."

"Turková is extremely light. She couldn't handle the jackhammer," I said. Orlík watched me carefully. "You think that Vavřinec brought me in so that he could use me as a pawn?"

"We call it a white horse," he said. "An outsider on whom they then pin everything."

"I have nothing to do with Renova or Turková, unless you count the slaps."

"So she did slap you after all! Is she up to attacking a man?"

"Do not misinterpret what I say."

"Look," he leaned toward me, "it is not officially murder. I, however, believe that it was."

"Why don't you call it a murder?"

"We don't want to end up being idiots," he growled. "Three specialists wrote a report that it was an unfortunate accident with negligent manipulation of the equipment."

"But—"

"No *but* applies. The only thing that applies is what's in the report with a signature and stamp." It was obvious that it all really bothered him.

"So after all, the poltergeist did it," I responded sarcastically.

"That's much more plausible than him impaling himself."

A few weeks passed and I slowly started letting it go.

According to the official version, the construction worker Vasil Hrymalskij died as a result of negligent manipulation of a demolition hammer. Another group of workers started working on the construction site, and a multidisciplinary team of historians and art scientists were examining the tiles. Maybe because for a while there was press coverage of the accident, people started becoming interested in the St. Wenceslaus Rotunda. So the legend about its origin, linked to the story about the murder of St. Wenceslaus, was unearthed. According to legend, the funeral procession carried the body of the murdered saint on a carriage from Boleslav—where the prince had been killed by his brother—to the Prague Castle. Nearing the castle, the procession passed a prison where the inmates were freed from their chains by God's power and led to their freedom. Later, right there, they built a chapel with a circle platform—the St. Wenceslaus Chapel.

I did not originally know the legend, and the person who acquainted me with it was Adéla Turková, the activist from Trace.

One evening, I returned to my apartment in Dalimil Street—one room and a small kitchen on the fourth floor in a house with no elevator, permeated with the smells of sauerkraut and stale laundry. When I opened the door, I immediately stopped in my tracks. I smelled something strange in the air. I smelled fresh coffee! I didn't even close the door behind me.

Adéla Turková was sitting in the dark kitchen in an armchair, a cup of coffee on the table next to her. "How's it going?" she greeted me.

I returned to the hall to close the door. Then I stopped—shouldn't I kick her out?

"Will there be slaps again?" I asked. I walked to the sink to get water.

"I was stupid—they saw you with a policeman and so I thought you were a cop. But you were just snooping."

"Maybe I'm a secret agent," I said, and sat down across from her. The dusk was becoming thicker. Outside, the lights came on, illuminating the whole of Dalimil Street, except for the lamp in front of our house; that one remained dark. I sat down at the dining table.

"Bullshit. I now know very well who you are and what you do. I found your articles and I read your blog about paranormal phenomena."

"Hmm."

"You're not a fool at all," she went on. "You could understand more of what we are about."

"We?"

"The Trace."

"Ah, the thread."

"Clearly, the thread," she shot back, annoyed. "You do know the history of the St. Wenceslaus Rotunda?"

"I'm not sure." I shrugged and then she rattled off the story of the miraculous halt of the carriage with the remains of the murdered saint. How the carriage stopped, and they brought in a couple of oxen but the carriage still didn't budge an inch. The murderer of Wenceslaus, Boleslaus himself had come to repent, and only then did the carriage with the body of the murdered saint start again.

"And what's the point?" I asked when she was finished.

"The thread."

"I don't get it."

"On that exact place, there used to be a pagan sacrificial site. A source of psychoenergetic power, do you get it? That's why they built the chapel there. Back then, people were much more sensitive and every church was something of a generator of psychic energy. Churches in medieval Prague are located in the key points of a magic polygon."

I nodded.

"Their position was important for channeling psychoenergetic waves. They planned it smartly; but otherwise, they were idiots," she explained.

"But of course," I retorted. The speed and clarity of conclusions made by these kids always touched me. "Caesar Charles IV was a huge idiot when he founded the New Town of Prague on a magic platform."

She didn't get the irony.

"You're right! Total idiot. He built Prague on the platform of a cross. He didn't get it at all that the strongest layer of energy is down there. It's hidden in the pagan underworld of Prague. What could Charles IV have known about that? An outsider from Luxembourg brought up in Paris. The Přemysl dynasty were so much more clever. Přemysl and Libuše were pagans! Their residence,

Vyšehrad, is totally magic. Then they moved the royal residence to the other side of the river. Where to? The Prague Castle is built on the place of a pagan sacrificial site. Its axis is the Brusnice brook. Do you know where the brook starts?"

"No," I mumbled. *How did this girl get into my kitchen?*

"At the spot where the Břevnov Monastery is located. It sits like a Christian lid on a pagan pressure cooker. The Monastery of Premonstratensians on Strahov is also such a lid. During the Kosmas times they were still having pagan rituals. But let's go further down: under the Cathedral of St. Nicolas is a boiler of magic powers. That's why the Prague Bambino holds such a power. The Jesuits knew the source of that power very well. That's why they built their palace on it and attached it to the Cathedral of St. Nicolas!"

This girl could be either hysterical or boring. She was getting on my nerves being either.

"How did you sneak into my apartment?"

"Through the door," she answered dryly. "I know how to open doors. Your dumb builder friend discovered the same."

I got up and turned on the light.

She squinted. "That was really unnecessary."

"What's unnecessary is breaking into somebody's apartment."

"So call your buddy the policeman," she grinned. "Listen, it is serious and I came to you because you are not as stupid as the others. You have an idea of what's going on here."

"Of course. It's all about the thread."

She waved her hands as a sign for me to stop joking around. "They discovered the Circle. Listen to me. If it's at all possible, tell them not to touch it—"

"Not to touch it?" I interrupted. At that moment, I did not realize yet what circle she was talking about.

"Oh, well, they have gone quite far already. Let them glue those tiles of theirs, they won't figure out the original structure of the magic pattern anyway. But the Circle—they must leave it be."

A circle made of marl; the outside natural, the inside sculpted.

Preliminary dating—the tenth century. It was being analyzed by the interdisciplinary team. They had a hunch that there was something else underneath it.

Perhaps some thread.

"What happens if they do not let it be?"

"What do I know? Maybe the end of the world. But seriously—the energy there is very strong. You saw what happened to that poor soul." She stood up.

"How did you get in here?" I repeated my first question.

"You have heard of telekinesis. Lock tumblers—that's child's play." She shrugged. "I was sure about coming here. I knew you were not home."

"Seriously?"

"Yep, I have a gift. When I want to, I know where a person is."

Well, that was something: a telekinetic who knows how to open locks, and a psychic to top it off. An exquisite piece had just been added to my collection of crazies.

She marched out of my apartment and I closed the door behind her. Just to make sure, I secured the door with the chain. But even that would not be a hurdle for a telekinetic.

I returned to the kitchen and put the kettle on to make coffee. Then my eyes wandered to the chair. And there, peeking from behind the cushion, was a ring of keys. One key was flat, very simple, the kind used to open hanging locks. Many such locks are used on construction sites to secure the perimeter fences.

I smiled. I had almost started to believe that there was something to her telekinesis and psychic powers—and here she was, the same kind of con artist as all of those I had met before her.

Then it hit me—what the keys meant.

I was debating with myself whether or not to tell on Turková when Orlík called. That was quite a relief. I harbored no sympathies for her, and in addition, those rumors about her slapping me were true. But then again, I did not feel like making accusations against some girl who did not weigh more then an empty bag of cement. Orlík asked me if I knew anything about Vavřinec.

I hadn't seen him for a good fourteen days. I told him so. "Listen," I added, "that Turková, that crazy girl from the Trace, she—"

"I couldn't care less about her right now. We're looking for Vavřinec. It's clear now that he syphoned off at least two million. He has a lot to explain. Once we're done with him, we can talk about Turková."

Okay then, I thought as he ended the connection. *I tried.* I had mixed feelings. I had not accused the girl, but on the other hand, there was the death of a human involved. Orlík did not believe it was an accident. Was it murder? If yes, then the perpetrator had to get inside somehow and then out. Through that lock.

I was pondering all of this while examining a small piece of tin on the key ring.

My thinking was interrupted by a phone ringing. I looked at the display—an unknown number. But the voice I recognized right away. It belonged to Turková.

"You're looking for Vavřinec," she said to me.

She was really getting on my nerves. "Listen, how did you—"

"I know where he is. Don't ask how I know, I simply know it. The main portal in the St. Nicolas Cathedral. In half an hour."

I checked the display. "Wait, it's seven thirty—"

But the connection was already dead.

I arrived five minutes late. She was standing in front of the locked door, a tiny figure in jeans and orange tennis shoes and a jacket with a hood. When she noticed me, she only nodded. She did not comment on my late arrival.

"It's locked," I noted. I pointed to a sign on the door. It closed at four p.m.

"It depends," she replied, and leaned her shoulder on the door. It opened. The evening Mass, I thought. A suffocating silence, permeated with the scent of holiness, was coming from the interior of the church. We slipped inside. She closed the door behind us and pointed to the left.

"Here," she hissed.

I looked up. The frescoes by Kosmas Damian Assam were lost in the darkness. The crystals on the chandelier in the form of a czar's crown gleamed in the dying daylight. There was no time to look around, and I hurried behind the small person heading for the confessionals to the left of the entrance. She slid into the first row and waved at me to follow her. Carefully, I inserted my head inside. At that point, the girl was pushing her palms against the wooden wall. It gave and revealed a passageway. A light flashed in her hand—the LED on her cell phone. The white light twinkled, revealing a narrow hall. We entered. The passageway door closed behind me with a rasp.

The hall was not long, and at the end, instead of a secret passageway, there was an ordinary door. In the small cone of the LED light I glimpsed an aluminum doorknob with an ugly plastic covering. I reached into my pocket and felt for the keys I had found on the chair. The girl, however, couldn't care less about any keys.

What was behind the door I knew very well—a large palace staircase landing—there, in the corner, the construction site begins. Soon we'd see the hanging lock.

It really was there, in its place.

It occurred to me—had she finally noticed she lost her key chain?

She aimed the light on the lock. I took out the keys from my pocket, fingered the flat tin one.

"These keys . . ." I tried to insert it into the lock. It did not fit.

"These keys are from my grandma's cottage. I left them on your chair. I knew they would confuse you, I enjoy a bit of entertainment too."

She took them from me and tucked them into the back pocket of her jeans. She simply clasped the lock in her palm. A metal click sounded. She released the lock, it opened, and we entered. She closed the door behind us and with the cone of LED light looked for the switch.

The glare of five halogen lights hit our eyes used to the dusk—as if we were suddenly standing on a podium, actors in a pitiless farce.

In the middle of the room there was a cement mixer, and from that hung the body of the construction manager, Vavřinec. Something rumbled in the machine and then it turned on—perhaps it was connected to the switch, that was my first thought. In the following moments, however, I forgot all about the switch and electrical circuits.

The mixer was on and the body was being tossed around like a puppet.

"The Circle," breathed Turková, and pointed with her finger.

From beneath a fragment of the floor, a circle segment composed of marl stones jutted out. In the sharp light of the halogens the stones shone, contrasting with the unearthed soil—maybe it was natural stone? The stones slowly yellowed and then turned red. They radiated warmth. From the corner of my eye, I glimpsed movement. I turned, and at the last moment I dodged a shovel. Nobody had thrown it at me. It started moving by itself, circling the working mixer.

We could hear sounds. It occurred to me that these were the sounds which the night watchman had heard before he woke up Vavřinec. One after another, boxes with tools came loose, the covers opened, and trowels, hammers, and tacks started flying. Sifters and pails and mortar tubs lifted off too. They all circled the mixer, and I noticed they were aligned with the circle of marl stones.

Stones that were arranged by human hands, in the times when Christianity hadn't yet reached the Czech basin against the flow of the Elbe and Vltava; when it hadn't yet conquered the Moravian Gateway. Arranged during the pagan times when no one knew about Thessaloniki and Cyril and Methodius.

I froze. Adéla Turková was standing beside me, her face white and eyes ablaze.

I read books about telekinesis and poltergeists, I myself had

written many articles on the topic—half skeptical, half apologetic—
written in the spirit of, *I do not believe but I hope I will see.*

Now I saw it—it was in front of me. Frightening, and at the
same time intoxicating. I felt the vortex carrying me with it.

I turned toward Turková.

"I believe you now understand . . ." she began.

Then there was a bang. One of the water risers cracked, then
another one. Water started to flood the room. The chaos increased.
The items had ceased to rotate in a regular pattern; the order was
lost; suddenly, there was just an ungraceful mixture of heavy tools
intended for masonry work. I staggered among the junk. A few
times I stumbled and fell, then something hit me in my back. In
the water maelstrom, I saw a dancing female figure. Adéla Turková
seemed to be rejoicing in the disaster; I thought I could see a look
of excitement on her face.

Then the lights went off, but not the sound. I fell down, and
something metallic and terribly heavy dropped on me and pushed
my head under the water.

I lost consciousness.

I came to in the intensive care unit. Orlík was standing beside the
doctor and a nurse.

"What about the girl?" I asked him.

"Which? Our friend Adéla Turková? I have no idea what's with
her. Should I find her so that she can bring you a bouquet of flowers? Or possibly a flask?"

"What's happened to her?"

"What should have happened to her? Your friend Vavřinec is
not doing well. Actually, extremely bad. He's dead. Well, at least
he's out of his pickle, that's a way to look at it."

He was watching me.

"I'll wait. I'll wait until you're better and able to talk about all
of this reasonably. I am very much looking forward to it. Right
now, I can't make any sense of it."

* * *

Sensible explanations didn't start until two days later, with the help of my lawyer. He listened to my account very politely. I understood very well how he felt. I used to listen this graciously to the tales of poltergeists and dancing things.

"I see it like this," he said, when I was done and he'd had a moment to think. "You visited your friend, the engineer Vavřinec. He confided in you about his work-related problems, and you advised him to talk to his superiors, or alternately to the police. You met at a secluded place—in his office—so that you wouldn't be interrupted. There was a breakdown of the water system, the lights turned off, and Vavřinec, unfortunately, lost his life. Or is the story different?"

"Something like that could have happened," I replied.

Write it down, sign, stamp.

It took a long time before I was brave enough to visit the former Jesuit Palace in the neighborhood of the St. Nicolas Cathedral. The restoration had progressed a lot; artists had replaced the construction workers. They were arranging those beautiful tiles in the form of hexagons, squares, and triangles; decorated with lions and griffins.

"What did you do with the marl circle?" I asked them.

"What marl circle?"

"It was right here." I gestured toward an area with dark soil and seemingly natural rock.

"Nothing like that was here," they reassured me. "It would be in the documents otherwise."

I wished them the best and was about to leave, but then I stopped short. There was a small figure leaning against the door-frame, in a jacket with a hood—a tiny, thin girl.

"How did you get out of it?" I asked.

"I know to be where I am needed, and I know not to be where I am not needed," she said.

"And the marl circle?"

"What marl circle?" she replied, and left the building.
I haven't seen her since.

Author's Note: The Jesuit Palace, now the seat of the mathematics and physics departments of Charles University, truly does closely adjoin the St. Nicolas Cathedral, and in its basement, in 2003, there really were discovered the remnants of the St. Wenceslaus Rotunda. With the help of a public collection, the remarkable historical site is being restored and reconstructed in a dignified manner. For more information, please visit http://www.naserotunda.cz/, or http://www.naserotunda.cz/en/about-project. You will not find the information included in Peter Wagner's statement. It is certain, however, that pedestrians walking around in the evening can hear strange sounds coming from inside the building, and that the magistrate of Prague closed the traffic on the Malostranské Square in case a rapid intervention of an unknown nature is needed to combat equally unknown powers.

THE CABINET OF SEVEN PIERCED BOOKS

BY PETR STANČÍK

Josefov

From time immemorial, a disparate figure has been roaming through the Prague ghetto. Nobody knows how old he is, but even the elders know him as an old man. Nobody knows his name anymore, but everybody knows about his curse. Nobody talks to him, nobody pities him. If someone wants to be exceptionally cruel, then they will give him some spare change or food.

Our story began on a Friday evening, the twenty-first day of the month of Cheshvan in the year 5626 counting from the creation of the world—in other words, the tenth of November, 1865 AD, exactly when Rabbi Flekeles was singing the tenth verse of Psalm 92 for the second time: "*But my horn shalt thou exalt like the horn of an unicorn.*" Golem entered the Old New Synagogue, yelled out horribly, and exploded all over the walls.

In the synagogue, they all should have been used to such things by then. Because a long time ago—back when the cavaliers would wear Spanish "virgin" pants with a raised velvet flap for their penises, and Prague was the capital of the Holy Roman Empire—Prague's own Rabbi Low, by uttering the name of the Lord, reenacted the creation of man from clay. Since he was not a perfect creator, his creation was not perfect either; it had a whole lot of strength but not much for brains. Therefore, the rabbi called him Golem, a.k.a. Dummy. One day, precisely when the rabbi began the Sabbath in the synagogue by singing the psalm, Golem went mad and started to destroy everything within reach. Rabbi Low ran outside, transmuted the broken Golem back into a mound of clay, then returned to the synagogue and sang the psalm one more time as if nothing had happened. From then on in the Old New Synagogue, at the beginning of each Sabbath, Psalm 92 has been repeated twice and so—as has been mentioned already—they should have been used to such things. But they were not, and they all shrieked in horror.

To solve this case, Commissioner Durman was summoned. Not really due to his detective skills, but more likely because he was nearby. More specifically—no other policeman was available.

Things went so-so during the day, but at night the police were afraid to go into the Jewish ghetto. The police superintendent Leopold von Sacher-Masoch himself was trying to win his force over; first by promising them an extra dose of office rum and new feathers for their hats, then by crudely scolding them and threatening them with reassignment to a rathole outpost. But it was all for nothing. Between dusk and dawn, patrolmen would circumvent the ghetto by a good distance, and it didn't even occur to them to enter it. In the dark, no laws applied in the ghetto—penal or physical.

The order mandating Jews to live only within the walls of the ghetto hadn't applied for a long time, but the ghetto remained. Those who could afford it had left to live in a better part of the city; only the poorest were left behind, plus various other wretches who filtered into the ghetto from all around the city. The ghetto had become a magnet for misery, madness, and crime; it became the final stop on the line, and there was no going back.

Alongside the ordinary poor souls, there were crooks, kabbalists, cheats, hucksters, mystics, pessimists, lusty murderers, ghost-hunters-for-hire and their demons who hadn't found their way back to the astral world, black and salon magi, wounded poets, old angel-hunting women, late alchemists, abstract painters, perpetuum mobile inventors, honey counterfeiters, Lilliputian prostitutes, forgers, cannibals (due to hunger or preference), door-to-door hypnotizers, and other lost beings lived there.

The problem was that nobody had ever drawn any reliable map of the ghetto. Maps of Prague that were precise for every other part of the city were of no use within the limits of the ghetto, because any and all streets led only to or from elsewhere. It was easier to get lost following the map rather than not following it. In addition, it was not clear where exactly the mistake had occurred. Somebody alleged that the surveyors had become intoxicated by hallucinogenic vapors from the gutters while working, or they were bribed by the degenerate Lithuanian prince Kazimieras Trupello—the father of Central European crime, who had been hiding for years from the authorities in Prague. Somebody else believed that the blueprint of the ghetto was fluid and ever-changing because it was a huge living creature in the form of a city, gestating there long before the founding of Prague.

Commissioner Durman, unlike all of his colleagues, loved the ghetto. It was a stone's throw from his bachelor pad in a small, flattened house built between two gothic buttresses of St. Anne's Church. He frequented pubs every evening after work—of which, per capita, the Kingdom of Bohemia had the most.

The ghetto's hygiene, the saying goes, was iffy. The streets had no pavement, only layers of stomped dirt, excrement, and refuse. The water and sewer systems hadn't infiltrated the ghetto. In wells, there was more bacteria than water. Those who—after they had been weaned off breast milk—didn't immediately start drinking alcohol were almost guaranteed to contract cholera or typhoid.

Therefore, there were not only pubs in the basement of every building, but almost everybody brewed their own beer or distilled their own liquor, and so there was always something new to discover in this area.

Restaurants in other parts of Prague had already adopted large steam beer brewing machines, and the ginger-colored liquid started to taste somewhat the same everywhere.

And while waitresses in Prague refused to let the regulars slap their butts—because the members of the Society for Women's Rights ("Kazi") had convinced them that men were always trying to enslave and demean them—to the hostesses from the ghetto (still called wenches), butt slapping was welcomed because it was concrete proof that the woman in question was liked by men. In addition, it helped circulate the blood in her tired limbs.

Thus, Commissioner Durman was automatically assigned all the ghetto cases. Just like now, when they found him in the picturesque Albatrosses pub, right by the synagogue where he was tasting a local specialty: an ale brewed from malt smoked in beech wood, which gave the beer a beautifully smoky aftertaste.

It occurred to the commissioner that crimes perpetrated outside of office hours should be punished with an especially painful sentence, but he kept it to himself, and commenced the investigation with vigor.

He ordered the remnants of Golem to be scraped off the walls and the arch of the sanctuary, and for them to be delivered to the morgue. Then he interrogated Rabbi Flekeles (who, as per usual, didn't know anything) and the other gathered Jews, with the same result. Finally, he carefully examined the site of the explosion, but in vain.

Therefore, he went back to the pub, but the vat with that exquisite smoked beer was almost empty and all the chairs were already turned upside down on the tables, perfectly aligned. The commissioner thus slapped Mrs. Albatross on her bottom, ate a bit of homemade onion soup while standing, wiped the tears from his eyes, and headed home to bed.

First thing in the morning, he took a coach and left for the General Hospital.

The morgue was cold and there was a sweet malodor of lifeless bodies. The pathologist, Doctor Tombs, as was his custom, addressed the dead: "You were a man, based on the completely calcified, swordlike spur on the sternum. More than forty years old. The cause of death was alcohol-induced fermentation. The murderer made you swallow so much yeast (probably baker's, using a mechanical apparatus designed for force-feeding geese) that all of your body tissues started to ferment. The pressure of fermentation gasses bloated your body so that you looked like Golem, and eventually your body exploded."

"What kind of apparatus?" Durman asked.

Doctor Tombs, after a short pause, took the commissioner to the adjoining morgue, where he and his colleagues had been fattening a goose in a wire cage amongst all the coffins. The bird was so morbidly obese that it filled the entire cage and swelled out of it through the wire loops. Doctor Tombs picked up an object similar to a gun, and forced it down the throat of the dead animal, inserting the iron tube into its esophagus first. From above, he poured potato dumplings into the funnel, and as he was turning the crank, the machine pumped the food directly into the goose's stomach.

"Today is the feast of St. Martin, so the bird is going into the pot," he called through the open door to the cadavers.

The commissioner was shaken by the image of the tortured animal. "Don't you feel sorry for the poor thing?"

Tombs put the apparatus back into its place, caressed the goose through the cage, and shrugged. "Pleasure is born out of suffering."

The commissioner searched the dead man's clothes, and in the breast pocket he found a small piece of paper. On it, there was a drawing of a square with a rhombus inside, and inside of that, another square. The space between the large and small square was divided by lines into twelve isosceles triangles marked by the Roman numerals *I* through *XII*. Inside the image were scrawled some words.

"It's a horoscope," said Doctor Tombs, who was looking at the paper over the commissioner's shoulder. "I know because I recently dissected an astrologer who had his horoscope tattooed on his heart."

Durman visited the nearest astrologer, and after much ado the man disclosed to him that it was the horoscope of a man born in Prague on July 27, 1824, and that he was supposed to die on November 10, 1865, meaning a day before his actual death. His name was not there. To divine the date of death from heavenly bodies may have been possible, but it was unethical; therefore, most astrologers refused to do it. This horoscope was probably developed by an astrologer named Detlef Murbach, because he did belong to those few black sheep who, for a few pennies, would predict one's death—in addition, Durman recognized his handwriting. Murbach lived somewhere in the ghetto . . . Wait a minute, it's right here: Thin Street, number 88.

And true, at the given address, Murbach had rented a small shack built, with enviable courage, on the roof of a building, on a plank between two chimneys. When Durman climbed up the ladder and heaved open the hatch in the floor that served as a door, he didn't find anything interesting inside. Absolutely nothing—except a bed, chair, table, plate with a spoon dried onto it, some frayed ephemeris charts, a small empty keg labeled *baker's yeast,* and a used feeding apparatus. In the corner there was a cage with a goose inside, similar to the one in Doctor Tombs's morgue. The bird was so fat that it could not get through the small opening in the cage, and Durman had to borrow pliers from the doorman and cut the wire. The emancipated goose was far bigger than the cage, and it held the form of a cube. The commissioner took it into his hands and threw it out the window.

The goose spread her wings, and for a moment it looked as if she would fly. But then her weight forced her down to the ground, where the fall broke her long white neck.

She died, but she died free.

The commissioner, based on the evidence, concluded that the victim of yesterday's explosion in the synagogue had been the astrologer Detlef Murbach. Now all he needed to do was to track down the murderer.

* * *

Durman sent officers to all of the parishes in Prague to copy from their registries information on all males born on the twenty-seventh of July, 1824. There were only three: Kylián Smell, baptized in the St. Steven's parish in the New Town; Baltazar Carbuncle, baptized in the St. Haštal's parish in the Old Town; and Matěj Snide, baptized in the St. Joseph's parish in Malá Strana. Snide had recently died of tuberculosis, and Smell was in the military in Halič, so only Carbuncle was left. The commissioner ordered a search for him around the entire city of Prague, and because it was evening already, he set out back to the ghetto, heading straight to the pub.

It was the feast of St. Martin, and everywhere there was the wonderful smell of roasted St. Martin's goose. The commissioner, after his terrifying experience with the force-feeding apparatus, did not want to taste the goose at first, but his reservations didn't last, and he finally gave up and ordered one entire goose without fixings. The lovely animal glistened like a golden crane gliding on a lake of iridescent grease. She was magnificently juicy, because during roasting she'd been continuously moistened with a stock of giblets. The crusty skin was decorated with feathers made of phyllo dough.

By the time he was finishing the meal, his eyes were bulging out of their sockets; still, he went for a goose period, or more like an exclamation point—a neck finely stuffed with mashed liver, fried in its own lard.

At the exact moment when the commissioner was ascending to the utmost apex of happiness, a man in a black coat approached his table. Quietly gazing at him with his bloodred eyes, the man simply stood there inhaling. The commissioner thought the man may have been shy to speak and so he kindly addressed him: "Would you like a cigar?"

At which point the man's body cracked like a walnut along his breastbone.

Chaos ensued. Blood sprayed, the guests shrieked, goose meat burned and stuck to pans. The commissioner covered the corpse with a tablecloth, slapped the most hysterical women, had the pub cleaned with a wet mop, and ordered a large shot of rum for everybody, courtesy of the police. The people calmed down and Durman interrogated them.

The dead man had come in from the street. Why he burst, nobody knew. They knew him very well here; he was a regular. Actually, a nightly one. His name was Hubert Anywho, and he made a living as a teller. Not in a bank, but as a fortune-teller.

Durman, stuffed with goose like a goose stuffed with dumplings, barely dragged himself home into his small home, where he toppled onto his bed and started snoring before falling asleep.

The third day was a Sunday—no working, no murdering.

The following Monday morning, the commissioner finally succeeded in digesting the St. Martin's goose and could continue with his investigation. According to the domicile registry, the suspect— Baltazar Carbuncle—lived on Wight Street, right at the gates to the ghetto. Furthermore, he discovered that Baltazar made a living as an organ repairman, but according to the accountant, he'd left his workshop yesterday without telling anybody where he was going and he never returned.

In the meantime, a postmortem report from Doctor Tombs came in: the murderer of the fortune-teller had shoved into his larynx a tube with a valve, so that he was able to inhale but not to exhale. The air pressure in the lungs increased with each breath until it ripped him apart. The same valves could be found in organ pipes, so that the air didn't return to the bags.

Then an undertaker came in, with a telegram: *ANOTHER MURDER HAS JUST OCCURRED IN THE GHETTO, RABBI STREET, NUMBER 391. —CRYSTAELO*

Durman immediately left for the given address. A still-warm corpse lay in a pool of its own blood, pierced with a stiletto which the perpetrator had left in the wound. According to the maid, his name was Crystaelo and he was a fortune-teller. He was a young, wealthy-looking man clothed in a violet silk smoking jacket, with a nightcap on his head. Investigating his domicile in the ghetto, Durman found a big and pricey cabinet filled with books, along with other volumes lined up along several bookshelves, and stacked in any free space in unstable columns, mountains, and steeples. The man had also used books as a defense against the murderer. From the door to the corpse, seven books pierced with the same weapon were scattered.

The commissioner picked up and aligned the books. The titles on their spines composed a curious poem:

Baking Desserts
Child Rearing
Milano Tour Guide
Rules of Jewish Fasting
Grooming Ginger Mustaches
The Second Czech King
Weathercock of the Candlestick Makers Guild

He had a feeling that a message was hidden in the connection between these books, but he could not figure it out. His pensive moment was interrupted by a manly mixture of spermaceti and the musky smell of hair gel that was used by only one person in Prague—his best friend and assistant, an autarchic detective, one Egon Alter. Egon brushed the book spines with an extended digit on the silver hand on the head of his walking cane, and declared in an operatic baritone: "The connection among the books carries tidings."

Alter, as it happened, had a peculiar talent of always finding himself in the right place at the right time, and often it appeared that he was able to read thoughts.

"The Czech king Vladislav I was crowned by the Holy Roman Caesar Bedřich I Barbarossa. And Barbarossa means . . ." Durman started thinking aloud.

"Ginger mustache!" added Alter, and continued: "The Czech army led by King Vladislav in the year 1158 conquered the famous city of Milan without a fight . . ."

". . . by roasting children made of dough in front of the city gates. The denizens of Milan believed that the Czechs actually devoured children and opened their gates to them . . ."

". . . which they should not have done because the Czechs robbed the city and thus acquired tremendous spoils. The most valuable was . . ." Alter let Durman pick up the thread.

". . . a menorah, a sacred candelabrum with seven branches from the Solomon Temple in Jerusalem. This temple had been destroyed twice on the same day on the ninth of the month Av; first in 586 before Christ by the Babylonians, and the second time in 70 AD by the Romans. To this day, Jews commemorate that horrible day with . . ."

". . . a fast," said Alter. "And where is the candelabrum now?"

"In the church treasury of the St. Vít Cathedral, obviously," answered Durman.

"And that's where the perpetrator hides, clearly. That's what the books were supposed to tell us. Let's go arrest him."

They were already on their way out, but the commissioner suddenly returned and skimmed the books one more time. "Dear Egon, look over here," he said triumphantly, and pointed to a circular stain on the title page. "This time your own genius has betrayed you. We're not going to any cathedral. The answer to the conundrum is here in the ghetto."

The friends hurriedly walked a few blocks through the winding streets of the ghetto. They entered the house, climbed up the creaky stairs, and knocked on a door.

The door opened a crack, and a surly face appeared in the small opening: "I do not wish to be interrupted."

The commissioner displayed his police badge, with the Byzantine eagle of the Holy Roman Empire. "Baltazar Carbuncle, I am arresting you for a triple murder."

"Well, come in."

They entered a small room with a view of a wall. The cracked mirror on the wall multiplied the little that was there: the dirt line in the sink, a small stove with a crooked pipe, and a worn sofa.

There was a momentary silence, then both Durman and Carbuncle spoke at once:

"Why did you kill them?"

"How did you find me?"

"When you answer my questions, I'll answer yours," the commissioner promised.

"Okay. The astrologer Murbach learned from the stars that I would die this year, 1865, on the tenth of November. I killed him because I did not die on that day."

"Why did you want to know the time of your death?" Alter asked.

"Because since my childhood, I have feared uncertainty more than death. Every day, I was dying of fear that it would be my last. When I learned from my horoscope when I would die, I finally got rid of that fright. But once it became clear that that prediction had been wrong, the terrible fright returned."

"And what about the yeast?"

Carbuncle shrugged. "It was simply at hand. Murbach applied it to his nose to treat the itchiness."

"And the fortune-teller, Anywho?"

"He claimed to know the future. So I tested him. I asked how he would die. He said: *While making love to a beautiful girl.* It was not true. That's why I brought the valve and rammed it down his throat."

"And the third one?"

"At the beginning, I thought that Crystaelo was a true clairvoyant . . ." The murderer sank into his memories . . .

When he went to the clairvoyant's house, he looked for the door knocker in vain. He was just about to knock using his fist when he noticed a small plaque with an inscription:

CRYSTAELO
Divination, prophecy, augury, clairvoyance.
Do not knock. If I do not open, I am not home.

Before he finished reading, the door silently opened and the inscription became blurry. The clairvoyant invited him in.

"I want . . ." Carbuncle started, but Crystaelo interrupted him with a gesture.

"I know, you want to know the place and time of your death. I know both, but I will only half fulfill your wish: I will tell you when you'll die though not where."

Carbuncle offered him money, all his possessions, but it did not work.

"If I want money, I'll buy a lottery ticket."

Carbuncle pleaded and prodded—in vain. Finally he started threatening to kill the clairvoyant, but Crystaelo only laughed: "You dummy, I lost interest in living a long time ago. I am denied surprise, curiosity, and suspense. I cannot play any game, happenstance plays no role in my life. The worst is—I will never know love, because with every woman I know beforehand what will happen to her."

Desperate, Carbuncle looked around and noticed a stiletto, casually placed in the umbrella stand. He picked up the weapon and attacked. The clairvoyant deflected seven thrusts with seven books, but the eighth time, he dropped his hands and let the steel tip pierce his heart.

"You'll die today at eight in the evening," he whispered, and then he himself drew his final breath.

The commissioner looked at his golden watch with an inscription from the emperor engraved on the cap. It was five to eight in the evening.

"Can I ask questions now?" the murderer asked politely.

"Of course."

"Why aren't you looking for me in the cathedral? Have you not discovered the secret of the seven books? The clairvoyant chose them on purpose to give you a lead because I had really wanted to hide in the cathedral. I recently discovered a secret hiding place there when I was repairing the organ. But I solved his riddle, and that's why I was hiding here in the ghetto where I have never been before, and nobody knows me here. I rented this room in a house, the number of which I decided based on a coin toss. What gave me away?"

The commissioner smiled. "Sometimes even a novice defeats the chess master, because he plays too simply. You found a message hidden within another message, but the true one was the first. Stenography inside out. The books were not pointing to the cathedral but here. All seven pierced books had a stamp on the title page with an address of the antique store of Isaac Goldschmerz, which is located on the first floor of this house."

In his pocket, Durman's golden watch played Papageno's "Aria" from Mozart's *Magic Flute*, and within moments the church bells from the surrounding quarters joined in.

Eight in the evening.

"Will you shoot me, commissioner? Or perhaps throw me out the window? Or suffocate me?" Carbuncle asked sprightly. "I have nothing to be sorry about. I wanted to get rid of the fear of uncertainty and I did get rid of it. Even now, knowing that in a short while I will die, I am happier than not knowing it and continuing to live."

"You can go—you are free," the commissioner said simply.

"How come? You're not going to kill me? Not even arrest me?"

"That wouldn't be punishment. In any case, you will die sooner or later, and I hope it's later. But if I let you live now, uncertainty will torture you every day and that is far worse than death. You said so yourself."

The villain blanched so much that under his skin, his blood vessels drew out as if in an anatomical atlas.

At the door, the commissioner turned and added: "The first ones were charlatans—good riddance. But the third one was a true clairvoyant. So *now* you know that Crystaelo lied to you, and why."

PART III

Shadows of the Past

THE LIFE AND WORK
OF BARONESS MAUTNIC

BY Kateřina Tučková

New Town

That building left on people strolling along the promenade the impression of an unsettling inappropriateness. At first sight, something about it was off—something on it was crooked, something was missing somewhere, or, on the contrary, there was too much of something—devil knows what. It emanated disharmony. One's vision became overwhelmed, as if one was looking into the distorted mirrors in the nearby Petřín Labyrinth. Passersby on the promenade usually looked at it searchingly—twice or even thrice—but then they gave up. After all, on the other bank of the Vltava, there opened in front of them the panorama of the Prague Castle that draws one's eyes so naturally that it cannot be resisted.

Therefore, only a very few deciphered that the apartment house in the shadow of the National Theatre seemed strange because each window on it was different. Each window had a slightly different stylized form: some were perpendicular, others had a semicircle or a triangle at the top, still others were divided by columns, but some windows were also doubled or tripled. In addition, each was surrounded by a unique ornamental decoration. But the difference was—and this was what was so confusing—in the details. The windows changed gradually, from one floor to another, sometimes broken off by a dormer window or a balcony which only contributed to the overall bewilderment of its disposition. That's why the building left the impression of disarray, disproportion, and discrepancy without anyone realizing the source of the impression.

The house was the work of the architect Gustav Papež, but more so than his invention, it reflected the builder's wish. Baron Mautnic, the last descendant of a family of industrialists, had a reputation as a man whose visions transcended his time, with a spectacular imagination and courage bordering on exhibitionism.

Twenty years before the birth of the future little artist and visionary Stowasser—and fifty years before he introduced himself in Vienna as Hundertwasser with his *Musty Manifesto Against Rationalistic Architecture*—Baron Maxmilian Albert Mautnic built a house about which he proclaimed: "It will be a building that will overwhelm the eyes of many, and the mouths of many will howl in enthusiasm or revulsion; it will be the most absurd building in Prague, the most celebrated in all of Bohemia, and the most talked-about in the entire monarchy!"

And now the house is theirs again. After almost half a century, they have it in black-and-white; the decision about the restitution of their property is glued to the front door to spite all the current tenants who, during all those years, behaved toward them as if they were mangy.

"Look, has destitution taught hard work to even Miss Baroness?" they laughed at her, as on hands and knees she trudged from one floor to another, hunched over a pail with a rag, cleaning the stairs of pink travertine. Nobody scoured them, or kept them up, except Hedvika and her mother. Even if the tenants were supposed to maintain and clean the property—which at the moment of nationalization became their commonly owned house—they all knew that if they didn't do their work, if they didn't wash the floors, didn't dust the original stucco, didn't polish the art nouveau lamps and forged banisters, the two women would not be able to bear it. And the following Sunday, they would trudge through the house and put everything in order that had to be put in order, wearing head scarves and sweatpants.

"A squad of baronesses," they laughed at them, instead of

thanking them as the tenants returned from their afternoon card games.

Their wives, smirking, would add: "Serves them right—otherwise, they would never know what real work tastes like."

As if they didn't know that she and her mother were no baronesses; that the title could be inherited only in a direct line which died off with the uncle and then definitely became extinct with the death of the aunt in 1974. They ignored it even if after the founding of Czechoslovakia, noble titles had been invalidated and she herself had a completely different name. Nevertheless, it was as if the hallmark of the Mautnic family was sealed on her forehead—and if not there, then definitely in her files where the personnel committee wrote: *Incompetent to study natural sciences at university.*

Thus, to experience what real work tastes like was something she certainly had plenty of opportunities to do. In the mideighties, she couldn't get into any other high school except an agrarian vocational school, and once she'd finished her studies in floristry she got exactly one job offer—at a crematorium. For five years she arranged flowers in the ceremonial hall, but also cleaned, moved chairs around, and, together with the eulogizer, moved coffins onto the catafalque when one of the staff responsible for cremation had nursed a bottle of schnapps instead of working, and left the freshly grieving family and friends impatiently shuffling outside the door. Then, during the first couple of post-revolution years, she held quite a few jobs: warehouse worker; miserly paid night watchwoman at a women's dormitory (when she thought she could attend university during the day); and postwoman, which is the job she still has today.

She had no choice—once the government returned their house to them, she had to forget her university studies and secure a regular income. The building, neglected for years and then flooded, required everything—her time, all of her money, and her full attention.

And so now, at four in the morning, she was already sorting

through mail. At five she ran out for her half-marathon through the center of Prague, delivering letters and bills, so that with ten kilometers in her legs already, she could commence her next shift. From nine, she cleaned and dusted, managed workers, and, most importantly, pleaded for money which this house literally hemorrhaged . . .

Hedvika exhaled, looked tiredly around her auntie's bedroom, one of only two in the apartment, where she had grown up with her parents.

The former private floor of Baron Mautnic was divided into two apartment units, between which they had fitted a common bathroom with a toilet. And then they moved them there—the auntie and Hedvika's parents—into the former study room with the uncle's collection on exhibit. The family of the functionary Knotek was moved into the salon and the smoking room—no questions asked, because back then the housing issues in Prague were solved without any discussion. After the Communist putsch, the auntie defended her property rights with great difficulty; she had no control over who would be moved into it.

And so one morning, apparently, there reverberated the rumble of jackhammers, a banging of hammers, and the ill-tempered shouts of masons, and partitions appeared in the beautifully polished hardwood and mosaic floors, dividing spacious rooms into small apartments for *the needy*. Those rooms with a view of the Prague Castle silhouette and the Vltava River were given to worthy revolutionaries; rooms with windows facing the courtyard were given to the no-less-worthy informers. The entire attic was taken over by Doctor Šimek—cold, taciturn, creeping through the halls like a ghost. This doctor of who-knows-what, who, in addition to having the key to his apartment, also owned the keys to the turret where, in an eagle's nest high above the roofs of New Town, the eye was enthroned.

The eye of a telescope—which from time to time would betray itself with a flash when people returning home from work would look up searchingly into the only window on the turret—that could easily watch the goings-on down along the promenade. No suspicious movement of locals could escape the eye. No foreigner who, for example, went to see the golden chapel, let alone one of the dissidents who used to meet in the nearby Slavia coffee house, where they were plotting to bring down the regime. Above and below, only a couple dozen meters from each other; ideologically, however, there was a distance of hundreds of thousands of light-years . . .

"What should I do with this? Store it or dispose of it?" the elderly foreman of the moving company interrupted Hedvika in her thoughts. Since the morning, they had been emptying the flooded first and second floors and moving furniture into an empty apartment one floor above, or, alternately, carrying it into the container parked in front of the house.

If there was any silver lining to the flood—which overflowed the dam on the promenade on one stormy July night and rose through the basement and the first floor, narrowly missing the windows of their apartment—then it was the fact that the restitution process sped up by weeks if not months. A bailiff delivered the notification (dated the day prior to the flood) on the second day after the disaster, thanks to which a third of the unwanted tenants had to move out.

However, the flood had caught Hedvika unprepared. She would hardly be able to finance the reconstruction of the decrepit house that had been neglected by the municipal authorities—flood or no flood. She now had to deal with the basement filled with mud, the dumpy walls on the first floor, and the mold climbing up the walls to the upper-level apartments. All the savings—hers and her mother's—she lost in the first days after the flood to pay for the cleaning. For the reconstruction, which could not be delayed even for a few days, there was nothing left. But the bank didn't care. Hedvika had a ridiculously small income as a postwoman, and her old mother plus a waterlogged house did not provide a sufficient guarantee to get a loan. Everywhere, the door was closed with the words: *We advise you to get rid of it fast, sell it even if you have to undersell it.*

Thus, Hedvika had not done well with banks, she didn't believe in under-the-counter "fast money" loans, and she didn't want to involve her friends. She had only one option left—to agree to the odious offer from Doctor Šimek.

That idea horrified her. She had been afraid of him her entire life. In past years, she'd unsuccessfully fought off his claws reaching to the offices of the court where the restitution of their house had been held up—and now, she should sell off half of her inheritance to his son? She recalled how he would smile at her unctuously from the depth of his wheelchair and say: "And maybe it could go further than just joint custody of the house!" She shook with disgust envisioning any closeness to Šimek Jr.—a chubby, incessantly sweating squirt, barely up to her breasts at which, during their every meeting, he impertinently gazed.

"I said, what about this?" the mover repeated. He was holding a big turtle shell, which for years had been lying on the cabinet together with other unsellable items from the uncle's collection which, in deference to his bequest, they never threw away.

"That's a shell from a hawksbill sea turtle, *eretmochelys imbricata*. This specimen of a critically endangered species was caught off of a coral reef in the Pacific Ocean. Especially interesting is the saw-tooth rim with a gorgeous black and red pattern on the carapace," Hedvika recited from the tag affixed to the abdominal plastron. As a child, she had spelled it out at least a thousand times.

The mover looked at her as if she had insulted him with the information, and then he lashed out at her impatiently: "Very well, but where should I put it?"

Hedvika felt her face redden as she stammered, guiltily, "Right . . . put it somewhere upstairs, please." She could only imagine what he must have thought of her.

Such a fine lady, nouveau riche—a house on the promenade falls into her lap and now she lectures and hustles them. Them, the former working cadres, not so long ago the pride of the nation, as they claimed in the news, on the radio and TV; hard workers who used to work with their hands to make a very nice living that allowed them to enjoy nice holidays and cars. And now, when all the privatized businesses laid off workers, they had to plead for a little money from people like this one. A good-for-nothing, gawping, too-clever-by-half heir, whose debauched ancestors amassed houses on the Prague embankment by wringing people like him dry. Where was the fairness in that?

From the hall shared by both apartments, she could hear a disgruntled moaning and a banging of furniture as the movers were taking out one piece after another. Hedvika turned her back to this abrasiveness and peered out the window.

The turtle shell, a stuffed stoat, and a frog that looked like a dried-up apple were the only pieces from the uncle's collection of zoological specimens which her auntie—after they had forced her in her own house into one small room—never gave to the National Museum. Her generosity back then was a virtue of necessity because the collection, consisting of many different exhibits, couldn't fit into the small apartment. Not one of the nationalized institutions was able to buy the collection from the aunt, so in the end—grinding her teeth—she gave it to the National Museum and thus buried it in their depositories. Exactly as the upper echelons had intended to do with his *wunderkammer*.

To the aunt's horror, the museum staff receiving the collection didn't even bother to check all the valuable objects. The papers with detailed descriptions, which the auntie had copied for them from the uncle's catalogs, ended up under a seat in the truck.

"Do you know how much of this we now have? Tons. You have no idea what those precious princes, counts, and barons had amassed, and how much junk we now collect in the interest of the people of Czechoslovakia," the driver told her as he was closing the truck's hull. The huge stuffed grizzly bear—which until that fated day had welcomed guests upon entering the uncle's salon—

was sticking out like a caught criminal; they secured it with ropes around its neck and paws. Auntie Magdalena later reminisced that its raised paws in the attacking gesture were rearing up like the hands of a despairing child whose wail—*Don't believe him, don't let me go, keep me home!*—died out in the roar of the truck's engine firing up.

"Don't worry, your stuffed things will end up in good company," an employee of the museum called after her before he left.

Aunt Magdalena didn't doubt that at all; she had an idea how much the state stole in those days. She doubted, however, that the state would take care of the newly amassed property as a good steward, which her husband Baron Mautnic—an amateur zoologist, botanist, and archeologist, and a passionate art and curiosities collector—certainly was.

It had taken him many years to assemble his collection, and when he built his house, one floor was specifically designed for it. He devoted the floor to science and the beauty of the arts; he furnished for himself a study, a salon where important scientists, thinkers, and artists of the day used to meet; he had his *wunder-kammer* and depository there. On the walls hung first-rate paintings and the casts of world-renowned sculptures; in the monumental shelving cabinets, of which only one piece now remained standing on Hedvika's left, the most interesting examples of zoological rarities had their place. The giant butterfly *attacus atlas* from the island of Ceylon, as large as a turtledove; the arrow frog *phyllobates terribilis* from the jungles of South America, which in the pores of its skin hid the most potent of poisons; the genuine feathers of the mythical phoenix . . . Uncle's collection was a shining jewel among all the Prague collections. They said that Caesar Rudolph II would himself have been envious of it.

No wonder Auntie, after all of the forced surrendering, fought fiercely until the day she died for the only thing that remained of Baron Mautnic—the family house on the promenade. She was relentless—she demanded information from the authorities who refused to provide it. She hired expensive lawyers who would go against her if she didn't have by her side the loyal J.D. Boháček, who was once the legal advisor to Baron Mautnic, but who at the time was working as a laborer, having been promptly stripped of his law practice in 1948. Thanks to his efforts, she always learned what she had to do (even if at the last minute) to take care of the house, or what to install in it so that they did not evict them due to neglect of upkeep, as was common in those days. And then she would come up with a piece of jewelry from somewhere, an antique painting or a valuable vase, which she was able to sell through a state company for a ridiculous, extortionately small price. Still, she was always able to scrape together the money she needed.

But that is also why she didn't escape the attention of the tenants, the national committee, and at last the state police. For a while, there was a revolving door of unexpected visitors.

"How did you come to own the painting you sold on November 7, 1959, to the state company Antiques for 1,900 Czechoslovak korunas?" men in gray trench coats would ask her.

"I have a few pieces left from my husband, you know. In the confusion of the move I didn't really know about everything he owned," her auntie would answer and open in front of them a neatly organized home accounting book.

They quizzed, investigated, and sometimes they would bring a warrant to search the apartment. They rummaged through the basement and attic, but did not find anything. Maybe a few trinkets hung on the walls, portraits of family members, a painting of the house above the aunt's bed, some antique furniture—things for which she had papers from the authorities confirming that she was allowed to own them.

Up to the moment when the Russians showed up, they had been satisfied with that.

But after two tanks had nestled in front of their house, on the exact spot at which Hedvika was looking right now from their apartment, each of their visits became pure hell filled with threats and intimidation.

Hedvika could not take her eyes off that place, where the riverfront promenade opened up into a small space in front of the National Theatre.

The view offered to her today was quaint. The afternoon sun was already above the castle and was shining on the surface of the river that idly flowed in its original bed as if it didn't want to leave the promenade, with its alley colored with all shades of the incipient autumn. This view differed vastly from the one she knew from the photographs dated to the late summer of thirty years before. Thanks to them—the small, slightly blurry black-and-white images—and thanks to her father's regular reminiscences which were de rigueur at every one of her birthday parties, she felt as if she herself had taken part in the event.

That night, just prior to August 21, 1968, both Auntie Magdalena and her father—who was supposed to bring in the newborn Hedvika from the hospital in the morning—did not sleep a wink. As if bewitched, they watched the street. With bated breath they listened to the radio where in an unending loop, an announcement was repeated: "*Yesterday, on the twentieth of August around eleven p.m., the armies of the Union of Soviet Socialist Republics, Polish People's Republic, Hungarian People's Republic, and Bulgarian People's Republic crossed the state border of the Czechoslovak Socialist Republic. This transpired without the knowledge of the president of the republic, the Bureau of the National Assembly, or the chief secretary of the Central Committee of the Communist Party of Czechoslovakia, who regard this act as contrary to all the fundamental norms of international law. However, they call on all the citizens of the republic to remain calm and not to challenge the advancing troops, because at this moment, to defend our state border is unfeasible . . .*"

Those two stayed up the entire night, in silence, and only at dawn—when they saw a stream of armored vehicles and trucks with very young Russian soldiers on the hulls, rolling through the promenade—did Auntie Magdalena speak up.

"Well, this is the end," she said in a voice that could break with each word, and she was right. At least as far as the Mautnic family dynasty was concerned.

For Hedvika, however, it was only the beginning. That morning, she entered the apartment in their house for the first time, and this momentous event was being saluted by the raised barrels of Russian tanks, aiming at the windows of their apartment, as is evident from the first images in her baby photo album. Father evidently had no idea whether he should first photograph the newborn or the tumult of the people swearing at the Russian soldiers; whether he should focus on the livid faces of the citizens of Prague or the confused faces of terribly young Red Army soldiers, which were taut with nervous tics and ready to crack. It would take so little for the entire situation to turn into a massacre. It would take so little for an excited Ivan to press something inside the metal belly of the tanks, and a shot would fly through the windows of their apartment and forever silence the quiet happiness of Hedvika's parents and the persistent defiance of Auntie Magdalena. That day, no shots were fired; no catastrophe took place—nevertheless, it visited their family soon enough.

First, her mother was called off her maternity leave back to work. Due to the noble ancestry of Auntie Magdalena, Hedvika's mother was demoted from the offices of a construction company to a cold screws-and-bolts warehouse, and shortly thereafter, they fired her father. Nobody would hire him, except the ironworks in Kladno from which he would return home progressively skinnier and stooping: month by month, he was disappearing right in front of their eyes until one day, he never came back. He got an attack of dyspnea and fell into the melting furnace. They stopped production because of him, and even though they cooled down the furnace as fast as possible, they of course did not find anything there. So they were sent from the ironworks a symbolic bag filled with metal shavings with a letter where the director wrote his condolences in one sentence, and also threatened that—should they discover that the father's carelessness was in fact a case of sabotage—they would demand from them the lost earnings incurred by stopping production, which the Czechoslovak people had been robbed of.

Just to ensure that all of this would not be insufficient, a year later they found the auntie lying under the basement stairs. Considering her age—she was then almost ninety—the doctor, pointing meaningfully at the cane lying nearby, concluded that the death was an unfortunate accident. The bruises on her neck and arms and her terrified, protruding eyes did not interest anybody.

To this day, Hedvika cannot forget the image. She was standing among them, then six years old, and was looking at the auntie's bulging eyes, at her mouth distorted with horror, at the face so dissimilar to the kind face—the one she knew so well—creased with wrinkles and framed with fine, always tidy white hair.

"Auntie is an elegant and educated lady," her mother used to say. "Listen to Auntie and always learn from her."

Languages, etiquette, natural history—she was supposed to learn all of that from her aunt, but the moment the door closed, Auntie conspiratorially winked at her and from under her bed, she took out a puppet theater folded in a large box. Entire Sunday afternoons, which her parents spent with friends, Hedvika watched puppets running on the headboard of her aunt's old-fashioned bed.

"Once upon a time, there lived one Baron Mautnic," one of Hedvika's favorite stories began. "One day he accepted an invitation from the Náprstkovo Museum to lecture about his collection of zoological curiosities to ladies and damsels from the American Club of Prague Ladies. One of them, an orphan, who was once taken in by the Náprsteks and who then later would take care of cataloging the museum collections, asked many smart and well-informed questions. And it was precisely those questions that brought the baron to look somewhat deeper into her eyes . . ." The eyes must have been the thing that captivated Baron Mautnic about her aunt.

Hedvika moved from the window to the huge shelving cabinet which took up one entire wall in the room. Some time ago, there used to be a showcase cabinet to exhibit Uncle's collections; today, there was a bookcase from which one of the movers—a youngster in an *I Love USA* T-shirt, with long, curly, greasy hair—was taking one row of books out after another and packing them into containers. Hedvika looked at one of the framed wedding pictures standing in the middle of one of the shelves.

A faded double portrait of the Mautnic newlyweds from 1908 captured an aging dandy with a bald crown, but with very ample sideburns and full lips, alongside a very young girl barely twenty years old, with boyish features and a severely tied bun. The only thing that caught attention in her simple, utterly unadorned face were her lively, earnest eyes peering straight into the camera.

What was it that the wealthy and respected Baron Mautnic saw in Hedvika's auntie, a girl from the orphanage of Vojta and Josefka Náprstek? She had asked herself this a hundred times. Did he succumb to her youth? Or was he interested in her encyclopedic knowledge in the field of natural sciences, her healthy common sense, and her calm disposition? Whatever it was, shortly after the construction of the house was finished, he brought her in, disregarding the rumors which the unequal marriage caused among the respected burghers bound by ossified monarchical morals. Nevertheless, he was celebrated that much more by the Czech Patriotic Association, which praised his good heart since he so magnanimously took under his wing an orphan with no dowry, and his forward thinking since the auntie was considered in those days to be one of the most emancipated and educated young women in Prague.

"It was truly a modern marriage. The young girl became not only a good wife to the aging scientist, but also an irreplaceable colleague with whose help he organized his extensive collections and published a few studies of exotic fauna," continued the puppets in the fairy tale. "Studying together compensated for their childless marriage, and if Baron Mautnic hadn't disappeared one day in an African primeval forest, where he went to follow up on his research, they would have lived happily ever after," Hedvika remembered what she always declaimed in unison with the puppets at the end.

Her thoughts were interrupted by the sound of something breaking. The photograph that she had just been looking at was now lying on the floor among shards of broken glass.

"Careful!" Hedvika shrieked, too late.

The young man, instead of apologizing, only grinned. "Nothing to worry about, madam," he said, and as he was putting the picture in the container, he added: "Besides—glass shards bring luck!"

Hedvika thought that his *madam* didn't sound at all as derisive as *baroness*, which the tenants still used to address her. Moreover, she needed good luck now more than ever.

Just a short while later, the bookcase was empty. The large shelving cabinet stood there suddenly naked, and the movers—who had already emptied the neighboring apartment—were now removing the last pieces of furniture from her apartment. Their steps echoed in the empty room as if in a cave.

"That painting—just take it down and lean it against the wall. I'll bring that one with me," Hedvika said when she saw one of the movers taking down the portrait of the house that used to hang above her aunt's bed. The portrait of the house as a member of the family, the portrait of the house as the focus of the entire world.

"So that's it, the floor is empty," the grumpy foreman eventually announced, his words vibrating for a while in the hollow space. "Everything is put away on the upstairs floor and everything that you marked we're taking to the dump. Here's the invoice." He inspected her with a cold look. Surely he must have thought she would now take out a thick bundle of korunas and hand him the cash with a dismissive gesture, as if to say, *Keep the change.*

But instead, Hedvika opened her wallet and sheepishly counted out the sum they had agreed upon in advance. Even if he wasn't that unpleasant and deserved a tip, she still wouldn't be able to give him one.

The owner of the house, and she's this stingy. She glimpsed the shadow of contempt in his face as he was tucking the banknotes into his pocket. Then he turned and left without a word.

Hedvika felt awkward, but what she really found painful was the empty wallet.

The moment when she would find herself out of options had just occurred; tomorrow morning the masons were coming, and she did not have a penny for them. Now she truly had no other choice but to climb up to the attic, ring the bell of the apartment in the turret, and agree to the disgusting offer of Doctor Šimek. That notion made her anxious; she was drowning in it just as her house had been drowning not that long before in the Vltava.

"When the going gets tough, look at this painting," her auntie used to say. "This is your home, your place in this world. This house is all that remains of the family line of Baron Mautnic. Soon it will belong to you. Take good care of it and it will take care of you in return."

Hedvika would really like to take care of the house. For her auntie and her mother, who had for years reproached herself for not being able to take care of the Mautnic home that she'd inherited from the aunt. They got her on the first try—due to a mandatory fitting of a lift—and they seized the house from her. *As a result of the incurred arrears of the reconstruction works in the amount of 1,215 Czechoslovak korunas that was not paid in full on the due date, the real estate thus becomes the property of the state*, the official notification read, over which her mother had cried many a night. To whom she owed this much—she never knew. The reconstruction was organized by the National Committee, and all the invoices they had sent to her she duly paid off—every last penny. Except the last one, which she had never received.

"That house has cost us so much already that it's high time it pays us back somehow," Hedvika said aloud to herself, and crouched down to the painting, which had been taken down and placed on the floor.

Against the blue-colored sky on the painting, the house soared with carefully rendered details. Garlands, tracery on balcony railings, every window different—exactly as it was in reality. And then she paused. She took a handkerchief out of her pocket and gently wiped a fine layer of dust off the painting. Then she bent over, and with her eyes centimeters from the canvas, she studied it thoroughly. And indeed—on the uncle's floor, the one she was crouching on at the moment—there was a figure standing in a window. Painted with the tip of a thin brush, a tiny figure of a young man with familiar features. He was looking at her through the window panes, red-cheeked with a rich thatch of black hair (which in his wedding picture was long gone from his forehead and only a white crown circling the top of his head remained), with a scarf tied like that of a romantic poet, and wearing a tight suit the color of dark-red wine. She had no doubts that it was Baron Mautnic.

From where, however, was he looking at her? Surprised, Hedvika glanced around the room. The light entered through only one window.

Again, she carefully looked over the painting.

There was no doubt—the corner room on this floor should have two windows, according to the painting.

A second later, a warm gust of Indian summer wind wafted in—the air smelled of the nearby water and the first rotting leaves—and Hedvika, leaning on the parapet like a gymnast on uneven bars, bent out the window until she almost fell out, curious what the façade would reveal.

Exactly where the space inside was blocked with the huge bookcase lining the entire wall, there was indeed another window on the outside.

It took her a few hours.

A few times she thought that she'd give up. That she would bring an axe the following day and ram through the bookcase to the other side. But then she found a lever hidden under one of the shelves so cleverly that it clung to the small cantilevered beam; she needed only to touch it lightly and it moved so smoothly, as if somebody had last used it just a day before. A portion of the bookcase opened up in front of her and uncovered a passageway, tall and wide enough that an adult could get through.

Hedvika hesitated for a moment but then, slowly and carefully, she entered.

The darkened room surprised her at first with dry air infused with old age and decay. It hit her nose with such vigor that her hands unconsciously covered her face. Then she groped about for the door and opened it wide so that fresh air could get inside. Along with it, more light filtered in and revealed a narrow room filled with various objects from the floor up to the ceiling—paintings, sculptures, furniture. At the far end she noticed a bunk on which there were carefully aligned boxes of various sizes in rows marked with letters of the alphabet. Beside the bunk there was a rocking chair, and in it rested something which seemed to be, at first glance, a tangle of bunched-up clothes. Only when Hedvika really focused did she see that from the tangle protruded a shrunken, dried-up head with empty eye sockets and a collapsed chin revealing a grisly, wide-open throat. Bony hands were tied to the back of the armchair and sticking out of the sleeves of a khaki suit; she noticed how, on slender ankles covered with dried skin, heavy traveling shoes hung on.

Hedvika shrieked and jumped back, hitting the back wall of the bookcase with her shoulder. A long belt with metal spikes fell on the floor with a thud, and around it, with a quiet sigh, photographs and newspaper clippings glided down. What in God's name is it—a mummy? And the peculiar installation that she just broke—what was it supposed to mean?

With a wildly beating heart, she looked away from the corpse in the rocking chair. While she was rubbing her shoulder, she scanned the collage sprawled around the backside of the bookshelf like a spider's web. It consisted of strange objects such as straps, whips, and handcuffs on a nail driven in near the door, and all around were affixed newspaper clippings and colored pictures ripped from calendars, or black-and-white amateur snapshots evidently taken in the room where she was standing. They showed naked young men, and some of them featured various creatively arranged groups of them—almost like a horse cart or a pack of hounds. Others revealed enlarged details of their genitals. All those groupings were dominated by the figure of Baron Mautnic with a whip in his hand, festooned with trinkets.

"Well, I'll be damned!" Hedvika exhaled in shock. What she had just seen stunned her more than the mummy sitting in the rocking chair.

Again, she glanced around the strange lair in astonishment. Slowly, the realization came to her that she had discovered an unknown chapter of the Baron Mautnic family; a chapter which the Sunday puppets never mentioned. *What—hidden from the world—happened here, what secrets did the Mautnic family have?* she wondered.

And then her gaze fell on a small writing desk under the window covered with transparent paper. Lying there, too, were small, haphazard heaps of magazine clippings, and more black-and-white pictures. Finally, a diary was resting on top of the pictures, right in front of the chair; all one needed to do was open it, grab a pen, and start writing.

Hedvika took a few hesitant steps toward the table and tremulously opened the diary.

September 10, 1925

It's shortly after his funeral. What a farce! The coffin without the body, the only survivor without sorrow. Sorrow! Ha! Disgust and hatred are what twisted my face during the ceremony, not pent-up tears. And in order not to have to pretend anymore, I avoid everybody. I instructed the staff not to interrupt my solitude and sorrow, and visitors are refused before they have time to introduce themselves. "The baroness does not receive visitors," I hear the footman's tragic voice from the entrance, "she is in mourning." And so finally I have time to gather my thoughts.

So first—I do not regret anything.

His death—and it was, thanks to that frog, fast and painless—is for me deliverance. No guilty thoughts encroach on my peaceful sleep at night; he got only what he deserved! How could I give that asshole any heirs when he would barely look at me, when he preferred to bring into his burrow boys from the neighborhood? Let him roast in hell for all those insults he would hurl at me, let him roast, the lecher!

And second—nobody will figure this out anyway. Mr. Boháček, JD, has fulfilled his mission perfectly, and the news he sent from that wilderness could not be verified by anybody here. And who would not believe the consular stamp? As soon as a document is kissed by a stamp, there's nobody here who would ever question the news certified by it. There's no hope, it said, so the officials clicked their heels, the baron was pronounced dead—and my life can finally start!

I will no more be just a faithful wife indulgently overlooking the bestialities of her husband. I will no longer be just a trained poodle, a walking card file, a handy secretary—the next study will bear my name and the world will finally learn that I too . . .

Hedvika trembled with excitement.

The history of the Mautnic family line suddenly changed, assuming different contours, and her uncle's mummy—the most peculiar specimen of his own collections of zoological exhibits, gaping at her from the corner of the room—did not mortify her at all anymore. The idea that he got what he had coming resonated in Hedvika's head when she turned again to the pages of her auntie's diary. There weren't many entries. It looked as if Auntie wrote in it only occasionally—perhaps only when she came in the room for a valuable piece to sell to prevent the nationalization of her house. It didn't take Hedvika long to make it to the final entry.

January 17, 1974

Šimek was snooping again. I know that he suspects something, and he knows that I know. But he won't find anything. This hideout is difficult to find, and while I am alive he won't get any opportunities. Let him sweat trying to figure out where I keep getting all the things which always, at the last moment, save our ownership of the house. Let him threaten me, let him keep on waiting for me in the niche above the stairs, let him try—he's not going to get anything out of me, even if he were to push me down those stairs. I will always try to do everything I can so that our little Hedvika can inherit from me as much as possible—so that she keeps the secrets of this house through her childhood, but also so that she can remember it when she really needs it. Our Hedvika, she is the future of the unfortunate Mautnic family; our Hedvika—a child with bright eyes and an open mind, who will one day finish what I have started. She will reclaim the collections, publish my studies whose authorship was denied to me by that pack of academics, chauvinistic sycophantic friends of the deceased baron. She will bring back to the house of Mautnic justice and order. Our Hedvika, she will pull it off one day . . .

March 31, 1998

It has taken a year and a half to be able to add this entry to the previous ones. But finally—the waiting is over. The house looks like new, everything has been restored to its original condition, and downstairs, where there used to be a shop with paint, I have opened an exhibition hall.

The exhibition is called "The Life and Work of Baroness Mautnic."

The opening was attended by many people from the neighborhood, but also complete strangers, and even the press. From upstairs, Doctor Šimek came too. Gnarled in his wheelchair, his face puckered like a rotten potato, shooting thunderbolts from his eyes—at the walls with exhibits, and at me as well. However, he congratulated me with a heartfelt zeal as if he has never wanted anything else but welfare for the Mautnic family. And so I offered him, with the same heartfelt smile, a glass of wine, and waited until the last drop slithered down his throat, tight with rage, and then I bent down to him and whispered: "How could you be so inept? It was all so simple!"

The profanities he wheezed out cheered me up, unlike the indignant visitors among whom the aghast goblin Šimek Jr. tried to maneuver the wheelchair back to the elevator. "I will show you yet!" he threatened before the door closed.

I worry that he won't get the opportunity to fulfill those threats. The magic of the thorn frog may have weakened a little through the years, but the heart of Doctor Šimek has weakened too. By the next day, the news of his fatal heart attack had spread all over the house. At his age, it didn't surprise anybody . . .

You would have enjoyed that evening, dear Auntie.

ALL THE OLD DISGUISES

BY MARKÉTA PILÁTOVÁ

Grébovka

I'm returning to Prague. The big return for the big bucks. But what am I doing here, really? I was Vilda's partner. And now I've been invited back here by his grandson. It's so unreal that it's almost ridiculous. I do not know exactly what it is he wants. He simply paid for my plane ticket. He only wants to tell me something. And I will not say no to a visit back to Prague, to the city where all the disguises are buried. I will walk through the Jewish Quarter; I will have a crappy cup of coffee in one of the coffee shops and then . . . we'll see. We'll see what the grandsonny wants.

I look like Robocop. I have always stood out. It didn't matter if my suits were tailor-made; however much they tried, I have always looked like a gorilla dressed as a man. "You're too big, try not to hurt anybody," my Mom used to urge me. And then later, when I hit puberty, I realized that in the big skull of mine there's much more going on compared to others. I realized it slowly but surely. I breezed through school with a thumb up my nose, but I looked like I could easily beat the crap out of Godzilla. So nobody ever suspected me of having more of a brain than themselves. Only the old physics teacher Macek realized it—he urged me not to be too vengeful, because I could easily cause all sorts of ugly things to happen.

I haven't been here for something like thirty years. Perhaps more—but who's counting? And when Vilda's grandson wrote me, I was not curious. I was not curious at all to see those melancholy stone houses and the pungent, murky river about which Smetana composed all that puffy music. I don't suffer from nostalgia or the desire to fart on the frozen dirt here. And my memory is very good. My mind palace, where I go to reflect and spit into the dirty water under the Charles Bridge. And if you do not know what a mind palace is, then go and read Cicero. I have no home, and that makes my job easy. And I have always been busy with work. No thanks to God. None at all—I'd rather do nothing and watch detective stories, or read Ovid's *Metamorphoses*. In any case, speculating with stocks had never appealed to me, nor translating Roman philosophers and quantum physics, which Macek wooed me to study. It was more boring to me than even organic chemistry. And then I discovered that I was interested only in being smart and getting paid for it. Vilda and I came up with a few new machines. We built a huge factory for those smart machines and had plans and branches. Everybody everywhere needed our turbines and metal blades. Finally, something that truly tantalized me.

It was a long time ago when we were building our empire . . . but Vilda was a Jew, and he did not want to move. Not even when it became clear that the Nazis had decided his time was up. I ran fast; he stubbornly stayed. And then I bailed him out of the concentration camp. Back then it cost us all our money. But it had become quite clear that nobody was interested in reporting on Buchenwald to the rest of the world, and so on his way to the United States, Vilda got finished off somewhere between Lisbon and Havana. Allegedly by an SS doctor who was sent on the boat with him. Apparently the insulin dose he injected Vilda with was a tad too much. It doesn't matter what had really happened, because when all the truth about the camps came out after the war, it became very clear that Vilda had no chance. In 1941, not one of those bastards was interested in some wealthy Jew—whose money ended up in their pockets—talking to the White House about his experiences in Buchenwald and Dachau.

And then I did not return back home. I quite simply cast everything aside—the war, Vilda, factories—and I started doing something completely different. Vilda would be surprised. He always claimed that I was a bit of a scoundrel and that I was wasted on business. In fact, it wasn't until after the war that I started doing what he always recommended I do. It didn't pay as well as when one engineers machines nobody else has ever designed; on the other hand, it was quite enough. I was able to dig around in languages, change accents, travel all around the world. I was so conspicuous that nobody was ever able to connect me with what I was really doing. *It's so conspicuous that it is rendered inconspicuous,* as my dear Sherlock Holmes might have said. Peculiar how we are always drawn to book characters we can never resemble. Maybe it's enough that we *want* to resemble them?

I had always lived exactly as I wanted. Mom used to say: "Never live according to others, because others have no good intentions." Mom was an innkeeper, almost as large as me; she smelled like goulash and stank like a spigot, and when one of the regulars slapped her butt, he was still collecting his teeth the following day. So she was certainly worldly, and I always took her advice to heart—if I did not, I could not sit down for a week. The only person who had always had good intentions with me was Vilda.

Maybe his grandson wants to hear this old history? What use would it be to him? I found out that he returned from the States to the wild East after the revolution in 1989, and worked as an economic consultant to some government minister with a violet tie. The clown had studied economics—Vilda would probably not approve all that much. He did not approve of schools; he detested educated people because he himself was not educated. He did like intelligent people, for sure, but naturally intelligent people who do not need to sit around reading books for five years to understand what they're supposed to do in life. Vilda started at his parents' shop with feathers, then he worked for my mom as a busboy, and all the while he was designing machines—coming up with technical improvements which, once he showed them to me, left me inspired. We both knew we were made for each other. And now his grandson has started to do serious business in Prague. He's bought a few Communist bars he wants to refurbish into posh establishments and maybe he feels he should get back his grandpa's factory. All options are possible as I have confirmed so many times. But I do not want to be surprised. I really dislike surprises. And so I keep on wondering, *What does this boy have on his mind?*

From the pictures I got, he is the spitting image of Vilda. Thin, a hollow face with black eyes; underneath, a hook for a nose. I am sure, however, that Vilda would hate him. But perhaps I am not being fair, allergic as I am to everything that belongs to Vilda's family. Still, Vilda simply never liked these careful, uninspired types. When I was looking through those pictures, I saw a guy who at once knew and didn't know the ropes. He didn't know himself. You can see that by the way he looks into the lens. The body language and all those observation techniques can be cut in half if you just look carefully into the eyes. Hands, body composure—all of that can be controlled and learned. Except eyes. Those who are self-possessed have calm in their eyes. This one's eyes are like gas burners incinerating him from the inside. And that's not good. But I am curious—that has always been my biggest problem.

He arranged a meeting with me in a tavern near Grébovka. That choice is already, shall we say, significant. Next to it was Vilda's villa, which contained that immense collection of sculptures, almost to the point of a fetish. He had to put all that dough into something. And then he stayed—because of his pride. Stupid pride. This all goes through my head as I order mediocre wine from local cellars, which they pour so proudly—this swill they make out of what has been growing here on the hill since Charles IV. Well, one should always taste what the locals are trying to make. I do like the view, though. Through the smog, I can see a piece of Prague as I used to know it. As I see it even today, whenever I reminisce. Sometimes I sketch Prague with a charcoal pencil and every detail is where it's supposed to be. Church spires and flocks of pigeons under cloud lines. The only thing I can't get into those drawings is the smell of the streets. That smoky, foggy scent with a tinge of the gutter, each spring colored with lilac. Light spots from the streetlamps are starting to softly circle around the park. It's still quite cold, which is further accentuated by a fine drizzle. In the park, fitness nuts are running about in colored jackets; in the late afternoon they swarm under the lamps like moths.

The tavern is stylish, but utterly empty. Perhaps people drink here only on weekends—like everywhere else, where during the week people make money so they can then pour it down their throats in the two days they are off. In any case, I am sitting here alone, gazing into the large jar full of corks that seems to be obligatory in every good establishment serving wine. He came up to my table silently, like a greedy tomcat. Expensive briefcase; cheap shoes. I didn't ask him how he recognized me, because everybody knows me. My hair is gray but my physique hasn't shrunk or dried up with age. We greet each other and I do not feel like telling him to get to the point. I enjoy long negotiations; I like watching people's eyes. How they change, how the pupils narrow or widen. I am, however, absolutely taken aback by his likeness to Vilda. How he moves like him. As if somebody stabbed me right in my heart with a thick, blunt, corroded needle, and thoroughly dug it in there. His son didn't resemble him this much. He's been dead for a long time; cancer got him when he was still young, and so it is possible that I actually do not quite remember what he looked like. The grandson is more than just Vilda's carbon copy. He even speaks like Vilda. First it confuses me. Then I get used to it. He makes too many unnecessary pauses and probably thinks that gives the impression of smartness and depth. The same mistakes. Can't those genes be distributed in a better way? He starts telling me something about himself, as if that should interest me. This type of information hasn't polluted my brain for a long time. I only listen to the manner of his speech. It's not like a greedy tomcat anymore. It's an anxious dog. I don't need to consider the inconsistencies in his life story to understand that he has carefully invented and designed it in his head so that he can later retell it at any time to anybody. "Well, thanks for the info," I say politely.

He's sitting and smoking. That does not quite fit his image of a clean-cut young man. Apparently, he heard that me and his grandpa . . . ehm . . . that we were very close. That, we sure were. "I didn't invite you here by chance. I mean here, to Grébovka."

"Even an idiot would be able to figure that out," I answer.

He just about sloshes the expensive wine on his cheap shirt. He doesn't quite know what to do with me. He'd like to come out with it, but I don't feel like hearing it yet. We're silent. "You haven't been here since the end of the war?"

"What would I do here?"

"I don't know, I wasn't born here—but the place has always draw me in. I wanted to know the places where Grandpa and Grandma lived."

"People are all different."

Again, a pause. In his eyes, the nervousness is starting to morph into anger. "Your Czech is still excellent."

"That's possible, I still read Czech news on the Internet."

"Apparently you're a polyglot."

"Not really, I just like Latin. Since my school years. And once you learn Latin, all the other languages are fun."

"They're after me."

And it was out. A bit too fast for my taste. He tells me he has a feeling that somebody is watching him.

"Why don't you hire security?"

"I don't trust anybody."

"But I wasn't your grandpa's bodyguard."

"I know; you were partners in your business. Grandma said that you also . . . that you were really close."

"Yes, we certainly were. Your grandpa went both ways, as did many others in those times. The time before the war was fiery, hedonistic . . . no careful consummation like now."

I watch his pupils. They have widened with disgust. Grandma surely informed him in much more detail.

"Why should I help you? Because of Vilda? Because you're his grandson? Don't be ridiculous. You yourself do not believe something like that could interest me."

"Allegedly you killed his murderer. Grandma said so."

"Yeah? And when did she tell you? On her deathbed? And even if I did—it was war back then. One Czech simply killed the Nazi who killed his friend. That's all. I cannot protect you, kid, because I don't even know why they're after you and why I should bother. But thanks for the talk and the trip to Prague."

He was right. I ferreted out Vilda's killer. For that, I used all sorts of skills. In Argentina, where that bastard with the syringe who gave Vilda an overdose of insulin ran for cover, I sent him over a cliff in Buenos Aires, behind the Centrangolo station. And maybe he didn't inject it; maybe he came clean, because my torture was a tad more effective than their war torture. Anyway, he fessed up, and even if it was under duress, I did not care—that guy worked in a concentration camp as a doctor. He probably wasn't really taking care of patients there. I shouldn't have told Zdenka. It only affirmed her belief that it was wasted money back then. I will never forget how she begged me not to rescue Vilda. *What will be left for us?* she whimpered like a kicked dog. I hated her. And she was right. She was left with nothing. But compared to me, she didn't know how to take care of herself. She had a hard time in the States. No longer young, with a child to take care of. I didn't care how she scraped along. I was not interested. She ceased to exist for me the moment she didn't want to save Vilda. And now I should save her grandson.

"So, get to it—who is after you and why do you believe that I could do something about that?"

"It's about that factory of yours here. All the land and the workers' houses. I would like to apply for restitution. With you, of course. And perhaps that's why somebody is following me. It's a huge amount of money."

"Did you say *restitution*?"

He uttered the word the same way a hungry dog eats a fancy piece of brisket. Every syllable in that foreign, hopeful word was full of mad desire. Now all I am interested in is how he wants to accomplish this. What his plan is. It's turned out quite nicely. I will let him utter the word one more time to make sure. Then I have to gain time. It's quite late, it became dark a long time ago, and this park is not very easy terrain—all uphill or downhill, and I am over eighty. I have to gain some time. I have to create it. And then I have to provoke this sweetheart. Hit the bull's-eye.

"I do not understand why it is that you should get anything back. You're a grandson; you do not deserve any of Vilda's or my money. You're a nobody who emigrated here from the States because you wouldn't have made it there. You are a consultant to a rookie who knows jack about capitalism, and you think that that's a career. And now, when everybody asks to be *restituted,* you should get something? Why? Because thanks to some cosmic irony your name is Šantavý?"

He's listening to me, his eyes burning with an enraged, cold flame. Vilda's eyes could burn like this before the war. Just a bit more, just a bit more oil for the fire and he will lose it, and I will learn how he has everything planned out. He doesn't have a gun, though: when he came in, I carefully looked him over. He is not the type who could shoot—too nervous to carry a gun. A small fish who has only started to attend the mafia day care. He'll have somebody do it for him. Somebody who has not come yet. He hasn't given him the sign yet. He still needs something. That's why he keeps himself in check. I have to get to the next step hellishly fast so that I can learn from his eyes where that somebody—who is going to do his dirty job for him—will be coming from.

But I better not hurry. I know what I want. And I know myself so well that I could take my finals on it. And I am proud that I can see through myself. Most of the time, everybody is just lying to themselves. I have learned not to do that. To others, I lie often.

Calmly, as I see fit—never to myself. Did Vilda feel the same? He would have said that he didn't want to lie to himself, that he didn't want to feel like vomiting because of himself. How I understood him then! He was beside himself with rage. From how everybody pretended that nothing was really happening, how they all retreated, how they groveled; then Beneš capitulated, the Jews did not defend themselves . . . How everybody, including me, scurried away like rats and spiders from a sinking ship. He did not pack his suitcases; instead, he started organizing resistance. Back then, I was not trying to dissuade him; I did not ask him to go with me, I did not push him into anything. I loved him, even with his laughable, dangerous pride, with his need to start a family and have everything. I have never tried to change anybody; perhaps out of laziness, perhaps out of disgust toward those tiny lies that people find in their pockets and then try to turn into some large truth about themselves. But that pride was not Vilda's lie, that was him; he was very proud and he paid for it. And then I tried to save him, because I did not care about money, but about him. I did not care that I shelled out six million to the Nazis, which today is more like six billion or trillion; it doesn't matter. I thought that money was absurd, just like Vilda's pride. And I knew they would never let him go. Despite that, I did pay that money. I wanted him to feel—even if only for a while— like a human being, and not like an animal driven into a corner.

So, young pup, what's the story? I want to kick him under the table. And suddenly I'm fed up. It's not impatience, but it's starting to get boring—this waiting for somebody who's supposed to come but is not coming, and the kid is growing a tad nervous. Or am I paranoid? Am I like those old curmudgeons who always imagine that everybody wants to steal their wallet, break their bones? Vilda used to say that the price for great imagination is fear. He always disapproved of my imagination, and he always made a decent profit out of it. I have a large but already fragile body. I can shove as much calcium down my throat as I want to, but I feel how it simply is not what it used to be. So I should take off; I should think of something. But I am starting to fear. Fear that I will not be able to manage anymore. I will not manage in the same city where I buried all that old and useless junk; memories of the fabulous prewar ride, of Vilda's wide shoulders and tailor-made white shirts—and the silky smooth skin underneath. I see in front of me his silhouette, his fashionably twisted cotton shawl; he stands over there by the park gate, leaning on the cracked wall, imagining his new villa, taking a drag on his cigarette. We used to come here often. Me and Vilém Šantavý. The beast and the beauty. At night, we would just sit around on benches or lie down under blossoming chestnut trees, smoking and holding hands.

Where did his bad boy of a grandson plan on ditching me? The trash cans by the park, or the tiny river flowing behind the fence? And would I then be found by a pooch being taken for his morning walk? Will they then assume the culprits are the young junkies sitting around behind the stone gate? Or the playboy Russians who go whoring in the houses not far from here? Or the tasteless coal baron who demolished Vilda's villa and built in its place a luxurious concrete bunker?

I nervously fidget my legs under the table, and I start to sweat. Perhaps I better inhale my own scent one last time, before it becomes clouded with cold fear. I smell the perfume Vilda used to give me every year for my birthday. It has been given so many names and so many labels, but the basics are the same—the heavy, musky smell of tiny deer that use it to mark their territory. Today, it is made synthetically. But before the war, everything was real—furs and musk. I sniff at my wrist, where every morning I have applied two or three drops of the perfume since Vilda gave me the first bottle. It may be more than just an aphrodisiac. Every morning, it gives me the feeling that I should still live. And I still do not quite want to kick the bucket even if this homophobic puppy in a cheaply cut suit—who dares to judge us and at the same time wants our money—believes he's got me.

But my plan is laughably simple—the kind that works the best.

I got it from Marcus Aurelius. I watch Vilda's grandson. He prat-
tles on about restitutions again—it sounds somewhat complicated;
with an air of importance, he discloses the names of his lawyers. He
rubs his hands, squirms in his chair. Then he stands up and goes to
the bathroom.

Now or never.

I too get up and follow him. On the way, I manage to upend
a chair; the noise echoes in the empty tavern like a cave full of
agitated bats. I'll wait until he comes out of the stall. I hide myself
behind another toilet door and when he's washing his hands and
drying them politely in the drone of the hand dryer, I put on secondhand kid gloves.

I stab very precisely. One motion. Clean job, just like in the
old times. When Marcus Aurelius had to be read in its original
form. He slides down like a rotten log. Dear goodness, I will have
to drag him to a stall! But he's not heavy. I position him so that it
will take a long time to discover him. And so that the blood flows
into the toilet bowl. And in my head, a quiet moment of power.

Vilda would for sure ask me: *What is it like, to kill somebody?* I
don't want to lie to him and so I answer him in my thoughts that
murdering his good-for-nothing grandson for money was as sweet
as doing in his killer. It gives me strength. The strength to keep up
the fight. Back then, I fought through life without him and his
body. And now I'm fighting getting old; the feeling of drying up,
vanishing, wrinkling. I need that strength.

Suddenly, I am in no hurry. And so I nicely wash my hands
and politely dry them up. I savor the fact that I have managed here
too. Even in this city done up in a grubby dress from a closet of
bygone fame. I pay. For both of us. And am I still afraid somebody
may come? Somebody hired by this kid? Maybe yes and maybe no.
The fear resulting from a compulsive imagination can be conquered
with time. So just go ahead and imagine whatever you want to! You
don't need to worry about me. I have a driver waiting for me already. The plane leaves in two hours. I still have time to get a stiff

drink at the airport—I deserve it. The lawyers whose names the boy so importantly listed will now have to really earn their money. But bribing cops so that they find a convenient culprit is not a problem at all in a post–Eastern Bloc shithole of a place like Prague. And all the restitution documents are ready. They only need my signature.

PERCY THRILLINGTON

BY MICHAL SÝKORA

Pohořelec

When Commissioner Mojmír Skorec retired, his colleagues knew exactly what farewell present would make him most happy. They all knew his life passion: his hobby was as renowned as his most famous cases. From an early age, Skorec had exceptional musical talent; in his hometown, he had acquired a reputation as the local Mozart, who by the age of twelve had become an attraction not to be missed at town events. Everybody foresaw a brilliant career as a pianist for him. He himself fully identified with this dream. His showcase became Beethoven's Fourth Sonata in E-Flat Major. During his concerts, he would always amaze and touch his audience with his precise interpretation of all the sonata's themes, with his subtle mastering of leggiero passages, with his contrast between the meditative second movement and the playfulness of the final rondo, delivered with a childlike naïveté.

After school, he went straight to the music conservatory where he piqued the interest of the audition committee with Beethoven's Rondo in G Major, impeccably capturing its rococo levity. At home, he was considered a genius. However, that was not the reputation he would enjoy at the conservatory, because he had achieved the limits of his talent at sixteen and he could not develop further. When, years later as a Prague detective, he listened to his juvenile recordings, he could clearly hear why. Even if every note was correct, every tone exact—there was nothing more. Technical precision was no substitute for feeling; lyrical passages sounded cold and unemotional.

But the young Mojmír did not know that. Spoiled by all the attention he had gotten as a child prodigy, he did not deal well with the fact that in the company of truly talented musicians, he could not astonish anybody. The feeling of being undervalued had germinated in him, and it was amplified by the fact that even though he was able to finish the conservatory, he couldn't get into a music college. An eighteen-year-old boy who had dreamed about the world of concert halls, only to realize that the future before him was one of a teacher of medium-talent pupils in the same backwater town where he was born. And to add to his depression, instead of a college acceptance letter, he received his draft papers. Due to his bleak prospects and to the harassment he faced in the army, Mojmír grew depressed and fell into unending despair. Fortunately, one of the officers took pity on him, and he told the young man that his service would shorten to five months if he applied to the police academy. This suggestion thus became the proverbial straw that the drowning Mojmír grasped.

At his new school, he shined—his love for music provided him with skills and allowed him to excel among his classmates. These skills also became fundamental to his successful police career. Precision, attention to detail, excellent memory. Just as he never forgot one note, his investigations were pedantic, with an air of abstraction and precisely executed administration. The love for music never left him, though. Skorec became famous for his collection of Czech classical music and his proclamation: *Nothing can make one happier than enjoying Leoš Janáček in peace after having solved a case.*

Therefore, when Commissioner Skorec was retiring, his colleagues got him a Swiss gramophone as a farewell present so that he could enjoy his collection of vinyl to the fullest.

It was a freezing Saturday afternoon, and fresh snow glistened as if two suns had risen that morning. A longtime colleague of Skorec, Martin Dráb, had brought along the present for the retired commissioner, which Skorec's colleagues had ceremoniously promised to him at the farewell retirement party two days prior. It was a pleasant duty for him; Dráb shared with his boss an interest in music, and he knew that once he set up the gramophone, Skorec would take out a rare LP and offer an in-depth commentary. Dráb had become enamored with classical music thanks to Skorec; and this led his colleagues to joke that the ideal case for him would be the murder of a female harp player from the Czech Philharmonic Orchestra. When Dráb set up the gramophone, the old detective had an unexpected surprise for him too: he opened a small cabinet under his TV, the contents of which had been kept secret until then. Dráb was not surprised to see more albums in there. He was surprised to see *which* records. Instead of Dvořák and Janáček, the cabinet contained a veritable mélange of illustrious foreign names.

"I haven't shown you this yet," Skorec said, and displayed to Dráb the most eclectic portion of his collection. He'd built the basis for it in the seventies and eighties, when in addition to classical music, he was buying American and British albums as well. Together, they read through the titles and Dráb was astonished: Armstrong, Cash, the Beatles, Genesis, Pink Floyd . . . At the end, Skorec produced a double LP of Paul McCartney, peered nostalgically at the dust jacket, and said: "Thanks to this LP I solved my first homicide."

Dráb raised his eyebrows in astonishment. Naturally, this bit of information could not remain unexplained. For now, the gramophone was turned off; they sat down in the living room and Skorec topped off tea for both of them.

"It was January of 1992," Skorec began. "That time was a nightmare for the police force. Plenty of people thought that everything was allowed, and when you insisted on upholding the rule of law, they would deem you a relic of the old totalitarian regime. Back then, we had to deal with a wave of suicides. Many people's dreams of entrepreneurship collapsed. They could start a business but they did not really know how to do it; they had to learn on the go and many went bankrupt. The famous aphorism of our first post-Communist premier—*Dirty money does not exist*—was interpreted by many entrepreneurs their own way, and thus the standard methods of doing business became *not* paying invoices, fraud, and all sorts of schemes. This case was, for that period, typical. They called us over to a construction company. The administrative assistant came in in the morning and found one of her bosses hanged in the office. Because it was a suspicious death, it became my assignment to investigate."

The construction company Kolář & Roman resided in the attic of a bourgeois baroque house in Pohořelec. The office windows offered an amazing view of the Hradčany panorama. Mojmír Skorec remembered very well the morning when he arrived to the crime scene: the historic army barracks, which dominated the square, were disappearing in the haze and smog; the slippery cobblestones glistened; the plaster on the old houses was flaking off and, in the claustrophobic blueish shade, the ruined memorial to Jan Nepomucký resembled a tombstone for a homeless person rather than a memorial for a martyr and a Czech patron saint.

"The suicide of one of the company's owners surprised their employees, because the deceased Miloš Kolář was very popular, and everybody believed that the firm had a bright future. When I got there, they had already hauled the body away. His office, exceptionally organized and aseptically clean, was a room in the attic—the ceiling was made of supporting beams and the window offered a breathtaking view of the old-fashioned roofs. From one of those beams hung a piece of nylon cord. Under it was a chair, upside down, and on the table we found a suicide note. According to the pathologist, the death occurred at approximately ten p.m.; nothing pointed toward a suspicious death."

Martin Dráb was looking sadly at Skorec. "Hanging is a terrible death," he said. Today's sunny afternoon, with a fresh layer of gleaming snow, could not be more different from that gloomy dark-blue morning. In the hangman's office, they had to turn on all the lights to counter that depressive desolation. The police pathologist showed Skorec the suicide note.

> *I can't go on anymore—this is the only way. I can't deal anymore with the loneliness and the incessant pressure. The company is not doing well and I am responsible for it. I am taking my own life after a long reflection; my continued existence would only cause problems for people I like. I am not able to live anymore with the remorse that, due to my mistakes, many people could lose their livelihood. I ask for your forgiveness. Adéla, forgive me, I wanted to be a better father but I failed.*
>
> *Miloš Kolář*
>
> *p.s. At my funeral, please play the following songs:*
>
> *The Beatles, Help!: "Tell Me What You See"*
> *McCartney, Tug of War: "Here Today"*
> *Percy Thrillington: Song no. 3*

The secretary gave Skorec all the details about the day-to-day running of the company. She had tearful eyes, and with a shaking hand she lit a cigarette—surely not her first one, as the air in her office suggested. The dead engineer Kolář was divorced, but he had been living with his daughter, who was studying at a school of education. The ex-wife had died of cancer three years before, and the daughter had moved in with her father. "But they really didn't get on well, and it troubled Mr. Kolář. But I had no idea how much . . ."

"Was this morning typical?" Skorec asked the secretary.

She inhaled more smoke, shaking. "What?"

"The door, for example. Was it locked?"

"Yes." The secretary dabbed her eyes with a handkerchief. "I wanted to put today's newspaper on Mr. Kolář's desk, when . . . I saw him hanging there."

"The door to his office was not locked?"

"No, he never locked his door. It was enough for him that the door to *my* office was locked."

Skorec looked back over his shoulder. There were three doors in the secretary's office: to the hall, and then two opposite each other—one to the office of the deceased; the other remained closed. "This door leads where?" he asked.

"To the office of the engineer Roman, the other business partner," the secretary said. "The poor soul doesn't know yet. He traveled on business to Tábor yesterday. Mr. Kolář"—a head movement toward the door of the deceased—"did it yesterday so that Mr. Roman"—she nodded toward the other door—"couldn't stop him, surely. They were friends."

"When does Roman come to work?"

"He doesn't know about it . . ." she repeated. "God, what is he going to do?"

Half an hour later, Mojmír got an answer to the question, when the partner of the deceased materialized, in the form of a tall man in his fifties, who could be considered elegant if he didn't come to his office in a dark-blue nylon tracksuit with the Puma logo on the pants, sleeves, and breast. The death of his partner devastated Mr. Roman, but he was still able to answer Skorec's questions. They started the business in 1990. Their jobs were divided—Roman was in charge of finances and contracts, while Kolář communicated with architects and builders. Until the previous year, they had been doing well. Then, however, problems started: clients wouldn't pay; meanwhile, they always paid their employees on time, and the business had been going slowly down the drain.

Roman sat in his office and narrated how his partner reacted to the news of business problems. "Miloš was devastated," he sighed. "I told him a month ago because I still believed I could solve it somehow. We had a horrible argument. Miloš thought it was my fault. Perhaps Zdena here"—he pointed to the secretary's door—"told you about the scene."

Ms. Zdena was a loyal employee, so Skorec admitted that she did no such thing.

"But it was not so bad that he had to kill himself . . ." Roman put his face into his hands.

"Did you know anything about Mr. Kolář's personal financial situation?"

"Miloš had a car, an apartment, and he was taking care of his daughter. The competition is tough, people do not have money, so we haven't gotten rich."

"He didn't have any other family?"

"No, only Adéla."

"His share in the business was 50 percent?"

"Yes, but now it will go to me."

"You?"

"We had an agreement. A partner was not allowed to sell or stop his share without the other partner's consent. The other partner had a preemption right and in the case of the death of one partner, the other automatically gets the share."

Skorec raised his eyebrows.

"Does it strike you as peculiar?" asked Roman. "You know, Miloš and I, we started from nothing. At the beginning, we invested mainly our time and labor, the initial capital was minimal, because we simply did not have any money. We did not accumulate any profit. Whatever we made went mainly to pay our employees and to buy the modest furniture we have here. Miloš was divorced, he did not have an easy relationship with his daughter; my situation is similar, thus we had an agreement so that should anything happen to one of us, we would not have to deal with any settlement issues. Adéla is aware of this agreement. According to Miloš, she has never been interested in taking on the company anyway. By the way—does Adéla know?"

"Yes, my colleagues informed her already."

"She is not a bad girl, she simply did not have a good relationship with her dad. Miloš was troubled by it. I will have to go see her, she will need money—she's still a student." Suddenly, he stopped and stared intently at Skorec. "It will be okay to do that, right? If I go to see her and give her money."

Skorec didn't have any objections. All that was left was to check a few last details.

"Everything pointed toward suicide. The investigation hadn't raised any doubts. The suicide note written by the hand of the deceased; no contradictions in witness statements; anybody else's involvement in the crime was ruled out by both the pathologist and forensic technicians. I remember I was sitting in my office, about a week later, reading through the reports and statements. That suicide was textbook; nevertheless, something bothered me. And then I read Kolář's suicide note again."

Dráb could imagine it all. Skorec, twenty-five years younger, sitting in his office furnished with particleboard furniture from the eighties, holding the evidence bag with the suicide note. Next to it, in another bag, was the fountain pen the deceased had used for the note. The lab report confirmed that the note was, in fact, written using the bagged fountain pen. The court graphologist confirmed the authenticity of the signature. Skorec took the note out of the evidence bag. Technicians had already looked at it so he did not have to worry about contaminating the evidence. He put the note as close to his eyes as possible. Nothing. He looked at it against the light. Nothing. Ordinary office paper with ink and a fountain pen. He took out a magnifying glass from a drawer and looked at every line . . . Yes, here. About a third of the way down it was obvious that the words *I am responsible for it* had been traced at least twice. Perhaps while he was writing it, Kolář's pen ran out of ink; he had to refill the cartridge and wrote the words over again. Was there anything interesting about this? No, but it was odd.

"Imagine," he posed, "you want to commit suicide, you are in a terrible psychological state, and as you write your farewell note, you run out of ink."

"I have never committed suicide, but it would probably make me mad," Dráb said.

"I thought the same. What would you do? Would you spend time inserting a new cartridge? I wouldn't. I would grab whatever was handy and continue writing."

"How do you know the deceased didn't do exactly that?" Dráb asked.

Skorec had removed the Parker pen from the evidence bag, unscrewed it, and examined the cartridge. And another peculiarity struck him. The cartridge was half empty. He couldn't have used up half the cartridge on a few lines. He took out a dactylographic report from a file which confirmed that only the fingerprints of the deceased had been found on the pen. Nothing about the cartridge.

The next thing Skorec did was to go back to the technicians with the note and the pen. His hypothesis was correct: the ink in the cartridge corresponded to the ink from the bottom two-thirds of the note. For the comparative analysis, they used a sample from the signature.

"Can you test the ink used in the upper one-third?" Skorec had asked the forensic technician.

"Of course."

"And one more thing—how much of the ink from the pen did you use?"

The technicians exchanged surprised looks. "Only a drop," said one.

"And then just a few lines on paper to compare the nib," added the other.

"Well, that was truly a puzzle," Skorec remarked to Dráb.

"If you didn't mention at the beginning that this was a murder, I would expect that this puzzle with the pen would be easily solved; that there would be a rational explanation. That it was not a mystery, after all."

"It was explained rationally," Skorec answered. "But it also *was* a mystery. It kept bothering me. He's writing a farewell note, yet he takes time to change the cartridge. But what cartridge? Half empty. Where did he get it? If he had another pen—why didn't he use it? "Maybe he did?" Dráb suggested.

Of course that had occurred to Skorec. As the forensic team was analyzing the ink, he set out to visit the company to look over Kolář's office again. The tidiness of Kolář's desk bothered him just as much as it did when he first noticed it. The phone. Orders, technical and fire safety reports, notes on projects, documentation. It is not a difficult task to review a pedant's possessions. Skorec himself had pedantic inclinations, so he understood Kolář. A portion of the desk was taken up by a writing pad. Near the edge, there was a picture of a girl—judging by the likeness, the daughter—and a meticulously organized set of stationary containers that, in the bluish light from the rooftop window, cast bizarre shadows. In the first container, there were highlighters; in the second, colored pencils; in the third, regular pencils; and in the fourth, mechanical pencils. In the desk drawers he found paper clips, a stapler with staples, a small bottle containing ink, a syringe, and then envelopes, paper, and folders. He glanced around. An entire wall was taken up by filing cabinets. On the shelf behind the desk, he found a tape recorder and a set of cassettes, all of them pirated Beatles recordings from Poland.

Kolář's partner had peeked into the office and looked around the room as if trying to find an explanation for Skorec's presence. "I can't imagine that somebody could ever use this office again . . ." he remarked when his gaze landed on the roof beams.

The secretary stood behind him. Her eyes welled with tears.

"Zdena, have you nothing to do?" Roman said sternly.

"Since you're here, I'll ask about a few things," Skorec interjected. "What did Mr. Kolář need the colored pencils for?"

"Some of the architects like to differentiate various construction aspects by color," Roman replied.

"I don't see a drawing board anywhere," Skorec commented.

"Miloš was a CTO, he had people to draw projects for him."

"But to his employees, he was always very nice," the secretary chimed in.

The look her boss gave her indicated that era in the company was over.

"I understand that to write, Mr. Kolář used a fountain pen exclusively," continued Skorec.

Roman and the secretary both nodded.

"Was it this one?" Skorec produced the evidence bag with Kolář's Parker. Roman confirmed this. "Did he have another one?"

"No, Miloš always carried this one with him."

The secretary discreetly dried the corners of her eyes with a tissue and nodded.

"Miloš loved fountain pens," added Roman. "Once he had similar pens delivered to all the employees. I myself have one. It was so nice to write with it."

"*Was?*"

"I broke the tip."

"Where did Mr. Kolář keep extra ink cartridges?"

"He was quite angry about how expensive the cartridges were. He would always say, *Five cartridges for a hundred crowns, that's a rip-off!*"

"He wasn't charging it to the company?" Skorec asked.

"Mr. Kolář was always against wasting money. He bought an ordinary ink bottle and he would fill the cartridge using the syringe," the secretary explained.

Skorec nodded: the presence of the syringe in the drawer was thus clarified.

"Miloš had his fancies," Roman said apologetically. "I, of course, have been buying the cartridges."

"And where is your pen?" Skorec asked.

"I carry it in my briefcase."

"Didn't Mr. Kolář borrow cartridges from you?"

"No. But I'd be interested to know what all these questions mean."

"It's just details for the report," Skorec replied dismissively.

Mr. Roman shrugged. "Anything else? I have to go back to work."

Skorec thanked him. Then both he and the secretary left the office together. "One more detail." He turned to the secretary at the door. "You said that Mr. Kolář gave all the employees fountain pens . . ."

"Yes."

"You have one too?"

The secretary opened a drawer and gave Skorec a box with a pen. "I do not use it, the ink would smudge all the time."

Skorec studied the pen. "But this is not a Parker."

"Mr. Kolář would not give a pen for which you have to buy expensive cartridges to anybody. This pen uses ordinary cartridges."

"It's starting to take shape," noted Dráb.

"It wasn't taking any shape yet for me back then," admitted the old detective. "It only confirmed my suspicion that this matter with the pen was curious. I brought one ink cartridge for our technicians and they confirmed that the first third of the farewell note Kolář wrote using that ink. In that moment, the half-empty cartridge became a conundrum."

"And you played Dvořák and pondered it," said Dráb.

"But first I visited Kolář's daughter."

Many survivors who are left behind deal with the suicide of their family member worse than with a violent death or a tragic accident; they cannot become angry at the perpetrator, be it a human being or mocking fate. Any suicide leaves the survivors with an unanswerable question: *Could I have prevented it?* When Skorec visited Adéla Kolářová, he found her in a state of emotional chaos and material disarray. He should have been prepared by the state of that apartment building with its precarious banister in the stairwell, and a small courtyard where a broken carpet duster and pathetic juniper tried to resist the oily dirt advancing from the neighboring railway.

The apartment was overrun by a shocking mess. Used clothing, dirty dishes, and empty wine bottles were scattered all over the furniture and floor. One did not clean there, one did not take out the trash; one simply mourned. A week of sorrow had taken a toll on Adéla's face: dark circles under her eyes, an unhealthy shine to her face, and, on her left cheek, the violet trace of an unsuccessful attempt to remove acne. The stained sweatpants and shapeless hoodie did not help the overall impression. Skorec already had an image of the deceased: a person loving order and tidiness. If the disorder ruling the apartment was a standard mode for his daughter, they would likely have brought each other to the brink of madness.

Skorec introduced himself and told the daughter he would like to talk to her and that he would also like to see her father's room. They sat down in the living room; the girl swiped down the clothes and kicked dirty socks under the table.

"I know you told my colleagues that you did not pay attention to the everyday running of the company," Skorec started the conversation.

"I was . . . not interested." Adéla sobbed and started crying. Regrets about her own disinterest.

"Did your father tell you he had any financial problems?"

"In the last month, he was angry with Roman. Once I even heard him yell at Roman on the phone, but why . . . I do not know."

"Do you know Mr. Roman well?"

"Yeah, he was here last week, right after Dad . . . died. He gave me some money."

"How much?"

"Twenty thousand."

Skorec pulled a copy of Kolář's farewell note out of his briefcase.

"I read it," Adéla said. "I had to identify the handwriting . . ."

"I would like you to read the letter one more time," Skorec said quietly. "And point out anything that strikes you as odd."

"*Odd?*" Adéla erupted and her voice caught. "Everything is odd. He killed himself. Why did he do it? Didn't he know I would be left alone?"

Skorec himself had asked the same questions. Silently, he handed the note to Adéla. "Please, have another look."

Adéla took the note and Skorec watched her teary eyes as they ran over those few lines. Then she shook her head. "He even chose the music for his funeral . . . He loved McCartney so much."

Skorec returned the note to the bag.

"Even though . . ." Adéla knitted her brows. "That's strange . . . That Percy Thrillington. Dad doesn't have that LP."

"He doesn't?"

"No, but Dad really wanted that record."

"The name doesn't ring a bell," Skorec said.

Adéla burst into tears again: "He told me so many times, but I wasn't listening. He was looking for that LP everywhere, he asked friends who traveled internationally to look for it . . . Dad was a fan of the Beatles and McCartney. He had all their albums."

Adéla had touched upon a theme where Skorec would forget professionalism. "Can I see it?" he asked, as if it was all standard procedure.

Adéla took him to her father's room. There was an impeccable order. The desk looked like a twin of the desk from his office. In addition to a bed and bookcase, there were a gramophone and sound system, and shelves packed with LPs dominated the room.

"What did he tell you about that Thrillington?" Skorec tried again.

Adéla shook her head: "He had been trying to get the LP for the last three years. Once we had a fight in Vienna. He would go into every record store and I was angry with him because I wanted to buy T-shirts." Again, she started crying. "I was such a dummy! If only I had known . . ."

The way Mr. Kolář organized the records on the shelf reminded Skorec of the perfect alignment of the pencil boxes in his office. Of course he knew the Beatles albums but he didn't know that much about McCartney's later music with Wings and his solo career. Yet he quickly understood that all the LPs were organized chronologically, from *Please Please Me* all the way to *Tripping the Live Fantastic* in both its short and long versions. "Are these all of the albums?" Skorec asked.

Adéla opened a cabinet and Skorec saw more LPs, a musical hodgepodge.

Again, Skorec took out Kolář's note. "These were your father's favorite songs?"

As could be expected, Adéla did not know. "I don't recognize them by their titles," she answered, "I would have to play them."

"So let's play them."

Kolář's first choice surprised Skorec. It was short and fast, a happy love song. Adéla's face revealed astonishment as well. The next song was a better fit for a funeral.

"There's still that Thrillington . . ." Skorec interjected.

Adéla couldn't take it anymore. "What's your problem?" she snapped, then ran out of the room.

Skorec found her in the kitchen, crying and cowering on the floor by the oven. He decided to risk it: "Adéla, I'm not sure that your father committed suicide. There are some suspicious circumstances."

Adéla wiped her nose with the back of her hand and with one shapeless sleeve, she brushed away her tears.

"That's why I'm asking about these things. Doesn't it strike you as odd that your dad wanted to play a song from an album he doesn't even have?"

"I don't know," Adéla responded with despair, "I was not at all interested . . ."

"Don't worry about that. It sometimes happens that we have no idea what it is that the people closest to us desire." Skorec helped her to get up. "Now try to remember which albums were your father's favorites."

Adéla did not remember the titles, but by the dust jackets she recognized what Kolář listened to most often. From the era of the Beatles, it was *Abbey Road*, from the solo albums, *Ram*. Skorec looked at the jacket of the second album, but none of the songs rang a bell.

"I am truly interested in where this is going," Dráb commented.

"In that moment, I was at the brink of depression. The inspection of the albums didn't illuminate anything—except my suspicion that something was off. I kept asking, *Why would somebody want to play a song at his own funeral from an album he doesn't have?* I was convinced that the letter contained something more, but I couldn't figure it out."

The old detective went silent for a while before continuing: "You have to realize that back then, there was no Internet. When you needed to figure out something, you had to show far more ingenuity. Percy Thrillington. I had never heard that name. I decided to ask for help from experts—I went to many music stores, but the clerks had no idea if a musician with that name had existed. I went to a library, rummaged through encyclopedias—and nothing. That evening, when Tereza came home from school, I asked her. She called a few of her classmates, but nobody knew him. It started to look like Thrillington had not existed. But why would Kolář try to buy an album that had never come out?"

Skorec took a dramatic pause.

"Do you know who finally figured it out? My daughter."

"Tereza?"

"Yeah. I was calling various people all day long. I called the university, the department of musicology, I tried music journals, but nobody knew the name Percy Thrillington. I didn't understand it at all, but I was becoming more and more sure that the key to the mystery lay in that Thrillington."

"And what is it that Tereza figured out?" Dráb asked.

That evening Skorec was sitting in his living room exactly as now, and out of desperation, he played some McCartney songs.

Tereza poked her head into the room at one point and the music piqued her interest. "Are you fed up with Dvořák?"

Skorec told his daughter about the problems he was having with Mr. Kolář's funeral song list.

"Will you show me that note?" Tereza asked.

He handed her a copy of the note. Tereza skimmed the page. "Do you think it's a cipher?"

Skorec watched her closely. That is it, that's what had made him nervous. It was silly to discuss a murder with a high school student, but he just needed help, a different view, fresh eyes on the problem, and his smart daughter seemed ideal. "Imagine, Tery, that somebody wants to kill you but wants to mask it as a suicide. And the person makes you write a farewell note."

"How do you force somebody to write a farewell note?"

"That's not the point right now. You decide to cipher into that note the identity of the murderer."

"Percy Thrillington." Tereza raised her eyebrows. "That's why nobody knows him. He is not a musician, he's a murderer."

Skorec shrugged: "It's not that easy. It has to be something that the murderer would not recognize. Percy Thrillington had to make a record."

Tereza was still staring at Kolář's suicide note. "Dad, look how he wrote it. Every line has a different form. It's supposed to be a list of songs. But with the album he doesn't have, he didn't remember the title of the song, only its order—number three. Isn't that odd? Everybody remembers the titles of their favorite songs, right? He doesn't have the album but he knows what songs are on it."

Right then, Skorec saw it: "Tery, it really *is* a cipher—read it."

"*The Beatles* . . ." Tereza started.

"In Czech. *Help!* 'Tell Me What You See.' Here and now. And who he saw we will find out when we listen to the third song from the Percy Thrillington album."

"Which we do not have," Tereza remarked, as if her dad had forgotten.

The Paul McCartney album finished right then and the gramophone stopped. Silence. Disappointment. Without the record, they would not progress.

Skorec got up, took the album, and put it back into the dust jacket. Then he played the third side of *All the Best!* Kolář's favorite singer launched into "Live and Let Die."

Tereza immediately reacted: "This is from a Bond movie, right?"

Skorec shrugged his shoulders. He was helpless. They stopped speaking and listened to the music. Tereza found the liner notes with a Czech commentary on each song. The first song finished and "Another Day" had started and right then—

"Dad!" Tereza was pointing at the liner notes. "Here's Percy Thrillington!"

Skorec took out the Beatles star's album with the inside dust jacket and handed it to Dráb. "I had it at home the entire time. Read the last line."

Dráb looked at the place the old detective pointed to: ". . . *McCartney released an instrumental version of* Ram *under the name Thrillington.*"

"That's why he was trying to get the LP. Without it, the collection would not be complete. And that's why nobody knew about it. It was just Paul McCartney's pseudonym and only a marginal recording," Skorec explained.

"Still—we don't have the LP," Tereza exhaled.

"But we have its original version," her father answered optimistically. In his notes, he looked up Kolář's home phone number and hoped Adéla would answer.

After the third ring, her tearful voice sounded: "Hello?"

"Good evening, this is Skorec. I need you to look at the album *Ram*. You told me yesterday that it was your dad's favorite. Find out the title of the third song."

Tereza excitedly listened in on the conversation next to her dad, pushing her head against the phone.

"Hello?" Adéla spoke tiredly after a short while.

"I'm here," Skorec confirmed.

"Did you say *Ram?* Third song?"

"Yes, Adéla . . ."

"'Ram On' . . . It's noted here that it means, *Let's go, let's start.* Dad has the Czech version."

Skorec ended the call. Tereza was looking at him with disappointment. "It was a Spaniard who killed him?"

"Tery, it's not a Spaniard, it's an anagram."

"It was a curious situation," Skorec told Dráb, "nothing like it would ever happen to me again. To investigate any murder, there are three fundamental questions—how, why, and who? Usually, *how* is not a problem—the question *why* is key, and to answer it, you need to know *who*. But in this case, it was different. We had *who*, but *how* and *why*—we had no idea. The pathologist and forensic specialists went back to work. They were looking for the slightest suggestion of violence, proof that it was murder. Nothing. The court graphologist checked the farewell note again. Nothing. Textbook suicide. But I knew that Roman did it somehow. So pro forma, we closed the case as suicide so that Roman wouldn't become nervous, but we continued with the investigation. *How* remained a mystery; we were looking for the motive. But the motive by itself proves nothing. We had to get Roman to confess."

Fourteen days had passed since Kolář's funeral. Prague was still immersed in a bluish smog haze. Mojmír Skorec spent those two weeks rummaging through Roman's finances, his team strengthened with a colleague from the financial crimes unit.

Mr. Roman sat in his office and looked worried. When the secretary ushered Skorec in yet again, the expression on his face was replaced by vacant astonishment. The detective informed Roman that there had been new findings in the case of the death of Mr. Kolář, and that they would like him to come with them to the station.

"What if this is not a good time for me?" Roman tried.

Skorec raised his eyebrows. "Then I'll call my colleagues and they will bring you in."

"Are you joking?"

"Do I look like I'm joking?"

The correct answer was no, so Roman gave up.

"You mentioned that you have the same pen as Kolář," Skorec said as Roman was putting on his nylon Puma jacket. "Could you bring it with you?"

"Why? You can't write much with it, it's kind of broken."

"Take it anyway. The cartridges as well."

"Cartridges?" Roman put the pen in his leather briefcase. "I don't like this, I'm calling my lawyer."

"I was just about to suggest that to you."

Engineer Roman's Parker pen was indeed "kind of broken." He had probably pushed too hard and the tip came apart, and when writing with it, the thin line would sometimes double. If Kolář had written the second part of his note with Roman's pen, everybody would have noticed the difference. Of course, Skorec knew he had no proof yet, but he understood how Roman's cartridge had ended up in Kolář's pen.

So he decided to bluff: "The day of his death, a little thing happened to Mr. Kolář. He got a paper cut on a very silly spot. That's why Mr. Kolář was wearing a Band-Aid."

Skorec could see how hard Roman, behind his stone façade, was trying to remember the Band-Aid.

"This detail problematizes his death. First—the cord on which he hanged himself. It was made of synthetic fibers and so we could get fingerprints. However, neither—not the knot on the noose nor the knot on the beam—had any fingerprints on it. On the places which Mr. Kolář held, there was a clear fingerprint of the index finger with the Band-Aid . . . Why would Mr. Kolář wipe off fingerprints from the cord which he wanted to use to hang himself?"

Roman's facial expression betrayed him. His gaze wandered to the upper-right corner of the office and the corners of his mouth turned down; he looked like a student who was trying to remember which answer the professor wanted to hear.

Skorec continued: "Second—in the middle of writing his farewell note, Mr. Kolář ran out of ink. A silly situation when you're trying to commit suicide. The person is being kept from committing the act."

"I have never committed suicide," said Roman impatiently.

"What he did was change the cartridge in the pen."

"When you run out of ink, that is what you do."

"Well, yes, but he always filled his cartridge himself."

"Oh, right."

"Where did he get the new cartridge?"

"Perhaps he had one in the drawer . . ."

"But that cartridge was half empty. You cannot store an open ink cartridge. It either dries up or leaks."

"So he got it from somewhere!"

"Third—Mr. Kolář refilled the pen, but where did the empty cartridge disappear? It wasn't in the trash can."

Roman could not answer.

"I cannot imagine that Mr. Kolář would rummage through somebody's drawer looking for an extra cartridge. I'd expect he would simply refill his own. Don't you think?"

"How am I supposed to know?" Roman was practically yelling.

"True," Skorec said. "The problem is that there are no fingerprints on the cartridge."

Roman remained silent.

"Which leads to only one possible scenario. Kolář could not have changed the cartridge himself." This was a key moment. The trap either works, or everything goes wrong and the murderer gets away.

"I understand where you're going," Roman snickered.

"That's good. At your company, nobody has a Parker pen—except you."

"But I wasn't there. Whoever changed the cartridge, it wasn't me . . . Damnit, say something!" He turned to his lawyer. "He can't put it on me because of one empty cartridge!"

"How then do you explain that we found Mr. Kolář's fingerprints on your pen?"

"I was showing him the broken nib. You have nothing on me!"

"Ah," Skorec remarked as if everything had become clear. "How is it possible to leave a fingerprint when wearing a Band-Aid?"

"That's ridiculous, Miloš wasn't wearing a Band-Aid."

"The secretary put it on him."

"I'm saying he had no Band-Aid!" Roman's eyes jumped between Skorec and his lawyer.

"One more question," Skorec said. "How did you make Mr. Kolář write that farewell note?"

"The interrogation lasted five hours and it was a collusion not only between me and Roman and me and his lawyer, but also between Roman and the lawyer. Then, finally, he told us everything; it was a relief for him. Roman had defrauded a lot of the company's money and the firm came under the threat of a hostile takeover. Roman unwisely invested in a fund that went bankrupt, and he forged signatures and borrowed from bad people, which is when Kolář found out that the company hadn't paid their employees' health and social benefits for four months. Because he considered Roman a friend, he wanted to come to an agreement—he would not sue him if Roman immediately corrected the situation and returned at least half of the stolen money—in other words, Kolář's share. But that was not possible. If the fraud was uncovered, the creditors would start breathing down his neck . . . Roman concluded that the only solution was to take full control of the company and finish the money funneling. A colleague from the financial crimes unit said that it was a standard MO: since he could not get rid of his partner legally, the only option was murder. Roman was familiar with Kolář's work routine; he knew that Kolář would be in the office alone in the evening. He came to his office with a pistol and prepared a noose, a canister of gasoline, and a plan in which he arranged everything in detail. When I think about it, Roman looks to me like a calculating, ruthless man. He told Kolář that he had a choice—either he would die alone, or both he and his daughter would die. Either Kolář would hang himself, or Roman would kidnap Adéla and burn her in front of him. *Miloš looked as if he was really afraid I would do it. He really believed I meant the threat seriously,* he told me when we were finishing up the interrogation. Ruthless, egotistic asshole!"

Dráb stayed silent. He had nothing to say—what had been entertainment turned into disgust. He knew that in certain situations, parental emotions would overtake professional police demeanor, and therefore he was glad that he'd never had to deal with a case where a cruel scoundrel beats a baby because he's bothered by its crying, or an unstable mother poisons her child with antifreeze because she wants to punish the father. He could imagine what in that moment Kolář must have been feeling, because he too had children. How long did it take? How much time did Roman need to convince his friend that he was serious? Skorec always said that murderers—however intelligent they may be—lack something, a certain type of emotional intelligence and empathy, because they do not understand the pain they inflict. Dráb pictured Roman aiming the pistol at his friend while giving him the "choice."

"I kind of understand that," the old detective said. "When somebody aims a gun at you, you do not really have a choice."

Roman pointed the pistol at Kolář, who was paralyzed by fear. So that no accidental spectator could see his actions, he turned the lights off and the scene was lit only by the outside lanterns on the other side of the street and, from afar, a neon advertisement on the front of a bank. The shadow of the hand holding the gun was projected onto the photo of Adéla on the desk. Roman spoke with a quiet, calm voice.

"I'll give you whatever you want, I'll sign anything . . ." Miloš Kolář had muttered with exhaustion.

"Please, I am not that naive. I know you and I know how you think."

"What will you gain by hurting Adéla?"

"Nothing. But *you* can spare her. It's your choice."

"How could he be assured that if he hung himself, Roman would spare Adéla?" Dráb asked.

"Interrogating Roman, I understood one thing. Kolář was used to listening to Roman. That's why it took so long for him to un-cover the fraud. Roman always had a good explanation handy and was able to convince Kolář. Kolář was in charge of the construction jobs; he communicated with architects while listening to McCart-ney; meanwhile, Roman was in control of finances and speculated with bonds. I would say that Roman was an able manipulator but, on the other hand, he would only dare manipulate those who were weaker. And Kolář was weaker. The success and prosperity of their company was based on the one hand on Kolář's meticulousness, and on the other hand, on Roman's lack of scruples. As entrepre-neurs, the two of them completed each other. I think they needed each other, but Roman didn't understand that without his partner he would never be more than just a profiteer. And Kolář had noth-ing else left but to believe him. Roman would gain nothing by Adé-la's death; once Kolář was dead, his share would automatically go to the other partner. During the interrogation, Roman took pleasure in how everything went according to plan. Kolář wrote the farewell note and then he put the noose around his own neck.

"Why did Kolář cipher the message in the LP in such a com-plicated way? Why didn't he simply write that he wanted the third song from the original version?" Even though it sounded like a question, in reality, Dráb was merely thinking aloud, as was his habit while discussing cases.

"He needed to make sure, just in case Roman checked the list. He thought Adéla would understand. That she'd be able to connect the two LPs. He had no idea how much his daughter was ignoring him."

They sat in silence for a bit longer, each immersed in his own thoughts.

"I'll show you something." Mojmír stood up and rummaged through his collection. Then he handed an album to his colleague. On the cover in a circular red cropping, between a palm tree and a music stand, sat a classically dressed violinist with the head of a ram. A white inscription on a black background in the upper-left corner told Dráb what he was holding. "A present from Tereza— she found it about three years ago in a market in Paris."

Dráb examined the LP.

"Tery told me that I could make more than my monthly income by selling this on eBay."

"So if you find yourself in need . . ." Dráb said.

"I could never," Mojmír replied. He took the vinyl out and showed Dráb the inside paper sleeve, where Tereza had written a dedication: *Dad, some experiences are unforgettable! T.*

"Shall we play it?" Dráb asked.

"You know, it's not that great."

"Right, Janáček is better," Dráb smiled.

"Something more fitting since we're reminiscing . . ." Mojmír hunted among the LPs, took one out, and showed the dust jacket to his younger colleague. Smetana's String Quartet no. 1 in E-minor (*From My Life*) played by Smetana's quartet, in a beautiful, well-preserved 1964 edition. Martin Dráb nodded contentedly. They were like two wine connoisseurs who were looking forward to a particularly delicious vintage. The old detective took the LP from its jacket, affectionately peered at the dark-blue lettering, and with a look of full concentration put it on the record player. A soft click, the static of the starting groove. With the first sounds of violins, Skorec raised the volume using a remote, sat down in the chair, and blissfully closed his eyes. The old LP crackled but the warm, deep sound of the new gramophone amazed them.

"Well, Mojmír, it plays marvelously," Martin said.

"Beautiful," Skorec agreed.

Outside, it became cloudy. The room filled with the sounds of the string quartet while thick snowflakes fell densely over Prague.

PART IV

IN JEOPARDY

BETTER LIFE

BY MICHAELA KLEVISOVÁ

Žižkov

W hat is that damn woman doing here again?

Felix saw her as he was smoking, leaning against the doorframe of his shop—Twenties & Thirties. His mood had been quite pleasant before she appeared. On his back he felt the cold breath of the spacious, unheated hall, with its high ceiling and concrete floor; from outside, a gust of warm air infused with the sun and spicy fragrances of the Indian summer sporadically caressed him.

The woman walked through the gate to the grounds of the old cargo station. She passed the old wooden train car where somebody had not too long ago opened a taproom, and walked on the broken blacktop road toward the former storage building that had been running to seed for years. But then, slowly, merchants had started to use the space—selling secondhand furniture and original pieces. Felix recognized her from afar thanks to her particular walk; she moved decisively, unwomanly. She wore the same trench coat that she had on her two previous visits. He rarely cared to notice what women wore, but her thin, light-brown double-breasted coat had caught his attention on their first meeting.

When he had first seen her in his store a few days before, he thought: *She looks like a cop.* He had the same feeling the second time. Not only due to the coat, which he—who knows why—linked subconsciously with plainclothes detectives; there was simply something off about her. The way she walked between the things on display but didn't really pay attention to anything; the way she pretended to be taking a picture of a chrome-and-leather chair, but she turned her cell phone so that he was in the picture too. He tried to convince himself that he was simply being paranoid. Cops would come in pairs, right? And they would most likely be men, or perhaps a man and a woman. His imagination ran amok. Marty had been right when he asked him at the beginning: "Are you really going to do it? You won't shit your pants?"

Simply put, Felix had never been the type of roughneck who'd think only about money. He liked the design of the interwar era, and so he had studied antiques. Then he rented this space and began selling antique pieces from his favorite time period. He was also offering trinkets such as ashtrays, vases, and wooden toys. People liked his cargo railway store and his design pieces, and he had built a devoted clientele base. Predictably, he never got his hands on all the truly valuable pieces—he was a small fish—though he did make a decent living. But since Alice and her son had moved in with him, he had started spending more and more money. To be precise: it was more than he could afford. He simply was not making enough to support two additional people—especially since one of them was an eight-year-old with a whole lot of expensive hobbies, and the other was an unbelievably demanding and lazy woman. How come this hadn't occurred to him when he took them in? What did he expect? Originally, he didn't even want to live with Alice. When she suggested that she'd let go of the sublet and move in with the boy, he thought: *Out of the question!* He was worried that their relationship would go sour, that soon they'd be at each other's throats. At the same time, something (some sixth sense?) told him that if he agreed—if he allowed her to barge into his apartment with her million trinkets and clothes, with all of her divining rods and books about healing with crystals—he would eventually thank himself. In hindsight, his sixth sense must have been making fun of him, or it had decided to ruin him on purpose. Alice made her living by cleansing people's chakras in a massage studio, but the money was far less than what she needed for herself and her son. And so he took one loan, then another one, then a third . . .

Over beers, Marty asked: "Listen, do you need money?"

A dumb question. Who doesn't need money? Especially if it's offered by a friend—a close friend from school.

Felix learned about the operation, then took a few days to think.

"You hardly have to do anything," explained Marty, "you simply offer space and keep your mouth shut, that's all . . ."

And so Felix had been doing exactly that for a few months. For Alice, and for the boy. Even if he grumbled, he was happy to have them both. If they went somewhere together, people thought they were a family. He was thought of as a father. A nice feeling. Warm. So what if Alice was funneling his money away? So what if her silly material needs were greater than her income? For the boy, he'd do anything. He didn't want to lose him; didn't want another man to bring him up, even if his life with Alice was—to put it gently—strange. And, most importantly, had no future.

While he was pondering all of this, the woman in the trench coat walked through the yard. Seriously—there was something wrong with her, but what exactly was it?

He stepped back into the shadows. She passed purposefully by all the other stores in the hall and was now nearing his. He started to distinguish her facial features—she was about thirty-five; her dark hair was up in a French chignon; she had an eagle-like nose, and along her mouth were two hard lines. Should he initiate a conversation? Ask her what had brought her to Twenties & Thirties, or what she was looking for? Usually, he didn't mind his clients all that much; he let them walk among the furniture while he took care of his orders and accounting in the small, well-heated glass coop. It was his experience that if he followed them around his store and asked them whether they needed help, it would actually discourage them. If they wanted something, they would ask him. But now he was going to be more active.

The woman entered the store, greeted him with a nod, and

continued walking among the furniture. The frilly hem of her skirt sneaked up her calves—a bit too muscly for a noble lady in high heels, it occurred to him. She had calves as well-defined as a professional athlete. Like somebody who worked out every day. Too hard. Slowly, she followed the aisle between a functionalist cabinet and cubist sofas deep into the hall. Again, she pretended to take pictures and aimed her phone at him.

He was, of course, used to window shoppers who never intended to buy anything. There were so many of them visiting his store. Most of the time he recognized them immediately: they'd usually come in pairs, and despite all the warnings not to sit on the furniture, they tested the upholstery on all the sofas with their bottoms; they touched every ashtray and paper weight and exclaimed to each other incessantly: *Yeeey, look!* or, *Oh my god, this is beautiful!* The woman in the trench coat was not doing any of that.

He moved toward her.

"Can I help you? I've noticed this is your third visit this week . . . Are you looking for something specific?"

She was standing by a battered cabinet with a cherry veneer which Marty had used not that long ago to transport his merchandise. Why did she stop right there? Did she know what was being hidden in the cabinet drawers and what shortly thereafter was further transported under the fluffed pillows of a leatherette sofa?

"No, not at all." She waved her hands around. "I'm just looking. Everything you have here is beautiful." She turned and peered straight into his eyes. "I feel like I'm in the period of Hercule Poirot. Your store has an ambiance, Mr. Keller."

"Do we know each other?"

"I know you. I read an interview with you in *Living*. Because I love the interwar period, I knew right away I had to come and see Twenties & Thirties."

And she came to "see" it three times in one week? Only because she's in love with the twenties and thirties? And why was she so inconspicuously taking his picture? He discarded the idea of asking her for an explanation; instead he asked: "Do you live nearby?"

She hesitated—only for a second, but still. She lowered her eyes toward the cabinet and then looked away toward the hall. It calmed Felix down. A cop would never become this unsettled. She would readily come up with an answer—anything.

Again, she looked into his eyes. "It doesn't matter. Do you think that—"

Felix's cell phone ringing interrupted her. She went silent and puckered her lips. Felix took the gadget out of his bag. Alice. Who else? She called him easily fifteen times a day. "Sorry," he said to the woman, and turned his back to her. It was out of the question to ignore Alice's phone call. What if she needed something important? Even if she could get on his nerves, she still remained one of the two most important people in his life.

He left the woman among the various pieces of furniture and closed himself in his little office. Alice started to babble on about a blister on her foot—she was walking with the boy from a training session, she was carrying a heavy bag, every step hurt, and she really couldn't walk anymore—couldn't he close the store for a while and come pick her up? She would also need to buy something on the way. After a short exchange, he capitulated.

When he came back out, the woman in the trench coat wasn't there anymore.

It was quiet for three days. He forgot about the woman. Marty used his truck to bring in an oak cabinet, its drawers filled with small sacral articles and a wooden sculpture—over one meter tall— of Saint Barbara, hidden in a rolled-up carpet. It was quite obvious there was something in that Persian carpet.

"It looks as if you're transporting a dead body," remarked Felix. Usually they carefully bubble-wrapped larger sculptures for transport and hid them in armoires, but Marty apparently didn't have any handy and so he had to improvise. Felix, his stomach tight, was trying to figure out whether somebody was watching them—either from other stores or from the pub in the old train car—and if yes, then whether or not the bulge in the carpet piqued their interest.

"I'm going to make one more run," explained Marty. "Probably a little before closing time, I won't be able to do it before. Just wait here, okay?"

"Okay." Felix helped him carry the goods to the hall. He put up a sign on the door that read, *Merchandise delivery*—which was, after all, true—and locked up. He unrolled the carpet. He estimated the Saint Barbara sculpture to be from the middle of the eighteenth century. It was an exceptionally nice piece; it wouldn't last long in the store. And the cut he'd get would be decent. Lately, when he was unpacking stolen antiques with Marty, he'd forget from time to time that he could easily end up in jail. It had become routine. Everything was perfectly organized. Marty would identify a village chapel or a church, and the actual stealing would be performed by two thieves. The stolen sacral articles would then be transported by more than one truck driving through forest roads. Then Marty needed a dry, well-ventilated storage space where the antiques could wait until their sale abroad. Felix provided the storage. The stolen goods were stored in a small area in the back of the store. For every antique, they had a copy made—thanks to his contacts, this part of the scheme was arranged by Felix too. They thus obtained an official certificate that the piece was a new copy of an old piece. The buyer therefore had proof, in case of a customs check, that he was carrying something of no value. Yet what was sent abroad—most often to Austria but a few baroque sculptures went to the United States as well—were genuine, centuries-old sculptures of saints.

It was a genius plan. Flawless, claimed Marty. The masquerade was perfect too. After all, who would be surprised that there were trucks often parked in front of an antique store where desks and cabinets were being unloaded?

Marty left. Felix kept the door closed—it was near closing time anyway. He exited through the back door, onto the concrete cargo ramp above the long-unused rails, and lit a cigarette. Being alone, as per usual, brought on anxiety. No, it was not at all normal what he was doing! It would not run this smoothly forever. One day they'd be found out. Felix was not an idiot, and he certainly was able to realize that for all the money he was making so easily, he'd have to pay a price one day.

Alice called—the ATM refused to dispense money to her. Could she borrow money from him? Actually, uhmmm, she had already done that; she'd noticed that under Felix's shirts in his dresser there were a few banknotes, so she'd taken one. When he got home, could he reserve plane tickets to Crete? She noticed they were dirt cheap right now.

He hung up. He lit another cigarette. Dusk was slowly enveloping the rusted rails overgrown with weeds and unused train cars. The pub and other stores in the cargo hall had closed up and all he could hear were the sounds of cars and trams on a busy street quite far away. A black-and-white cat ran across the rails, but otherwise nothing moved. Felix inhaled the cigarette and pondered whether he really wanted to live like that. That foreboding that a life with Alice would make his life better . . . what foolishness was that? Or was his life already better and he was not able to appreciate it? Was *this* a better life?

He looked up at the shoddy iron bench above the railways and swore under his breath. She was there. The woman in the trench coat. Right above him. He hadn't heard her come, so she might have been standing there the entire time. Watching him from above. In the dusk he couldn't quite see her face, though he thought she was smiling. That was the first time it occurred to him that she might not care about stolen antiques at all, but only about *him*. Did he have a stalker? Was it possible that a crazy person would fall platonically in love with him based on the picture printed alongside his interview in a magazine? He smiled—such silliness. Cigarette in hand, he waved at her, but she did not move. So he stamped out the cigarette, went back in, and locked the store. Should he call

Marty to tell him not to come with the last load? Or behave as if nothing had happened?

As he was waiting in the quiet unlit hall, watching the contours of the furniture becoming more pronounced in the growing darkness, he made himself a promise. If all was going to end well, if that woman could disappear from his life without anything bad happening, he'd announce to Marty that he was done; that this lifestyle was simply not for him.

Things ran smoothly for the next few days, but Felix couldn't shake the feeling of being an outcast. Maybe it was for real that cops were paying attention to him, and that woman worked for them. Her flirting around Twenties & Thirties could have been part of some sort of tactic. What did he know? Would she try to entice him, and then get information out of him? What if she installed a bug in his store? When he was driving to work, he kept checking the rearview mirror to see whether anybody was tailing him. A few times he thought a car was following him, and so he suddenly turned onto a side street and stopped, only to see, with relief, the car continuing on its way. He didn't say anything to Marty just yet—after all, nothing had happened so far. But maybe he should tell his friend. And they should start discussing certain things in the washroom with the water running—not in the store, where the cops could hear their every word. Or should he inform Marty right away that he was done? He had decided already, after all. What was he waiting for?

One afternoon, he looked up from his office computer and saw the stalker woman enter his store, and it actually pleased him. He'd wanted to see her again. He needed to clear everything up. So he opened the door to his small office and walked toward her.

She was looking at a stone bird fountain. "My grandma had something similar in her front garden," she said without any greeting, as if they were already friends. But she did not look very friendly, more pensive. "She had a beautiful villa in Vinohrady. I loved that house, you know? I felt home there. And in the end, I lost it." It seemed like she was talking to herself more than to him, and the last sentence she hissed through her teeth.

"What happened to it?"

"My brother inherited it. He threw out my things. He changed the lock. We don't communicate."

She peered at him with anger in her eyes. A lot of anger, considering the situation. This could not be a cop, it occurred to him. Only if she were an excellent actress and this entire performance had a point—but what would it be?

"I am so sorry," he said, though he could care less. "Maybe if you try to call him and ask him for a few things from your grandma—"

"That would only make him happy—that it still hurts me," she snorted. "He always mistreated me. Even as a small boy. He mistreated me horribly. But why am I saying this to you?"

He would like to know too. "Well then—at least buy yourself the bird fountain," he suggested. "It's from the garden of a first republic villa in Nusle."

She shrugged. "No thank you. It's exorbitantly priced." And after a short pause: "Listen, would you have coffee with me sometime?"

In that moment, with great relief, he started to understand. Or at least he believed he understood. The woman was truly interested in him—only and exclusively in him, not in sculptures of saints in his back storage room. She might be a bit crazy, and for some reason she had decided to seduce the owner of the Twenties & Thirties antique store. Perhaps this was related to a bet she made with a friend? Or maybe she wanted to buy the furniture she was used to in her grandma's house but she couldn't afford it, so she was looking for a way to get a discount?

He didn't really want to have coffee with her. He decided to stall. "I'm still expecting merchandise today and then I have a thing I have to go to, so I'd rather—"

His cell sounded. Alice was calling, surprisingly, for the first time that day. She talked for a long time: her throat had started to hurt and also her back, then one of her molars—lower right—joined in. And Felix would surely never guess what her colleague dared to tell her! That she's a hypochondriac! So rude! Maybe it would be good if he closed the store for a while and went to pick her up from work. And he could also buy some buckthorn tea—she thought it might improve her mood—would he be so kind?

He agreed to everything—he was seriously starting to worry about her—and hung up the phone. He noticed that the woman in the trench coat had been listening in on the conversation. "Sorry," he said, and slipped the cell into his pocket.

"Your wife?"

If he said yes, perhaps he could simply get rid of her, but he realized that only after he replied: "My sister."

She raised her eyebrows. "You have a nice relationship. Well, it sounds like it."

"We're twins. She's a single mother of a small boy, and last year another—probably the eighth—man left her . . . and I had just gotten divorced. So we live together, but it might be even worse than a marriage." He smiled. "My friends keep telling me it's perverse."

He assumed she'd enjoy it. That she would smile. She was his stalker, right? She kept coming to his store; she watched him from the bridge above the rails; she wanted to have coffee with him—surely she wanted him to be single. But instead of satisfaction, a strange emotion scurried behind her eyes. She looked almost disappointed. Bewildered. He didn't understand.

"So you love her."

"Sure," he shrugged. "She's actually quite horrible, but . . . I would do anything for her."

She nodded, then changed the topic back to the bird fountain. Distracted, as if she were thinking about something else. She didn't mention the coffee anymore. Soon thereafter, she started to leave.

When she turned at the door to say goodbye, something in her face told him he was seeing her for the last time.

* * *

Three weeks later he was starting to believe that his premonition had been right. His stalker hadn't appeared again, and anything that could illuminate her visits hadn't happened. He was sitting at home watching television, slowly sipping whiskey. Why was he so afraid of her? She was simply crazy. Perhaps she'd really wanted to seduce him, but once she learned he lived with his sister, she lost interest. He remembered his own decision—if he got rid of her without complications, he'd send Marty packing with all the saints. Should he do it? Was that really a good idea?

As he was pondering this, he kept changing channels absent-mindedly. *The Big Bang Theory. Solid Gold.* The news on the trashiest TV station: *"A businessman was found brutally murdered in his villa in Prague, Vinohrady."* His picture accompanying the details. *"At the time of discovery, the body had been dead for quite a few weeks and was badly decomposed. Since he lived alone and was supposed to be on holiday, his relatives were not worried. It was the smell of the decomposed body that eventually indicated its presence in the first republic–era villa . . ."*

"That guy looks like you," commented Alice, who had just entered the living room holding a cup of buckthorn tea. "Seriously, look—if your hair was shorter . . ."

"Wait!" he yelled, and turned the volume up. "I'm listening!"

". . . what's striking is the strong physical resemblance of the victim to the man who was stabbed yesterday in the late-evening hours in a park in Žižkov where he was walking his dog." On the screen, two passport pictures appeared. Both men had dark, longish hair, narrow lips, and a hollow face. In his mind, Felix nodded to Alice's comment: they both looked like him. The hairs on his neck stood up. *"The likeness of the victims may not be accidental. An unnamed source informed us that the police are working on a theory about a serial killer . . ."*

"That's weird," said Alice. "You better get a haircut. Or color your hair. So that the freak doesn't finish you next time."

"Shut up for a minute!" A chilly realization was taking shape in Felix's brain. A first republic villa in Vinohrady. Two murdered men who looked just like him. That could not be a coincidence. Or could it?

"... *the wife of yesterday's victim stated that a week before his death, a strange woman took pictures of her husband on a mobile phone. He intended to report it to the police, but he never made it. A webcam near the murder site did record a woman who was already identified by a few witnesses as the sister of the first murdered man. Tereza S. from Prague* ..."

"Some kind of freak," Alice uttered huskily. "I would cut your hair military style, really. Otherwise I'm going to piss on myself worrying about you being her next victim. Can I?"

Instead of answering, he laboriously swallowed.

"... *the woman had been having arguments with her brother for a long time, and this year she was hospitalized in a psychiatric facility from which she signed out against medical advice. The unnamed source informed us that according to one of the police reports, Tereza first murdered her brother, and then a completely unknown man, because of his physical likeness to her brother. The police are asking witnesses for any information about the movements of this woman. You are now watching the webcam recording* ..."

Felix stood up so violently that he slopped some of the whiskey on his shirt.

He knew that walk. He knew that wavy hem on firm calves.

He looked at his sister and after a long time he felt something like gratitude.

ANOTHER WORST DAY

BY PETRA SOUKUPOVÁ

Letná

While she's making tea for herself, Hladík looks around the room. A typical nice home. Naturally, a few pictures of cute children, and of her and her husband as well. Attractive people; they both smile and look happy. Toys on the floor. Bookshelves full of books on history. It's clean here. Maybe it will be different this time.

Finally, the kettle clicks and she makes the tea. She sits down across from him. She really is pretty. Pretty and sad.

"We have about an hour before Gabi wakes up."

"Did anything unusual happen yesterday?"

She watches him for a while as if she doesn't understand what he's talking about.

"No, I mean before. Before your husband disappeared."

"It was a usual day, usual evening." There's frustration in Radka's voice. She has said this already, hasn't she? She's already described the day to them minute by minute. There's nothing suspicious, nothing even interesting about it. What could there be? Peter didn't leave her, he disappeared; they didn't fight; he didn't behave strangely; he came home from work and went on his run and he didn't return. Through the night she didn't sleep for one minute, and then she took the boys to school. Filip was happy, as if nothing had happened; Matěj needed a bit of assurance—*Dad will come back, he'll be back home soon*—and Gabi, she doesn't know or understand anything. She's asleep in her room, and Radka's hands are shaking, and this Captain Hladík with the greasy spot on his hoodie—since when do detectives wear hoodies? Since when do they look as if they got their clothes from the trash? How is she supposed to believe this man; believe that he is doing his job well when he looks like this?

"Please start one more time, Mrs. Fišerová."

"Start where?"

"Where you think you should," answers Hladík.

Radka tries, she really tries hard; she doesn't sigh noisily, doesn't yell even if she wants to, she only carefully exhales.

"So start from yesterday's breakfast."

"It was a morning like any other. We woke up; we had breakfast; Peter took the boys to school; they left at seven thirty."

"Did you set an alarm? What happened during breakfast?"

Radka watches him. Why all these questions? Her husband is lying somewhere, hurt or kidnapped, and she is supposed to discuss their breakfast?

"Yes, we wake up using an alarm. I use it because I wake up easier than Peter. I also go to sleep earlier."

"So you don't sleep together?"

Now she's had it. "Of course, sometimes, yes. Sometimes we spend an evening together and we talk and then we go to bed. But sometimes Peter works at night. He has a lot of work. And I know what he does—he doesn't do anything I wouldn't know about; he doesn't have a lover with whom he communicates at night, and he doesn't go anywhere at night alone; he doesn't come back from work late . . . Peter doesn't have anybody, Peter is not like that. But I've been telling you this, Peter is good and we love each other and we have a good relationship, unlike others. So go and ask other people who know him if you don't believe me! Peter keeps no secrets from me, I don't keep secrets from him, and we also sleep together!"

Hladík nods. "I understand."

But he doesn't, he doesn't understand anything; Peter is the best thing that ever happened in her life. He's her ally, her soul mate, the best man in the world. He would never hurt her—and he would never ever cheat on her. He would never endanger the family; he would never hurt the children or her. It is her solace; everything in the world is defined by Peter being simply a great guy, and their life together being good. If they were not so intent on wasting time by asking her to describe the breakfast, they could have started looking for him and might actually have found him. Even if they don't sleep together as much as they used to at the beginning (but who does?), so much else in their life is beautiful and fantastic; sometimes they just look at each other and they don't have to utter a word to know what the other is thinking—that's really important.

"Do you understand that this is not what you think it is? That it is not what it usually is? I checked on the Internet, I know how it goes when an adult who is psychologically healthy disappears. But that is not the case here, you're wasting time."

"Mrs. Fišerová, I really do understand you. I also believe you. Nevertheless, I still have to ask."

And so Radka describes how they had breakfast; how two days ago she baked an apple pie which everybody had for breakfast yesterday; the boys had fruit tea, Gabi still drinks milk; she and Peter had tea as well, but ginger, also pie—she had only two pieces, Peter three—he ate the pie as if it was the best pie in the world even if it was nothing special.

"Did the children like it?" Hladík asks.

Radka looks at him in disbelief; she can't remain silent—what kind of question is that? "How will this help you find him?"

Hladík gestures as if in apology. "Fine, continue."

She is quiet for a while. "They ate it—Filip had seconds but not Matěj. Gabi had one piece. It was no special pie. Wait a second—I still have a piece, would you like some?"

Hladík shakes his head. Then he points to his belly. He's fat. "I'm trying to lose some weight."

Radka realizes that she was already up to serve the pie, and so she sits down. For a a few moments, she's unsure what to say. She described the breakfast—nothing out of the ordinary happened during the breakfast; when the children go to school there's no particular moment to enjoy—everybody's in a hurry. I have to remind everybody to eat, to drink at least something . . . Why don't they enjoy it more—that they're together? Why is everything only a hurried routine?

"Then the boys went to dress and I prepared snacks. Peter dressed as well. Gabi remained with me—she enjoys helping me—then they left." Radka remembers: Peter kissed everybody goodbye and it was not just an obligatory kiss, it was a true kiss, even with the boys. Peter had a nice farewell with Gabi too, as always. He hugged her and they kissed each other and then they left. Radka has tears in her eyes because when he came back from work that evening, Gabi was already asleep, he didn't see her, and now . . . now.

"And then what did you do?"

She swipes at her eyes. "Then I went out with Gabi. We go out almost every day in the morning, sometimes to the playground, but I also go and buy groceries for lunch . . . the children don't eat at school, they don't cook well. Or healthy. It doesn't matter—I'm home anyway."

"So you haven't gone back to work yet?"

"No. I knew it back then that I wouldn't come back. And Gabi is not yet enrolled in kindergarten—she won't be three until February—and I didn't want her to go to a private one, I wanted to spend more time with her. And Peter supported me, he makes enough money. But that's not the point really, I take care of the children, of all of us, and I do take time to make sure we eat well . . . and I would like to have my own business. Something like a coffee shop, a bistro, a small business. So now I'm looking for information, and once kindergarten starts, I want to go for it. I want it to be nice. I bake a lot. In the store, I would like to sell homemade pies and such."

Hladík nods his head. "So you went grocery shopping and then you cooked lunch. And then?"

"Then nothing. He called me during his lunch break—just a usual phone call—we tell each other what we're up to and how our day has been so far."

"Did he say when he'd be home?"

"No, but that means it'd be as always. Somewhere between seven and eight."

"And that is usual?"

"It's the end of the quarter right now, it's always like this. In April, for example, he comes home at six; even picks up the boys from after-school activities."

"Does he like his job?"

She becomes silent for a while, then shrugs. "Well . . . as much as anybody else. Just normal, I'd say."

"Perhaps he wanted to quit the job?"

"No, not at all!" Suddenly, Radka bursts into tears. "Why aren't you looking for him? Please go and look for him, it's cold and raining and he's lying there somewhere."

"We're already looking for him. My colleagues are looking for him, do not worry."

The detective puts his hand on hers as a calming gesture. Radka doesn't flinch, even if she may want to. His hand is sweaty. Then it hits her. The sooner she tells him everything, the sooner she gets rid of him, the sooner she can start doing something herself. Go looking for him again.

Because naturally, last night when Peter hadn't come home, when she tried to call him and couldn't reach him, she had put on her running gear, including a jacket and hat because it was raining. It had started raining a short while after he'd run outside and it's been raining since, sheets of water; the kids in their rain jackets in the morning. She rang her neighbor Hana's bell—*The kids are asleep and I'll be back within an hour, please check on them a few times*—Hana stared at her dumbfounded, it was ten in the evening—*I'll explain it to you later, Hana, don't worry*—and Radka ran out.

Leaving the building, she started to jog, following the path

Peter used to run most often; the one they sometimes run together
. . . even if—when was the last time—perhaps at the end of the
summer, when the kids were at her mom's, they ran together before
breakfast, ten kilometers, a shower together, sex included (since the
kids were not there, they had to take advantage of it), and then had
breakfast together. It was actually a nice day, she tells herself, while
she's running in the dark and rain. She has to find time to run with
him—they both enjoy it after all. She will stop being lazy and will
run with him. But what about the kids—well, she'll figure that out,
they can run when the boys are in kindergarten and somebody will
simply babysit Gabi. Maybe her brother, he would probably watch
the kids for as long as an hour—on the playground, over the weekend, for example, and she and Peter could go run together.

She doesn't know right now what exactly she thinks has happened to Peter. Perhaps he twisted his ankle on a side road where
now, this late, not many people walk by, and now he's waiting there.
His phone is dead. She's imagining how she'll see him in a while,
she expects him to appear around every turn in the road, but she
runs their entire route and it doesn't happen . . . and she runs a bit
longer around Stromovka, but she's getting hot in the jacket and at
the same time, she's soaked. If she stops, she'll get cold right away;
but she doesn't stop, a few people walking their dogs are still out
even after eleven p.m. and she has no idea anymore where else to
run. Her legs are starting to hurt because she can't even remember
when was the last time she ran this much. In addition, at the end
of a long day, she is tired—and Peter could have run along the river,
but she doesn't really think so—so she takes out the phone, somewhere in the middle of the empty park under a tree, and wants to
call him, but then she tells herself, I better run back home. What
if Peter, in the meantime, has returned. What if he decided to go
for an especially long run—he's training for a half-marathon and
he likes to run in the evening . . . Yeah, of course, that's what it is.
So with renewed energy she runs home—you're such a fool, Radka,
you should have waited at home and not run outside; you'll get a

cold, then the kids will get it from you. Peter is surely home by now—in the shower. She speeds up so that she gets home as fast as possible. On her way, she knocks at Hana's door—*Sorry, I'll talk to you tomorrow, this was a bit foolish* . . . Hana doesn't understand anything; Radka invites her for a cup of coffee tomorrow along with the kids. But now she hurriedly unlocks the door—she is so sure that Peter's running shoes will be right there. She stops at the threshold—Peter's slippers, silence, the kitchen clock ticking.

Radka's heart starts beating fast and she takes out her phone, she should have done that right away, she's lost an hour acting on her silly idea to run around outside.

They listen politely to her. She must come down to the station. She tells them she has nobody to look after the kids. "You probably can't take them with you, right?" says that male voice—sounds young. It's half past eleven at night; Radka says she'll find a way and come.

She takes off the wet running clothes and leaves them on the bathroom floor. She takes whatever she can grab from the top of the laundry basket, slightly dirty—the jeans she wears only when she takes Gabi outside, the T-shirt she's worn today—and as she's putting it all on, she notices Peter's nightshirt—she picks it up and smells it; it smells like Peter. For the first time, Radka starts crying, loudly, and the traces of her tears are visible on her shirt.

A sweater, jacket, shoes . . . and she knocks on Hana's door again—she doesn't want to ring this late. Robert opens the door—"Anything going on?" And she says, "I have to go to the police station, Peter hasn't come home, please—the kids are asleep, could you or Hana check on them, I have to go talk to the police, they will not come here, I have to go there, but it's not very far, I'll be back shortly." Robert stops her; doesn't ask anything, takes the keys—he informs Hana, and then goes to Radka's apartment so that Radka can leave, telling her not to worry, to calm down, it'll all get straightened out.

And so again she runs outside this late at night, it's still raining, an empty tram goes by, she runs to the police station, everything takes forever—until somebody comes to sit her down in a badly lit room, it stinks like smoke and old paper; Radka explains what has happened—her husband came home from work, he ate, talked to the kids, changed into his running clothes, went out for his run, and didn't return. Maybe he fell into the river. Maybe—she doesn't know—but maybe he got hit by a car; the phone is turned off, probably dead, no he didn't go anywhere else, they do not have any problems, they didn't argue . . . "Look," Radka says as calmly and mildly as she can, "please believe me, my husband hasn't left me; my husband has disappeared."

The policeman says, "Do you have a recent picture of him?"

She takes her phone out and peruses the picture gallery—the biking weekend in Moravia; Peter and Filip and Matěj dressed in their cycling gear; Peter and the kids eating snacks in the forest; the kids, the kids again; she and Filip; she and Matěj, who makes silly faces; Peter holding Gabi the Saturday evening they went out for dinner—Peter looks handsome, he wore a shirt she likes.

She shows the picture with Peter to the policeman; he nods.

"And what now?" she asks once she's signed the forms and described Peter's jogging route.

"Now go back home; we'll have patrols continue the search."

"That's it?" she says. She's supposed to just leave?

"Calm down, Mrs. Fišerová, just go home to your children and try to sleep. You'll feel better."

Radka doesn't run anymore—she can't. At home, Robert sits on their sofa, he doesn't ask anything—perhaps he can see it on her face. He only says, "Ring the bell in the morning if you need anything—or do you want Hana to sleep here?"

She shakes her head—she wants him to be gone. She sits down on the sofa, starts crying again . . . tries his phone again, the thousandth time, she goes to lie down in their bedroom . . . but it's impossible to sleep . . . so she goes to check on her children. She'd love to take them all to her bed, but she can't carry the boys anymore, so she takes just Gabi and puts her in their marital bed. She puts her daughter on Peter's side and watches her sleep.

She knows she still won't be able to fall asleep. She keeps thinking about where Peter could have run. She has to tell someone where else he could have run, where they still have to go and look for him. She gets up and writes it all down; she'll call them first thing in the morning.

She lies down one more time.

Again she gets up, takes the sweater, and stares out from the balcony. For the first time the question of what she'd do without him, how she'd live, runs through her mind. She didn't expect such strong anxiety; it hurts her heart, and she's feeling sick. Quickly, quickly she stops pondering it all.

Wait until morning. Until dawn—which may not come since it's so overcast outside.

"Your husband doesn't have another phone?" Hladík interrupts her thoughts.

She shakes her head. She lists his friends. Close colleagues. Where they go for holidays, for weekends. Where Peter likes to go. As she speaks, she can see that Hladík is starting to believe her—that she did have something special with Peter. Since yesterday evening, this is the first time Radka feels a slight hope; now this man believes her, he'll take this investigation seriously, not like the overreaction of a crazy wife.

She gathers her last vestiges of energy to smile at him as he's leaving; she'd like to tell him that she trusts him, that she relies on him. Suddenly, she can see it in his eyes—he's not bad or dumb; he'll find Peter—but she says nothing.

Hladík is happy to leave. Always the same atmosphere—that tragic undertone, even if they offer him coffee, the household is on the threshold of chaos—which will inevitably come if the investigation is not resolved immediately.

Hladík knows that she too will go out to wander the places where her husband used to go. Let her do it. It's an extra pair of eyes and legs. She called her mother to help with the children.

Even though it's still early in the process, Hladík hazards a guess. She repeated everything three times, the entire day prior to his disappearance, and each time it was the same story. If she's lying, well then okay. But probably not. Probably it happened—her husband disappeared and she thinks he's hurt or dead. Hladík, however, sees him alive, sitting somewhere in a pub, shaking off their latest argument which she hasn't told him about yet, and then the husband will go home. It's almost always the same.

In the end, almost everybody reappears. Nobody kidnaps normal adult people. Neither do they fall into rivers and die. If he wanted to run across some tracks and a train hit him, they'd already have him. The Vltava will have to be searched. But he slips and he can't get back to the bank? A man who runs half-marathons? Hardly. It could happen. But it usually doesn't.

When they don't suffer from depression, they don't kill themselves. This one probably didn't suffer from depression. Or she didn't know about it. But she *would* know about it. Did they share their schedules? Damn, he has to check. They did share their accounts. Spouses. Nothing unusual in their accounts, she said.

Next time he'll ask whether he left all documents and other papers at home. She will cry again and she will look at him again as if she doesn't understand anything. Perhaps she'll swear at him. Okay, maybe Hladík does not understand it. He does not understand relationships—that some people make it last, some do not; it is all like magic and he does not like that. He himself prefers no ambitions and therefore no accomplishments. Only one child, by mistake—fifteen-year-old František, with whom he has sporadic contact that nobody enjoys and serve no purpose.

So yeah, it could have happened, it could have been an accident, in which case he is dead and their happy relationship will last forever and Hladík will let it be—as of now, he knows very little and cannot conclude anything.

Usually, a cheated wife sits across him—she admits that her husband cheated on her, says that it has not been good. But because of the children—perhaps the three best children in the world, for whom she would cook spinach for lunch and all three ate it, supposedly—Hladík is sure that she speaks the truth and this type of disappearance is his first. But it does not make him happy either.

Children who eat spinach.

Surely later, something ugly will come out.

But it makes him feel sorry.

He wants to tell the station that he's on his way and find somebody who knows how to talk to children to come visit them later, but when he steps out of the building, suddenly, without knowing why, perhaps because of her eyes, the expression she had when she talked about her husband, Hladík decides that he will go check Stromovka, after all.

He covers his head with the hood, the weather is disgusting, but the walk will do him good, and maybe he'll see something that will prove to be helpful in the investigation. He doesn't know what, but that doesn't matter. Sometimes it's good just to walk.

He lights a cigarette, covering it carefully so that it doesn't get wet.

At the food stands, he decides to buy something small. He buys bread and sausage—he really is very hungry—gobbles it down right there, and then he feels heavy. I will never lose any weight like this, he's berating himself, but does he have time to eat normally?

She'll stay in the quiet apartment. She'd very much like to wake up Gabi, put her in the stroller, and go outside to walk Peter's route again, but she must stop—she must behave normally. She has children, she has to take care of them, can't go nuts, and has to cook lunch. The dishes from breakfast are in the sink. She has no energy to put them in the dishwasher. But soon Gabi will wake up, she has to cook at least soup, there's still something in the fridge after all—just hold on for a bit longer, Mom will be here soon, then you can go out . . . She starts peeling carrots, Peter does not like carrot soup, if he comes back today, she must cook something else that he likes. She'll make chili; Peter loves it.

For a moment, she imagines that Peter will come back home as he always does, that he praises her for the chili and then they both sit down on the sofa with the children, that nice moment after dinner before the children have to take their baths and go to bed, they'll put on an animated movie for them, twenty minutes that Peter and she have for themselves, so they can talk about their day.

The sound of keys in the lock—Mom is here, Radka becomes alert—tonight, she'll sit here with her mother, whom she does not want to see at all; she's a miserable substitute for somebody who really understands her. Even if nothing is actually her mom's fault, Radka nevertheless feels almost hatred, but she puts down the peeler and wipes her hands to go welcome her mom.

"My little girl," Mom says immediately, and Radka jumps into her embrace and starts crying. "Don't worry, this will be all figured out, they will find him, nothing has happened to him."

"And how exactly will this be figured out," Radka asks.

Her mother is silent.

"Mom?"

She shrugs. "You never know anybody completely."

Radka pulls away. She'd love to hit her mother.

"I know Peter is not like that. I didn't mean it like that."

No, you *did* mean it, Radka thinks, but says nothing. Mom is bitter and thinks that all men are like that; that all men will eventually leave their wives, because Dad left her.

"Gabi's asleep but she'll be up soon. Will you make lunch? I have to go out."

"Of course," Mom says. "What time should I go pick up the boys?"

"At half past one. And then they need to be driven to the theater at four p.m. They'll stay there for an hour and a half."

"Have you eaten anything?"

She nods yes, but she's lying. She hasn't eaten anything and she won't be eating.

In front of the house, she inhales the clean air; it's still raining, she's put on her running shoes again; she'll run slowly, but will manage more. The shoes are still wet from yesterday but Radka takes this discomfort—just like her hunger—as an offer to a god or universe so that Peter will be returned to her very soon.

She sees the first policemen right away. The next ones, not until half an hour later. Then she runs on the cycling path along the Vltava River, and the rain becomes stronger and the dusk intensifies. The most unpleasant days of the year—the end of October, dusk, she can't go on anymore—more cops, they pass her, talking to each other, and she catches a snippet of their conversation: *She simply thought it was green, get it* . . . Radka continues running, looks back at them—they have no idea who I am, they just talk to each other as if they're on a stroll; Radka is still running but she slows down until she stops. She turns around and starts running toward them.

"Excuse me, hello. I am Radka Fišerová."

One gapes at her, the other one gets it. "The missing one . . ."

"Yes, that's my husband."

"I am so sorry," says the policeman.

"You're not supposed to be sorry; you're supposed to be looking for my husband."

The one gaping glances around nervously. She understands—he's worried that she's going to make a scene.

"But do not worry, lady," protests the other one. "We're looking for him."

"You should go home," says the first one. "You must be cold."

She really is cold. She realizes she is shaking. "Why don't you go down to the river? What do you think you can find here?" She gestures with her hand toward the bushes along the river.

"Don't worry, there are many other policemen."

"And divers," says the other one.

She understands that they're talking about Peter's dead body possibly caught somewhere in the river; suddenly, she can't take a breath, she is shaking, she can't take any more, and the first policeman collects himself, catches Radka so that she doesn't fall down. "Go get the car," he says to the other one. "Hurry and call an ambulance."

"No, let me be." She wants to jerk away, she must run more, but he won't let her.

Radka starts crying, she can't hold it in, and she falls into the policeman's embrace for a moment. She registers his frightened look, hears herself crying, but it's as if an animal's crying; she wants to apologize, but she can't speak—and then she faints.

Hladík is sitting at a coffee stand under a canopy, smoking. It is raining terribly. In the distance, the wailing of an ambulance. His phone rings. They have found the phone belonging to the missing person.

A drunk homeless man is waiting for him at the station. Shit, it'll stink here for two days again; he opens the window even though he's cold and wet.

"I found it in a trash can," repeats the drunk again and again. "It's mine, you can't take it."

Hladík checks the iPhone; it's dead, nobody has a charger; he checks for the SIM card, it's missing.

"It wasn't there," claims the drunk. "I will show you the trash can. Nothing else was there, only this."

"So let's write it all up."

"And will you give it back to me? Look, inspector, I could at least call my friends . . . You won't give it back? So go fuck yourself, you shitheads, you dicks!" he starts yelling.

Hladík points a finger at him. "Look, how about we write it up tomorrow? You'll get a good night's sleep before that, all right?"

The guy doesn't stop yelling. Hladík can see he'll learn nothing from him, so he has him taken away and goes to look for a charger.

Mom mentions moving for the first time the next day, right after she starts to feel somewhat coherent after all the drugs they injected her with. She can't believe that Mom really said that; Peter has been gone only two days and she's already talking about them moving away.

Mom says she didn't really mean moving *away*—more like a change of scenery until . . . it all clears up.

Radka shouts at her: "You are alone, Mom, so you want us with you so that you feel better, but we are a family, we belong here, and together, so stop talking about that, please, never again, whatever happens!"

Mom gets insulted—perhaps she's right, but Radka is so angry, as if Mom hopes Peter will never come back.

"Silly girl, of course I want Peter to return."

"But you think he won't."

"Yes, I think he won't come back. That he has left you. That he is a coward and an asshole."

They look into each other's eyes: Radka hates her, her mother can see it.

"You'd prefer him to be dead?" Mom asks, and Radka can't answer so she goes to pick up the boys from school and then takes them to their tennis classes.

She is cold there; during their one-hour training session she feels the flu coming, her entire body hurts. She has to be thankful for her mother and her help with the kids, with whom she has almost no strength left to talk. So far, however, the children have been calm. *Daddy is missing, but the police are looking for him. No, nothing bad has happened to him.* The police talked to them as well. For Gabi and Filip, it's a diversion. Matěj is a bit scared but pretends not to be.

The boys play tennis the way they always do—they laugh and joke with their friends. She takes them home and goes to lie down. She uses two covers. Now, she could get some spicy Chinese food—Peter would go and get it for her—sure, Mom would do that too, but she would grumble about how she'd rather make her some chicken soup and tea with honey. Radka feels sorry for herself, then at night she gets a fever and has wild dreams about Peter—he is alive, laughing, they swim together in the dirty Vltava until his dead, pale corpse floats toward them and the alive Peter says, *Just push it away.*

Then, physically, it gets better. The fever stops. Weak, she lies in bed. The children visit her in the bedroom—darlings; Mom manages everything, no problem. Radka reads—pretends to read—she still thinks of Peter, she keeps on remembering everything she can think of. She tries to remember a fight, something unpleasant; tries to convince herself that it was nothing special, but it's not working. TV. She makes herself watch boring and silly shows.

And on Sunday morning, she wants to make tea to fill up the thermos to keep it hot. The thermos is nowhere to be found. The children know nothing about it, neither does Mom. She checks all the rucksacks, the entire closet.

It's nowhere.

It can't just be a coincidence that the thermos disappears a couple of days after Peter disappeared.

Since Radka's been in a searching mood, she starts looking around the entire apartment. She doesn't quite know what she's looking for.

In one of the drawers, among photo albums, she finds an A5 envelope and inside, 800,000 korunas. In large bills. It horrifies her. Was Peter embroiled in something?

There's nothing suspicious about the phone, so he must have had another one. The same with his computer—nothing. The background—a preset landscape. In his office—a framed picture of his family, ceremoniously dressed, sitting at a table, all smiling, strained, into the camera.

At his work—nothing. His colleagues, polite and ordinary, only shrug their shoulders. No, nobody knows anything about him wanting to quit. Then she calls. She says she's found something peculiar at home.

It's been four days. The weekend during which winter officially begins. It's dark at five now; just before people draw their curtains, Hladík peers into apartments, illuminated rooms—an early family evening; safety and togetherness. He goes with it for a moment even though he knows much better—there is no safety.

Hladík arrives. She is sick, lying on the sofa; she looks horrible. She is almost unable to talk, her mother is there pretending that she's not interested in anything, but in reality she wants to tell him everything. She takes good care of the small girl who's watching Hladík through her thick glasses, but Hladík can feel the unpleasant atmosphere.

She, even if she can barely get off the sofa, will not leave him alone with the mother, and when the mother tries to get her to sleep, she starts yelling at her not to send her away, that her mother can feel free to talk with her present, that she knows very well that she thinks Peter left them so just feel free to say so to Captain Hladík. And she should also feel free to tell him why she is so bitter and mean, and then she cries again. The bespectacled girl starts crying as well and Radka's mother calms her down—she's calming down both of them—the small girl and Radka—and then she sends Radka to the bedroom to put the girl to bed.

Then the mother says to Hladík, "You see, my husband left me." And no, she does not think that Peter left her daughter and her grandchildren, but she is simply able to entertain the idea that it could have happened. What does Hladík think about that?

Hladík does not know. The body hasn't been found. They're still looking for it, but—and this Hladík does not say—the case doesn't involve a lost child, so there is no helicopter flying above the park in Stromovka.

The mother continues behaving quite rationally. Does Hladík

know the stats? How fast the probability of finding him is decreasing? Hladík does not know. But he can find out.

The doorbell sounds, the mother goes to open the door, and the boys come in; handsome blond boys, they look at him with curiosity and greet him politely.

"You are the one looking for Dad?" asks one.

Hladík nods.

"Dad hasn't died," says the other one.

Hladík shakes his head, "Of course not, don't worry, boys."

"I'm not worried," says the first one.

"Maybe spies kidnapped him," says the other one.

"Boys, go to your room, we're trying to figure something out here," says their grandma, and they obediently leave. "You'll find him or you'll somehow close the case; it's impossible to live like this."

Hladík says nothing; four days have passed, the real hell hasn't started yet, but how are these people supposed to know that—how are they supposed to know how hopeless and futile it all becomes after a couple of months, and how they will forget his face after a couple of years?

Radka, ill, comes out of the bedroom. "I have to tell you something even if it may mean nothing—I couldn't find the thermos. *Our* thermos."

Hladík looks at her and has no idea what to say.

The mother sighs; she's probably worried about her daughter's mental state.

"Can you come here for a bit?" She's inviting him into her bedroom; Hladík feels strange—not that he hasn't seen plenty of bedrooms. He follows her, she clears a chair for him, and she herself sits down on the edge of the bed.

"It's not only the thermos."

She then shows him the money. Peter must have been caught up in something, otherwise where would he come up with all this cash? Perhaps he hid the money for somebody, and then those whose money it originally was learned about this somebody (about whom Radka knows nothing) taking their money, and so they kidnapped and killed Peter.

Hladík watches her while she's explaining this conspiracy theory; of course he will check it out—he'll ask at his office, but right now it really doesn't look like he was involved in anything. It looks much more like he was diligently saving money.

"And hasn't it occurred to you that perhaps Peter left the money here for *you?*" he asks.

She stares at him. "No, not really." Simply because that is not what it is. If he chooses to understand it this way, then he'll never solve the case, doesn't he get it? Does Hladík understand? Hladík nods, he definitely understands.

"Don't worry, we'll check it out. Really."

"Do you think I'm crazy?"

Hladík shakes his head. She blows her nose.

Then they both fall silent. Hladík worries she'll start crying again, but her mother peers into the bedroom and asks if he'd like to stay for lunch. Hladík wants to refuse, but the mother says she's made dill soup. He will not say no to dill soup.

At lunch, as he sits with all of them at their big table, the mother helps the youngest with the food and Radka discusses plans for the next weekend with the boys; the atmosphere is actually pleasant, perhaps for the children, both women are trying very hard; in fact, Hladík tries too, and for a second it seems to him that he is the father and the husband here. Then he wants to leave as soon as possible.

Hladík is not quite sure why, then, on Sunday, he is taking a train to Křivoklát. Yes, it's one of the places where the missing person used to go with his family often; plus, this castle is his phone wallpaper—but that's all.

He is not sure whether this sixth sense is the reason he became a policeman, or whether it is a consequence of him being a policeman, that the years of experience branded some equation in his brain. He doesn't know.

He's riding a train to Křivoklát and watches the passing country. He doesn't know where he's going to get off or why; so first he gets off in Beroun and sits in the station the entire Sunday and watches people—nothing happens and so, once it gets dark, he returns home. In the evening, František e-mails him that he's sick and so he's canceling their meeting on Tuesday, and Hladík is relieved, and at the same time he is also ashamed that he is relieved.

He wants to go again. Although he does not know why he's doing it: perhaps he feels pity, maybe something in her eyes touched him. It's raining again on the weekend; it's terribly windy and leaves are flying on the streets and there are already Christmas ads on TV. Hladík's throat hurts so he lies down with a book. He has a feeling he'll probably let it go. She has something special about her, but he is a policeman who's investigating her husband's disappearance. He will always be a reminder of the worst thing that happened in her life.

But in two weeks he's again on the way there, the same route, though he gets off elsewhere.

And then—nothing. A visit to a psychologist. Antidepressants, sleeping pills. The kids afflicted with a cold, one after another, Mom with them, she's caring for them wonderfully; her perfume takes a spot in the bathroom and then Peter's toothbrush disappears. Radka cries over it; she weeps during this fall season a whole lot—over a whole lot of things—but then she has to buy presents and prepare for Christmas. Mom tries unceasingly to keep her busy with work and activities; the boys understand, each in his own way, that Dad is not here and will not be here . . . And Christmas—all that they used to do with Peter is now done with Mom. And after a few days she has no energy left to defy her mother when she says that they should move into her house in Unhošť. So they move, and the next semester the children start school there and Radka and Gabi go to the playground in the town, nobody knows anything here—and then one of the mothers asks her, and she says my husband died; she does not know why she is saying that. Maybe she doesn't feel like explaining that he disappeared; she doesn't want this mom to think he left her; she says it out loud for the first time and she has tears in her eyes; the mom apologizes, Radka apologizes—sorry, but it is hard, simply hard. Zuzana, the first friend in her new life, hugs her. A week later, they get drunk on red wine while their children, Zuzana has two, lie on mattresses they put together. And her husband has a night shift at the hospital where he fucks some nurse, says Zuzana with a crooked smile, and Radka thinks that she and Peter never had it like this, that everything was okay with them, nice, and that's how it would always remain, and suddenly she feels at peace—so this is how it is to be a widow, it occurs to her. Of course, it does not mean that from that moment she will never want to cry . . . when Filip draws a picture of their family and Dad is there on the side, apart from them, or when Gabi sings children's songs in their entirety alone or when she starts working in the bakery for the first time and puts on the apron. Peter will never see her like that, but somehow, somehow she moves along, maybe time really will heal all of this . . . the worst proclamation she used to have to listen to in the fall: Radka, you'll see, time will help and heal; how she wanted to kill everybody who said that, and suddenly she's actually living it. Time does help; of course, sometimes she still wakes up in the morning and wants to turn to Peter and hug him tight but then she realizes the reality and she is able to inhale calmly, get up, wake the children, and kindly greet Mom who is already preparing breakfast.

Hladík continues to ride the train on the same route—these have become trips for him where he mainly observes people. They checked Peter's business—he was not involved in anything; on the contrary, based on his bank accounts it is clear that the money he left her he had saved. He probably saved more so that he'd have some money to live off. But no clear trace. Nothing. He simply disappeared.

And then, one spring day, Hladík is sitting at the Roztoky station near Křivoklát, watching forest workers, and one of them is cleaning his glasses with a handkerchief, carefully and deliberately.

Every person keeps acting the same way, always, even if he wants to become somebody else. Places we like we continue to like. When we sever all ties, we want to keep at least a thread. One's habits are not easy to change. And so on. Hladík even lets him go, without talking to him, the first time he sees him. He approaches him the second time. Peter smiles sadly when Hladík introduces himself. Then he lights a cigarette. *My husband doesn't smoke and never smoked, he finds it disgusting and I stopped smoking the moment we met*, Radka had said to Hladík.

Now the only thing left is to inform her.

She is hanging clothes in the garden, the children are outside, the boys somewhere with their friends . . . this has all happened smoothly, this transition . . . even though they do not have a fencing team, they have a tennis team and also painting classes; Gabi is going to school next year, for now she's with Mom when Radka works. She may have put on some weight since she started working in the bakery, but the girls have a lot of fun together there . . . Anyway, meeting so many people is not bad at all and Radka still sort of believes that one day she will have her own bakery—maybe right here. She won't return to Prague, Mom is here, it's better for the children, it's better for her even if only for the reason that there are not many reminders of Peter. In fact, there are almost no reminders of him.

So when Muf starts barking and she turns away from the clothes and sees Hladík standing at the gate and notices his expression, it is not a good feeling. Some news, and it is not pleasant.

"Come in," she tells him, "he won't hurt you, he's still a puppy. Mom and the kids wanted him; the neighbors ended up with three puppies so Muf lies on the sofa every evening with them." Radka picks up the little dog and Hladík opens the gate himself.

While the coffee is being made, she says nothing; she knows she should ask but she is afraid—have they found his dead body? Have they found him alive—has somebody been holding him hostage? Will he return home different? Will he return home at all?

She gets a cup of coffee for herself too, even if she already had one earlier. "Wait," she says as she sits down and gets up again.

From the pantry, she brings two pastries—one with custard and the other with chocolate and liqueur. "Eat it, really. I have plenty, as many as I want, I work in a bakery, it's a good job, you know. One day I'll have my own . . . Sorry . . . I am simply scared to ask why you came, what happened. You . . . have you found him?"

Hladík watches her attentively; she's put on a little weight—but that's not it, she is somehow different. Before all of this, she was in charge of her home—but there was somebody to be in charge of; now, it's all on her shoulders, she had to grow up. Mistress from the bakery. A widow with three children. Mother who has to help her. The memory of the best husband. Hladík can see Peter's sad face—*I left them all the money, I thought it was clear. I'm not going back. I thought I would start missing them. But I don't miss them. Not even the children. So tell me how I could live with them.* And Hladík can now see himself—he also left his family, he was in the same situation, he does not miss his son, so what could he ever tell him?

"He's dead, isn't he? And I will have to identify him?" she asks, then suddenly she gets up brusquely and walks to the window, opens it, a gust of cold air blows inside, she reaches into a pot on the windowsill and gets cigarettes; she lights one.

"Do you want one too? Or do you want to go to the porch? We can smoke there . . ." She taps a cigarette.

They move to the porch.

Hladík obediently lights a cigarette, even if he's had plenty today and doesn't feel like it at all. She smokes too.

I was preparing . . . to do something, that's why I left the money for them, but on that day I simply wanted to go out for a run. But as I was running, suddenly I couldn't go back. So I threw away the phone. And kept on running.

Hladík wanted to ask him what he was thinking, but when he looked at him, he knew, he understood why Peter did it, the futility of all that effort, work, children, cycling weekends, getting up in the morning and going to work, kissing your wife, waiting for the elevator, every single day for the rest of your life, changing tires, preventive visits to your dentist, cleaning your shoes, reading political analyses, working long hours, helping the kids with their homework, eating healthy, the long lines at the post office, the looks your wife gave you when you didn't put up shelves, the dead fish in the tank, not forgetting to vacuum behind the sofa too, waiting in lines and listening to the inane talk of the radio host, scraping car windows, trying for something—to live right . . . it's pointless—everything.

I simply want to be alone—like this. I don't want anything I used to have, Peter had said at the end. Another worker was asking whether Peter was interested in a donut. He called him *Petrsi.* And Peter hollered back at him, *I hate these sweet things, dude!* and then he smiled at Hladík the way he used to smile at his clients, politely but impersonally. *I have to go now.* And Hladík only said, *So you don't like sweets?* And Peter became serious again—*Precisely, not at all;* then he got in a tractor with the other worker . . . and Hladík watched the tractor swaying on the rough forest road and then disappearing into the forest.

When Hladík came the following week, the workers were still there, but not Peter. *He said he needed to get out,* a gypsy with no front teeth divulged to Hladík. *Does he have problems?*

Not really, Hladík shook his head, and decided to go visit Radka right away. In that moment, he pretty much knew what he'd tell her.

"So what's going on?" she asks firmly as if the cigarette has helped her recover her strength.

"Nothing," Hladík replies. "Only . . . I came to tell you we don't have anything."

"Ah," she says, though there's only a small bit of disappointment.

"It's been a long time . . . I just wanted to tell you not to expect too much."

She doesn't say anything.

Neither does Hladík.

Don't come here anymore, this is a life where you do not belong; this is my new life, my husband is dead, and you just get the hell out of here, her eyes say.

Hladík knows he won't come anymore. He finishes his cigarette, his coffee, so hot it burns his tongue, and leaves. On the way, he gets a text from his ex-wife asking him what time he's coming. Hladík realizes he—again—forgot about František. He answers that he'll be there in half an hour.

OLDA NO. 3

BY IRENA HEJDOVÁ

Olšany Cemetery

A scream wakes me up. Softened by the glass in the windows and the slow daybreak above the streets of Žižkov; subdued by the drops of rain falling on the window, but still distinguishable from a dog barking or the squeaking of the neighbor's door. I open my eyes. A hangover is splitting my head in half. In the neighboring room, my son will wake up soon. And in my bed, there's a strange guy lying with me. There are only scraps of memory from last night in my head; my cell shows 6:37 a.m. and a text from my mom: *You looked terrible!* I remember that upon my return home, I tried in vain to cover my drunkenness and ended up feeling just as bitter as I used to when I would return the same way as a teenager twenty years before. I also remember that I slyly hid the guy who is snoring beside me under the duvet. He was able to come inside after Mom finally left the house. Pitiful.

It's drizzling outside, the Žižkov television tower is completely hidden in the mist as if it's not even there. Only the red light on the top flashes through the darkness, like a lighthouse beacon for all those who are drowning and who have drowned. Beside the bed, the dog whines—he wants to go out. All I need in this situation is a dog! I think about how to manage everything logistically—take the dog out, take Peter to kindergarten, get rid of the guy. I shake his shoulder—he doesn't budge. When he wakes up he will probably have the same terrible headache as me. And perhaps it will be better if I don't have to witness that. I write a message for him to close the door behind him. No intimacy—I was never big on it—and why, anyway? I don't even know who he is. I put the pencil quietly down and sneak out of the bedroom.

Little Pete is asleep—he always looks so sweet and innocent when he's sleeping. He has on his favorite pajamas with spaceships. For a second, I yearn to be one of them, to be shot up far away into the consoling quiet of the universe, without the snorting dog at my side, without the hangover, without the unwelcoming apartment from which Olda has already taken his half of things, and where everything seems to be falling down on me. Pete squirms a little and opens his eyes, looks at me for a while, and then turns on his side and closes his eyes again.

"Pete, get up—it's time."

I know very well that he's pretending to be asleep—but behind his closed eyes he's pondering whether or not to make his getting up today unpleasant for me. Recently, he has behaved atrociously toward me, but maybe it's my fault—in his eyes, somebody must be responsible for that terrible divorce, and Peter has chosen me.

"Pete . . ."

"You stink, Mom. Haven't you brushed your teeth?"

"No. Neither have you. Chop-chop—get up!"

I managed to push him out the door in record time, despite the hangover and the impatient dog. Luckily, I kept the guy in my bed hidden—I have no idea how I could possibly explain him away to my son.

It has been raining all morning. Pete splashed in his raincoat and boots with the dog—both of them jumping into puddles like they were nuts. At that moment, I did not care. I was focused only on the banging hammers in my head and trying in vain to piece last night together out of my fractured memories. I brought Pete to kindergarten and got excited by the idea of falling back into bed when I got home. But the reproachful look the dog gave me and the strange drunk in my bed pushed me farther into the rain instead of back home. I traversed Vinohradská and entered Olšany Cemetery through the main gate.

* * *

It may seem peculiar, but graves are linked to many significant and happy events in my life. Olda and I had our first rendezvous right here, he asked me to marry him here, and it was here I told him I was pregnant. During our divorce last year, I spent a lot of time in the cemetery contemplating many things, Pete asleep in a stroller parked beside one of the shabby benches. I have been walking this terrible pooch here for the past five years—from the moment Olda brought him home as a puppy. I feel good in this place, it's quiet and peaceful—you don't even hear or feel the rain as much inside. As if one has found oneself completely away from Prague in an otherworldly dream shrouded in ivy and spiderwebs, where sidewalks are covered in bugs and lined with unending rows of tombstones.

The dog happily runs between the gravestones, being surprisingly respectful toward the actual graves, as if he knows it's not polite to step on them, pee on the baroque angels, and gnaw on the flowers. I walk on the center line and do not take much notice of him. Here and there, he finds a stick and fights for it with an imaginary foe, throws it on the ground and then proudly takes it a bit farther until he finds a new and better one. It's after the rain, drops of water dripping down from the treetops above me, one or two falling right into my collar and stinging unpleasantly like a persistent memory.

Of course the divorce is still weighing on me. I never thought I would ever go through this, the hell of absurd accusations, petty fights, the subtle tugging for our child and our accumulated possessions of which there are not so many. But—it has happened, I cannot change it, and actually I do not want to; I am doing well being only with Pete and having periodic babysitting offered by my mom. I hope that Olda will finally come and take this idiotic poodle too. He keeps promising that once he has better accommodations he will immediately free me of the dog, but I have a tiny suspicion that he will leave it with me forever. I call the dog when I notice an alarmed look on the face of an old woman walking by with a water can and a dirty sickle in her hand. Why would she water anything when the rain has just stopped? I look back at her but she's disappeared behind the tombstones like a ghost, so I free the dog again and walk on.

Between the treetops with leaves glistening from the rain, the television tower lights up—it has broken through the mist and shines as far as here. Mist is like alcohol—it mercifully hides a lot, but once it's gone it reveals even more. I feel pitiful, like a small kid lost on her way home from school—damn, I'm thirty-five but it feels like what's inside my head hasn't changed. I look around, searching for the dog—everything is eerily static, only those slow raindrops drip on the tombstones. I call the dog, but not even the smallest branch moves. I stop and listen—I can hear the trams jingling on Vinohradská, but my dog (well, Olda's dog to be precise) is nowhere to be found. For a moment I ponder whether I wouldn't be better without him. I would not have to clean his stinky paws in my bathtub and suffer his licking and stale breath. Dogs are like men—they are so much work and it's all for nothing; they only occasionally smile at you, and quite stupidly.

Again I look around, and suddenly I'm gripped with anxiety. Cemetery anxiety mixed with a bit of fear—who wouldn't be afraid in the midst of thousands of corpses even if they're covered with wet dirt and riddled with earthworms and God knows what else? I turn toward Vinohradská and start to walk back, with a spring in my step which soon shifts into a gentle run; one more look back— of course nobody's there, but just in case. From one of the graves, the woman with the water can lifts her head and gives me a penetrating look—perhaps disapproving of my undignified running in this sacred place. She chops the overgrown grass on the grave with her sickle. I smile at her idiotically and keep running.

The gate into the cheerful and carefree earthly world is right in front of me; I am almost out—except my path is hindered by . . . the dog. Dirty and wet from his ears down to his tail, which he wiggles happily. He runs to greet me, I am dreading that he's going to jump up at me, but he doesn't come too close. He stops about a meter in front of me, peers at me somewhat foolishly, and then drops his spoil. In this, Pete and the dog are similar—they keep bringing home sticks. I find them everywhere—in the cutlery drawer, among toys, one was right there with the toothbrushes and another one was cleverly hidden behind the toilet. This latest spoil is unusually small, and I would not have noticed it if it didn't fall into my hand. A glitter made me stop, bend down, and look at the small stick. Then I straighten up sharply because this is no stick.

I enter the apartment, put away my keys, soggy jacket, and shoes; I send the dog to the bathroom and put the poop bag with the mysterious object on the chest of drawers in the hall. The dog, as is his habit, leaps into the tub; I clean his paws, so focused that I become startled and jump up a little when I hear a sound behind me. I turn around quickly—in the doorway, the guy from my bed is standing there. What is he still doing here?

"Hi. You've been outside?" He asks as a husband would; I suddenly find him obnoxious. He leans toward me, wanting to kiss me—I quickly dodge.

"You're not gone yet?" I reply coldly.

"I don't have a shift until ten p.m. so I thought maybe you'd like to have breakfast with me, Marti," he says, smiling. He acts annoyingly familiar, which is something I hate among even my closest family, let alone a virtual stranger. The dog scrambles to get out of the tub and snorts with disgust. I quickly dry his paws with a towel and let him go; I remain in the bathroom with the man alone.

"What shift?" I ask, and he smiles broadly.

"Do you not remember anything? You berated me for the parking ticket. I said I would help out somehow." He smiles.

"What am I supposed to remember?" I keep my distance—I am a champion at keeping a distance, especially from my nighttime acquaintances.

"Okay, a recap for you: You were in the bar with a friend; I invited you for a drink and then some more; we went to another place to dance and then we walked home. It was raining and you liked it very much. You danced in the rain, then you fell down, and I carried you all the way here. On the stairs, you were hiding me from your mother, then I put you in bed and fell asleep before my head hit the pillow. Right—and I am a policeman. Traffic unit. Olda."

"Olda?"

"Like your ex, right? You thought it was so interesting last night. Come on, I found something in the fridge for breakfast." He strolls out of the bathroom as if he already lives here. Jerk.

We're sitting at the table eating breakfast—he did quite well with it. Olda talks about something, laughs, so I smile from time to time too; I bite a roll and mechanically nod my head. Through all that confusion, the thought of the poop bag in the hall flashes in my head. When I took the object from the poodle and stuffed it into the bag—the only thing handy—I had no idea what I would do. I could have left it there, but in the haze brought on by the hangover I felt guilty that it was my dog (Olda's) that brought the abomination to me, so I quickly hid it. I could have thrown the bag in the first trash bin on the way, but I was worried somebody would see me and immediately become suspicious—of what, exactly? So now the small bag rests inconspicuously in the hall. I get up in the middle of another one of Olda's rambling sentences, grab the bag, and push it across the table toward him. He shuts up and looks at me. I watch as he takes it and dumps it on the table. A few clumps of hardened earth fall out. Olda examines them suspiciously.

"Is that a finger or what?"

"Yup. And it even has a ring, see?"

It was precisely that golden circle that had caught my attention at the cemetery—I remembered how Olda and I, a long time ago, exchanged wedding bands and promised each other the moon. All that's gone now. On the table in front of Olda No. 2 is a strange finger with a wedding band on it. And I have no idea what to do about that.

"Have you noticed that it's not on a ring finger but a pinkie? Odd, right? And did you look at the ring? Maybe there's something engraved on it."

"The poodle found it. In the cemetery. I haven't even touched it."

He stares at me, exhales, and then takes the finger into his hand and slides the ring off. It requires some tugging, and I feel quite sick. He cleans the ring using a corner of a napkin. He snickers and hands it to me. I refuse to take it, but I look. On the inside there's a flowery inscription: *OLDA 2015.*

"What are the odds—Olda No. 3," Olda No. 2 laughs, and reminds me so much of Olda No. 1, who in the final stages of our relationship I hated so much that when he laughed I had to leave the room.

"Who could it belong to?" Olda asks ponderingly, playing the role of a hard-bitten detective.

"Perhaps to Olda?" I counter. "You are a cop—so find out!"

"Didn't the dog unearth it from a grave?"

"The dog doesn't step on graves, he only runs on the sidewalks. And I find it weird that somebody who got married only last year would already be six feet under, right?" Even hungover, I feel like a champion investigator.

"It takes all kinds," the folk philosopher says, and glances at his watch. "I will bring it with me and have a look." He stuffs the finger with the ring back into the plastic bag.

"In between handing out tickets and testing drivers for blood alcohol levels?" I remark, feeling incredibly witty.

"I'll call you."

"You want the number?"

"You've given it to me—five times already."

I am embarrassed for my drunk cuddly self until Olda No. 2

and Olda No. 3 leave the apartment. Then I finally lie down and blissfully fall asleep.

The advantage of working from home is that you don't need to make any excuses for your hangover. Still, I feel somewhat guilty when I wake up to the ringing of my cell phone. I look at the clock—it's 12:02; I have three hours before I need to pick Pete up from school. I answer the cell.

"Hello, Marti? Good afternoon. Were you asleep?"

I look out the window. It's started raining again, drops beat on the glass, the dreary light permeates the apartment, mimicking the dreariness in my head. Olda and I used to call mornings like these "pajama days," and we had no problem lying in bed all day long. That was, of course, before Pete.

"Who is this?"

"Well now—Olda! Olda No. 2, ha ha."

I do not laugh—I just silently wait with the phone to my ear.

"Do you have a headache too, Marti? Probably yes, right? What are you doing? Sleeping, right?" It's marvelous to meet a guy who can answer all of his own questions immediately. So I pig-headedly remain silent, and when the silence becomes unpleasantly long, Olda speaks again: "I don't want to bother you—but I found your Olda."

"He is not *my* Olda!" I snap, and am reminded of my ex-husband yet again. That Olda who used to be mine and who I thought he would be mine forever but . . . that was not to be.

"I am so sorry. I too am divorcé, you do know that, so I understand. I am allergic in the same way to the name Judita. Fortunately, there's not too many of those. There's not too many Oldas either—but a bit more than Juditas. Do you have a piece of paper handy?"

"Why?"

"So you can write something down, dear. Go get a pen and write: *Oldřich Černý, Koněvova 295. Oldřich Strašák, Bořivojova 21. Oldřich Maděra, Lobkowicz Square 9.* Got that?"

"Got it. But I don't understand—"

"Listen, these are all the Oldas who got married last year and live near the cemetery. They all live in Žižkov, just like you. Beautiful, no?"

"And what the hell do I do with them?"

"You're going to visit them. You still have three hours before you have to pick up Pete; one lives right near you on the square and the other two a stone's throw away. So go visit them and check out their hands. And then we'll know."

"What will we know? Prague is full of married Oldas, why would the finger belong to somebody from Žižkov?"

"The probability is very high, and asking around won't cost anything, dear," he says, and it irritates me. The same way it irritates me that I brought him home, that I let him stay until morning, that I went to the cemetery and found the finger belonging to Olda No. 3. It irritates me that I showed it to this idiotic cop and he now gives me orders.

"I am not going anywhere—you find him yourself. Even if I find him—what then?" I watch how the alarm clock hand slowly moves ahead, toward the time when I have to pick up Pete, take him to the playground, cook dinner, and put him to sleep, which takes forever. "Look, give me a break. I want to rest. You look for Olda yourself, I don't care at all," I say, and end the call. To make sure, I turn the cell off and fall into the bed again.

The alarm clock lifts me from a sleep filled with confused dreams shortly before three p.m. I just have time to go pick up Pete and take him to the playground, listen to all the mothers talk, go nuts inside from all that talk while nodding my head sympathetically. When I step outside, I glance up at the sky. It is overcast again, it looks like rain, and like spring may never start. A drop falls on my nose, and from the road there sounds a horn blast. I flinch and peer straight at Olda No. 2 in the car in front of me. I walk up closer to him.

"What do you want now?"

"I found him. Look, he lives on the same square as you, isn't that a coincidence?"

"How about the other two?" I cannot hide my curiosity, silly woman that I am.

"Intact fingers."

"I have to go to the school," I say, and turn my back to him.

"I'll wait at the playground—you're going there right afterward, aren't you?"

"Not when it's raining," I say.

"It'll stop." He smiles broadly again.

He irritates the hell out of me; still, his interest in this crap with a stranger's pinkie (and in me) is also entertaining. Olda No. 1 was never this interested, not even in the beginning. So I look at Olda No. 2 again, nod my head, and his smile brightens. I turn and go to pick up Pete.

Pete suspiciously gauges Olda sitting beside me on the bench. Olda is the only adult man on the playground, so he attracts quite a lot of attention. We probably look like some happy family even with Pete's scowl. He walks up with his truck full of sand and dumps it right in front of us.

"This is a tractor that will drive over you," he says to Olda.

"This one couldn't run me over me, Pete. Try a bigger one, okay?" Olda replies.

Pete looks at him challengingly, then walks off. I watch him—his slender back touches me, probably the vestiges of the hangover. Then I examine the sky above us even more earnestly, and a moment later I examine Olda No. 2.

"So what do we do about that Olda?" I ask the cop beside me, and he shrugs.

"I rang his doorbell, but nobody was home, I guess. We can try again later—it's that white house over there." He points through the blossoming treetops at one of the unassuming tenement houses across the way.

"And if it turns out to be him? What then?" I watch him, his profile, and suddenly I remember him sitting beside me at the bar last night with the same expression on his face—staring straight ahead, with a slight smile on his lips. I couldn't take my eyes off him.

"We will know that he's alive and that nothing bad happened to him—other than losing his finger. It's good to calm one's soul, right?" He turns toward me. And then we look at each other for a while and then we kiss. And it is a long kiss, so long that my head spins. And then Pete throws one of his sand patty cakes from his truck into our faces; suddenly, there's sand in my eyes and it makes me cry; I cry grains of sand and that empties an entire boulder from my head.

We are at Lobkowicz Square 9, an unassuming tenement house like all the others, like the one where I live right across the way. The three of us stand there—me, Pete, and Olda No. 2—and we ring the bell with the name *Madera*. And nothing happens. So we turn to leave, when the speaker rattles and a female voice sounds.

"Hello?"

We look at each other—what now?

Olda coughs. "Good day, is Olda home?"

The speaker transmits silence, it feels almost oppressive as it flows through the cables from who knows which floor down to us.

"He's at work—but he'll be back any minute. Should I leave a message?"

"You don't have to. Thank you, we'll come back later," Olda says, and his deep voice soothes me; pushes away a peculiar hunch that's overtaking me. The voice from the apartment goes silent and we're walking out through the square toward my apartment when I poke Olda's shoulder. An old Škoda has just pulled up to the sidewalk from Vinohradská. A man disembarks and locks the car. On one hand, there's a dingy bandage covering his fingers. I stop breathing and grab Pete's hand, as if I just saw a ghost.

"Police—your driver's license and papers, please." Olda No. 2 shows Olda No. 3 his badge.

"Me . . . what? Why?"

"The vehicle seems unsafe to drive, I'm going to check it in the database. Your documents, please," Olda repeats, and he's terribly sexy—like a cop from an American movie. Olda No. 3 starts to reluctantly pull out the documents and gives me a quick glance. Maybe he thinks I'm another victim of police coercion. I smile at him guiltily. I glimpse the name *Madera* on his driver's license. Olda No. 2 walks to his car and I look at the bandaged hand of his victim.

"What happened to you?" I ask innocently.

Reluctantly, he turns away from Olda's car. "I stuck my fingers where I shouldn't have, miss," he answers snidely.

I don't know what to say, so I look quickly at Pete, who is poking a stick in a puddle on the sidewalk. I realize that the poodle has probably peed vengefully all over the apartment in my absence, and that I have no idea what to make for dinner. Olda is returning from his car and hands the documents to Olda No. 3.

"All in order," he says curtly, and pretends not to notice the surprised look on the face of his adversary, who now brightens up; it almost looks like he's going to fall on his knees before Olda.

"I . . . really? Well . . . you're really nice! Thank you! Thanks!"

"What happened to your hand?" Policeman Olda asks nonchalantly, and Olda No. 3 looks at me as if to make sure we aren't ganging up on him, and I act casual. Olda No. 3 exhales.

"A bit of a turmoil—I lost my finger, you know?"

"How?" Olda and I don't even breathe. Pete watches us in confusion.

Olda No. 3 probably doesn't really feel like explaining, but he relents in the face of a man of law: "Well, we had a small disagreement with my mom about a grave. She divorced my dad when I was a small boy, and it was very hard for her. Dad died last week, and she refuses to put him in our family tomb. We didn't agree, we had a scuffle over the key and she is quite something. She's an angry woman—she hacked me with a sickle she always takes with her to the cemetery. And the sickle cut off my finger. Unbelievable, right?"

I remembered my morning walk at the cemetery and the encounter with the old woman holding a water can and a sickle. "And when did it happen?" I asked.

"This morning. My wife doesn't know yet, I have to come up with more believable bullshit, she won't believe the real story. I wore my wedding ring on that finger, can you believe it? It was the pinkie; I have gained weight like a pig, I can't put it on my ring finger anymore. Fucking food. Oh well, I should go—again, thank you." Olda No. 3 looks back at Olda No. 2 and they exchange understanding smiles.

Then the door closes behind Olda No. 3. Well, almost—right before it closes, Olda No. 2 sticks his foot in the door. We wait awhile, then Olda, my Olda, enters the house and finds Madera's mailbox and stuffs the dingy bag in it. He exits the house and smiles at me. I smile back a bit stiffly; I reminisce about the old lady from the cemetery and then a question occurs to me—would I let Olda No. 1 lie in our grave? It terrifies me when I come to the conclusion that I probably wouldn't. I don't even notice that Olda No. 2 has put his arm around my shoulders and is walking me through the square back home. Neither do I notice when Pete gives Olda his hand.

I recover when a ray of evening sun touches my face. Hopefully the rain is done. Hopefully spring is here. I squeeze Olda's hand in mine, and start thinking about what to make for dinner. Perhaps I could also clean up and air out the apartment, wash the curtains, and check the status of my cemetery payments. Just for peace of mind. We never know what life has in store for us.

EPIPHANY, OR WHATEVER YOU WISH

BY PETR ŠABACH

Bubeneč

H e was sitting in a train station that was no longer a station, since years ago somebody decided that trains would only pass through here on their way to the new and rather ugly stop on the left bank of the Vltava. He was sitting on a wooden bench; on one side was a hill, on the other a crumbling building named after one of the most famous poets of all time. *"Ah, fate of man, how you resemble the wind . . ."* He thought about Goethe's verse, acknowledging the pathetic *ah* that he added to it himself. Purely to emphasize his utter despair.

This place had always drawn him in. It had the allure of the Wild West, and the fact that it was situated on the border of an English park with police on horses only added to this impression.

Beside him, casually resting against the wall, was his mountain bike. He was sitting and imagining what would come after he'd killed himself. If anything. He was hoping for nothing . . .

At first he didn't pay attention to any of it. As a working title, he called them "flashes," and he had no intention of sharing them with anybody. After all, it was nobody else's business. It used to happen, for example, when he was cleaning knives. In particular the largest of the set—the handles, aligned by size, stuck out of the heavy wooden block right beside the old toaster. This knife always unsettled him. He couldn't define it. He couldn't describe it. It was, simply, just a very short "flash." He started to be afraid of those knives, but at the same time, they irresistibly attracted him.

To avoid thinking about this, he got used to covering them with a dishtowel. He didn't realize that these "flashes" could have been premonitions of murderous thoughts, until the time when he and Helena were waiting for a subway train to arrive, and in one of his flashes he envisioned his wife falling onto the tracks in front of the first engine. Silently, without a scream . . .

Now he was sure. Almost all of his thoughts slowly changed into lines converging toward one point. To murder Helena. Until now, he had thought he loved his wife. At least that's what he had claimed to everybody. At the same time, he understood that the only way to prevent it all was to act faster—to kill himself before he could do something foolish; if murder can be described as foolishness. This could not be suicide; this was supposed to be only a preventive murder of self. Rational suicide. Of course he was afraid, but because he was unduly polite, he could not act any other way. He decided to proceed carefully. He waited until his wife went to bed. He sat down at his writing desk, and in the light of a replica green-shaded bank lamp, he wrote a sentence on a clean sheet of paper, with very neat, almost calligraphic handwriting: *ADVAN-TAGES and DISADVANTAGES of life after death.* For a short time he sat stiffly, and it was only when he became somewhat more alert that he added under *ADVANTAGES*: *I won't weigh anything.* And with this statement—because nothing else occurred to him at that moment—he took a sleeping pill and read until the letters in front of his eyes started undulating like wheat fields in the summer breeze.

He knew he would do it, but he didn't have any idea yet as to how. Because later, everything was supposed to look like an accident. That meant he needed to eliminate anything that could give rise to any possible questions and jeopardize the reputation of his family. That was a priority.

He pondered, purely theoretically, what form of suicide he would choose under different circumstances. Probably pills. He liked those the most. If just one could put him to sleep for an entire night, what would an entire package do to him? Twenty floors, twenty levels under his sleep, there must really be that large nothing—the majestic, dark nothing. A hundred times, a thousand times more nugatory than sleep without dreams.

It must look like ordinary absentmindedness. Later, they could all blame it on—and they probably would—his being overworked, his fatigue, perhaps burnout . . . who knows? The safest method would be to step out in front of some large truck or train, somewhere it would cause only minimal problems. He eliminated the subway right away because that was obvious—whoever decided to jump there, they certainly knew exactly what they were doing. And then there would be all the complications . . . After all, he didn't want anybody to become embroiled in his problems, and just the idea that it would block traffic for a few hours and thus complicate life for many innocent people as they were trying to get to work was so horrifying to him that he broke into a sweat. For the same reason, he rejected suicide by gas.

When he was small, in Dejvice—the Prague neighborhood that is so quiet that even a car accident becomes an event—there was a gas explosion in a large apartment house, right across from the Hotel International. The havoc this caused is hard to imagine. Fifty meters from the site of this catastrophe, the building's custodian ended up there on the tracks after she apparently ventured out holding a candle to find out what the smell was that had been bothering her at night. Even though he never saw this, he always imagined the poor woman, with gray hair up in a chignon fastened with a small comb, and with genuine astonishment in her wide-open eyes.

Therefore, an accident. Nobody who wants to commit suicide rides in front of a train with a bicycle, he realized with relief, and so he went to the cellar where for years his slightly beat-up mountain bike had been leaning against the wall. An older model which today would have no market value, and probably wasn't even worth stealing. He checked the brakes and the tires, of course, and the rest of the evening he spent looking for the air pump, which he later discovered in one of the ski covers.

"I'll go for a bike ride tomorrow," he later said to Helena. She didn't respond. She had no opinion on the matter at all. "Tomorrow . . ." he repeated.

He walked toward his work desk, opened the first drawer, and took out the list with *ADVANTAGES* and *DISADVANTAGES*, and under *ADVANTAGES*—with *I won't weigh anything* already there—he scribbled, *Definitely Helena!!!*

Well, I can't change what God has in store for me, he thought bitterly, when he learned that on the following Sunday his daughter was bringing her new—and by his count, third—boyfriend to meet him.

"Oh well," he sighed when his wife informed him about it.

"Why *Oh well*? Why do you say *Oh well* when you haven't seen him yet?" his wife said angrily.

He kept quiet. Could he tell her at that moment that he planned to commit suicide the following week? And specifically because of her? One thing was clear—he did not wish at all to spoil for his daughter her so very important day. He would never forgive himself. More precisely, he would not forgive himself in the little time he still had.

The young man who on Sunday really did come to visit looked to him a bit tipsy, addressed him as *Pops*, and what was worst of all—when Helena asked him whether he wanted a roll or a piece of bread with his soup, he asked for *bread but no crunchy crust*. His name was Pavel, and that same evening there appeared under *I won't weigh anything* and *Definitely Helena!!!*—*I won't see Pavel anymore!*

They say bicycle rides are unforgettable, but when he came out on the highway and started riding down the hill, it was not any grand experience. He rode slowly around the park, and after about half an hour he became brave enough to enter a busy street to ride among all the cars and trams. Once he made his way to the outskirts of Prague, he decided to ride along the riverbank. When he was returning in the evening and hit the lights that announced civilization, it took a lot out of him to navigate that chaos. He kept himself in the bike lane, which seemed to him impossibly narrow, and when he got close enough to see his apartment house it started to rain on top of everything, and the asphalt before him glistened like a river. No wonder his head was spinning; he was winding through a bunch of almost stationary cars, in a panic, trying not to scratch any of them. Riding on the sidewalk, as many others would, he considered to be highly inconsiderate.

He now coasted in a low gear, pretty much standing on the bike, when suddenly he tried to turn right. But as he maneuvered, he started wobbling until he couldn't hold on anymore and fell sideways. Directly behind him brakes squealed. He didn't even perceive much of the physical pain. His only thought was to get to safety with his bike as fast as possible, in a way which would not bother anybody.

The car that had almost hit him rolled up and one of the windows slid down. The driver—who had to lean over the passenger—asked him if he was okay. He nodded his head and gestured with his hand that they should continue driving, and to prove that there was nothing wrong with him, he laboriously picked up the bike and offered a friendly smile.

"You have no reflectors on the back!" the driver yelled at him, shook his head and drove away.

"That was close," he muttered, and for the rest of the way he walked, pushing his bike.

Before he put it away in the basement, he found out from the tachometer that he had ridden over twenty kilometers that day. It surprised him and also cheered him so much that he wanted to announce it to Helena and their daughter. But the wife was already asleep, and the daughter was who knows where. He took a shower, then settled down to read his book. Before he killed himself, he wanted to finish it. It took him awhile to remember the thread of the narrative where he'd left off and, lying on his back, he thumbed through the detective story. Later, after he turned off the lamp, he was thinking in the dark about what was going on with him. *How many of us are there? At this moment, on this night?* he said to himself, and in his somnolent thoughts, there scurried a memory of a news report about a desperate suicidal man who had hammered a nail into his head. *And am I doing anything different?*

He dreamed about Helena and himself drowning. He, not far from her, smiled while whisking his right hand against the waves and the flat pebbles beneath them. And then came the flash with the knife. That was, naturally, worst of all . . .

The following day Helena announced that in a week, he had to take her to visit her parents.

"We're not discussing it!" she preemptively declared, even though he—except for an exhausted look he inadvertently gave her—hadn't uttered a word.

So again, a postponement, he thought, and it occurred to him that if he kept being so considerate to everyone and everything, he could just end up dying of old age.

He suffered through the wedding anniversary. His father-in-law got completely drunk and laughed at him the entire evening for how little money he was making.

The following day, in the early morning when everybody else was still asleep, they set off on their drive back. At home, he succinctly added the word *Father-in-law*—surely it's not difficult to guess into which column.

It's not just that he was a polite person—he had been born out of politeness. Unlike many of us who were born out of love or boredom, he was born out of pure politeness. To explain—his father, many years ago, had met his mother through an advertisement. They had a date in a bar, and at the moment when this young woman—who would later become his mother—took cigarettes out of her purse, his father jumped up to her and in a flash, leaning gallantly toward her, struck a match. Unfortunately, a small part of the head from this cheap Czechoslovakian match fired directly into her eye, where the little piece of hot sulfur burned her cornea and iris with a hiss.

A fast transfer to the nearest hospital and surgery followed. The doctors took a long time to announce that they were able to save the mother's eye. And since the father was just as polite as later his son would later be, he asked this woman to marry him, because even if the eye turned out to be okay in terms of its function, after all the suffering, her visage had become a bit twisted, which bestowed upon her the look of a slightly cross-eyed young woman. More like *fetchingly* cross-eyed. There was a wedding and later a pregnancy, and even if the father already felt a bit old for children, he took it all in stride, and without any protest he began to prepare for his new role in life. And so Boris was born.

The last event he had to suffer through was Christmas. That would really be inappropriate—to kill oneself in the midst of the holiday hullabaloo. After all, it's the time of the birth of the most important—even though, technically, only half the most important—of us. He bought presents as he had done every year, which basically were just small trinkets for Helena and Klára. Some cosmetics, which, as always, the store clerks helped him choose. After that, he didn't sweat it. From Helena he got some underwear and handkerchiefs, and Klára told him that her present was still on the way. Naturally, he later added under *I won't weigh anything, Definitely Helena!!! I won't see Pavel anymore*, and *Father-in-law*, the word *Christmas*.

And then the new year came. Finally, he decided on Epiphany—that magical twelfth night after the birth of our Savior. He put all his things in order. In a few folders tied with bows in the bottom of the drawers in his writing desk, there were all of his grade school report cards—from kindergarten up to his university diploma, rolled up in a scuffed blue tube, along with his birth certificate, marriage certificate, and even his old vaccination card. He didn't write a will (as he barely owned anything) but in the envelope with the word *vacation* cleverly scrawled on it, he left twenty thousand korunas, which represented his life savings. According to the information he had, that should suffice for a very modest funeral, and perhaps Helena would even get some money from his insurance, though he didn't know much about that; it was more like wishful thinking. Truthfully, he wasn't even sure he had signed up for any insurance. That had always been Helena's thing.

Once he had assured himself that he had taken care of everything in this regard, he started looking after miscellaneous stuff. He returned all three books to the library that he had borrowed some time ago, and then he attached his library card with a rubber band to his credit card and ID. This small, tidy package he then placed with all the other documents.

Every afternoon now he spent riding his mountain bike to the Bubeneč station. There, sitting on a bench, he watched trains passing by without stopping. Not only watching, he was actually monitoring trains with a notebook and a watch that he held like a stopwatch—he was checking their punctuality. In the end, he decided on the train going north to Děčín which passed by every day at nine in the evening, reliable almost to the minute.

On the D-Day—like every morning—he shaved and showered, put on clean clothes, and read until lunchtime to learn how that utterly gripping book would end. But soon he lost the ability to concentrate enough on the book and so, with a sad sigh, he returned it to the library. In the afternoon he went out for a walk; he stopped in a half-empty coffee shop on the main street, then lazily returned home where he prepared a simple dinner for Helena and Klára. He himself didn't eat. He was not hungry. Around eight in the evening, he changed into his sports clothes and put his helmet on. By half past eight, he was already at the station. He stood there leaning against his bike, looking around, and it seemed that except for him there was no other living soul. In a moment he wouldn't be a living soul either, it occurred to him.

Waiting for the train, he amused himself by watching the moon and stars, as the sky was exceptionally clear that evening. He knew his constellations pretty well. He checked whether all the stars were in their rightful spots, and when he assured himself that indeed they were, he couldn't help but succumb to a moment of anxious regret stemming from the simple fact that he would never lay his eyes on this beautiful and majestic spectacle ever again.

At the turn, a train appeared. It was approaching fast and surprisingly quietly. His heart started to beat wildly and he couldn't catch his breath, but he hoped that this would serve him well for his last few steps. Something hit him hard in his chest, and suddenly he merged with the single and singular, Beautiful Nothing . . .

He was woken up by a subdued, blinking light. It took awhile for his absentminded consciousness to calm down, and then such a wave of bitter sadness and despair washed over him that he almost choked, because he realized that the first entry from his column *ADVANTAGES* did not apply. His body still had the old earthly weight. There was nothing on this earth that could possibly get close to the disappointment he was experiencing. No eternally long and blissful void existed. That absolute nothing that was his last hope now appeared to be just another reality in which he was lying helplessly on his back, breathing with difficulty. In addition, he was horribly cold. He tried to move his hands. He shifted his head to one side and discovered that if he remained in that position, the light became a bit more bearable. Drool leaked out of his mouth, slowly moving down the left side of his chin. He wanted to sit up but something was preventing him from doing so. As if he were tied up. *Perhaps this is how it is in hell,* it occurred to him. From somewhere nearby came an entire sequence of short, sharp hissing sounds, similar to the sounds rubber soles make on linoleum.

And then, right beside him, he heard something very much like the old noisy alarm clock, and somebody yelled: "One moment! I have no signal here! Hold on! I'll step out for a second!"

So this probably isn't hell, he thought. *Because surely in hell no-body discusses signals. Everybody knows that hell has walls forty thousand kilometers deep.*

For God's sake—I'm alive! he realized in horror.

While he was helplessly fighting with the fabric in which he was entangled as if he were a mummy, he could hear that male voice talking to somebody: "Dude, don't even say that—I've just brought in a guy after a heart attack—the same age as me! Well, buddy, our peers are starting to kick the bucket, there's nothing we can do about it!" It sounded like the guy was almost laughing. He was good at guessing voices. More precisely, he had a talent for imagining quite accurately the owner of a voice based on what he heard on the phone or radio. Most of the time, he got the weight, height, and the overall look of the person he had never seen before quite right. This voice belonged to somebody who loved boiled pork, a large unshaven man nearing fifty.

Finally, he freed himself from the fabric. He sat up and rubbed his eyes. There were two other bodies lying here under sheets. Startled, he watched them for a while and then quietly jumped down to the floor. His head fizzed a bit but he didn't fall. It took a little while to catch his breath and then he wrapped himself in the crumpled sheet. Under the monotonous buzzing of a fluorescent light, he dragged himself toward an open door. Carefully, he looked out. He heard the man again but he didn't see him. He tiptoed to the other side of the hall. He came to swinging doors with opaque, grainy glass fitted in the upper half. He thought something moved behind them. He had barely pushed himself against the wall when the doors flew open in front of him and something wedged through—something that slowly grew and acquired volume, and after a while there was no doubt that he was gawking at a woman's behind. And what a very nice behind it was. As he found in the following seconds, it belonged to a young and very pretty cleaning woman who was now standing in front of him as if on display.

Without moving, she watched him, flabbergasted. It almost

looked like she was going to say something, but then a frightening shriek sounded behind him, accompanied by a strange rattle. She came out of her swoon, slammed a bucket with a broom on the floor, and in a cute feminine way started running toward the morgue. He opened the swinging doors in front of him, peered in, and then, tiptoeing, started through the freshly washed hall. Moving like a wading bird so that he would make the fewest steps, he proceeded along the wall toward where he supposed an exit should be. Some ten meters farther, after a few turns, he found himself in front of a wide staircase. With relief, but also worries, he looked at a sign on the wall. *Exit*, it said curtly. As curtly as the doctor who announces, *Exitus,* after he takes his very old stethoscope out of his ears.

He smiled bitterly, and then started walking up step by step, shivering as he held the icy sheet close to his body.

Above, he looked around quickly. On the left, he noticed the reception desk where two people talked quietly. He approached them cautiously and in a way that would not alarm them. A gloomy doctor and an infinitely kind priest were blocking the narrow corridor with their bodies in such a way that it was impossible to pass around or between them.

"Excuse me," he whispered with embarrassment as he shuffled near the two men.

"You excuse *us!*" they called after him almost in unison, yielding to him sideways. And when he disappeared out the door they continued, uninterrupted, in what was assuredly a very learned debate on the topic of what exists in the space between heaven and earth.

ABOUT THE CONTRIBUTORS

CHAIM CIGAN is the former chief rabbi of Prague and currently the chief rabbi of the Czech Republic. He began his career in the late sixties as a screenwriter and playwright. In 1977, he signed the dissident declaration Charter 77, converted to Judaism, and shortly thereafter moved to West Germany where he furthered his Jewish education. He returned to writing in 2014 when he published the first book in his series *Where the Foxes Wish Goodnight: Altschul's Method*. He followed up with *Piano Live* in 2015, *Puzzle* in 2016, *Outsider* in 2017, and has also written a collection of children's stories, *The Small Mister Talisman*.

MARTIN GOFFA is a former police officer who has published seven critically acclaimed crime novels (*The Man with Exhausted Eyes, Christmas Confession, Without Body, Between Two Fires, The Swimmer, The Child in the Fog,* and *The Hunting*), and one short story collection (*Living Dead Man*), in the last five years. Thanks to his police career, he empathizes with both the detectives and the criminals in his hard-boiled thrillers.

IRENA HEJDOVÁ, a screenwriter, has received several awards for her work, including a special mention at ScripTeast at the Cannes Film Festival for best adapted screenplay (from Petra Hůlová's 2010 novel *All Things Belongs to Me*), the Sazka prize for her screenplay *Children of the Night,* and the RWE/Barrrandov Studios prize for the screenplay *Legs Up* (not yet filmed). She has also published numerous short stories.

MICHAELA KLEVISOVÁ is a highly acclaimed crime-fiction writer who has published five novels, and won the Jiří Marek Award for best Czech crime fiction for both *Steps of the Murderer* and *The Solitary House*. Her stories often involve middle-class characters who become embroiled in comprising situations, with a focus on their relationships rather than traditional police investigations and narratives.

ŠTĚPÁN KOPŘIVA is an author and screenwriter who combines hard-boiled action with science fiction and fantasy elements, as well as a large helping of dark humor. After publishing the successful novels *The Killing* (2004), *The Asphalt* (2009), and *The Black Frost* (2010), he turned to noir with his latest novel, *Rapid Fire* (2015), which was well received by both critics and readers.

PAVEL MANDYS is a Czech journalist, book critic, and organizer of the annual Magnesia Litera book award. He has written numerous book reviews as an editor of the online literary magazine *iLiteratura.cz*. In 2012, he published the book *Prague: The City of Literature* (in Czech and English) to support the city's successful bid to become a UNESCO Creative City of Literature. In 2013, he published the encyclopedia *2x101 Books for Kids and Young Adults*. He currently lives in the Prague neighborhood of Smichov.

MIRIAM MARGALA earned a dual doctoral degree in linguistics and English literature. She has been translating literature and other texts for the past twenty-five years and teaching in the field for the past ten years. Margala's translations (poetry and prose) have been published in Europe and North America; one of the poems she translated was nominated for the Pushcart Prize. She has also published interviews she has conducted with literary/intellectual figures in the United States and Europe.

ONDŘEJ NEFF is a living legend among Czech sci-fi writers and incorporates elements of hard-boiled noir into his novels and short stories. His most lauded work is *The Darkness* (1998), and his short stories have been included in numerous collections, such as *An Egg Inside Out* (1985), *A Zeppelin on the Moon* (1990), and *God, Ltd.* (1997). His novel *A Glimpse of a Dirty Trick* (2007) has elements of both science fiction and conspiracy theories.

MARKÉTA PILÁTOVÁ writes stories set in the Czech Republic and Latin America. Born in 1973, she has published four novels, one book of poetry, and five books for children. Her book *Tsunami Blues* (2014) was inspired by Graham Greene's novels: set partly in Cuba with elements of a spy thriller, her characters struggle with the past of Czech and Cuban communist secret services. Her work has been translated into six languages, including Spanish and German.

JIŘÍ W. PROCHÁZKA is an inventive sci-fi writer and was a Czech pioneer of the cyberpunk genre with his popular short story collection *Time Creators* (1991) and the novel *Star Cowboys* (1996). Later he moved to the action-fantasy genre with the Agent JFK series, but his latest novel is the crime story *The Dead Beast* (2015).

PETR ŠABACH is one of the most popular contemporary Czech writers and has published thirteen books, mostly humorous novels, novellas, and short stories, usually set in the Prague district of Dejvice. Some of them (*How to Sink Australia, Jackal Years*, *Shit Burns*, and *ID Card*) have served as inspirations for movies. His latest novel, *Rothschild Flask* (2015), is a variation on the classic "sting" genre.

PETRA SOUKUPOVÁ has published five novels and two children's books which have been translated into several languages, and she also writes screenplays for TV and film (a feature film she is working on will premiere in 2018). Her best-selling collection of three novellas, *To Disappear*, was a national best seller. She primarily writes about complex family relationships, incorporating elements of mystery.

PETR STANČÍK is one of the most imaginative contemporary Czech writers. He began in 1992 with his baroque fantasy *The Both Spring*, and continues writing playful, humorous, and slightly weird stories for adults and children. His novel *The Mummy Mill* (2014), a tragi-grotesque noir fiction set in Prague in 1866, won the Magnesia Litera prize for prose and was popular with both critics and readers.

MICHAL SÝKORA is a literary theorist at Palacký University in Olomouc who is acclaimed for his crime fiction as well as his books on Vladimir Nabokov and Philip Roth. His novels *A Case for an Exorcist* (2012), *Blue Shadows* (2013), and *Not the End Yet* (2016) were inspired by contemporary British procedural crime novels. All three have been or will be adapted into TV miniseries.

KATEŘINA TUČKOVÁ is a best-selling author whose last two novels, *Expulsion of Gerta Schnirch* (2009) and *Godesses of Žítková* (2012), benefit from well-constructed plots based on modern Czech history. Searching is the key idea: for the life story of a lonely, young, single German mother after World War II, or for the secret traditions of the pagan woman healers in the mountain villages persecuted by the Communist police. Her novels have been translated into fifteen languages, including English, Italian, and Arabic.

MILOŠ URBAN is a writer and translator who rose to international fame through the Spanish edition of his Gothic novel *The Seven Churches* (1999). He has written several thrillers and short stories set in both contemporary and historical Prague (*The Shadow of the Cathedral*, *Dead Girls*, and *Lord Mord*). His ecological thriller *The Waterman* (2001) won the Magnesia Litera prize for prose. His suspense novel *She Comes from the Sea* (2014) is set in England and was inspired by Hitchcock movies and the novels of Patricia Highsmith. His books have been translated into thirteen languages, including English, German, and French.